The Song of the Nightingale

By the same author

A Concise History of Irish Art
A Singer at the Wedding

The Song of the Nightingale

Bruce Arnold

HAMISH HAMILTON · London

First published in Great Britain 1980
by Hamish Hamilton Ltd
Garden House 57-59 Long Acre London WC2E 9JZ

British Library Cataloguing in Publication Data

Arnold, Bruce
  The song of the nightingale.
  I. Title
  823'.9'1F   PR6051.R6/

  ISBN 0-241-10497-1

Printed in Great Britain by Bristol Typesetting Co. Ltd,
Barton Manor, St Philips, Bristol

FOR IRENE

'. . . no one makes a study of himself, no one has the courage to keep an accurate record of all the thoughts that come into his mind, all the feelings that agitate his heart, all his sorrows and joys. In this way century after century will go past without anyone knowing whether life is a good or a bad thing, whether human nature is good or evil, and what makes up happiness and unhappiness.'

Denis Diderot

'Have read over a very practical page of my Diary where I say that we must not confuse perfection with perfecting, and must strive towards both by negative means. My chief shortcomings are idle habits, lack of order, sensuality . . . will struggle against them.'

Leo Tolstoy, **Private Diary**

Chapter One

I

'The nightingale,' said the Gaffer, 'here reaches the borderland of its visited territory.' He made a vague, expansive gesture with his hand towards the window and the night sky. 'It is rarely encountered westward. An occasional, and therefore accidental, visitor to Wales, it never goes to Ireland. Nor Scotland.' He paused, and I could hear him gently sucking his teeth. He spoke lugubriously, as though his was the responsibility for the fact that the nightingale had fixed the confines of its migration among these soft hills, long before man made any mark upon them. In the deep, late twilight of that summer evening, we waited for him to continue.

He was a dusky presence at the end of the dormitory, a still and shadowy figure standing before the deep cobalt blue of the night sky which outlined faintly the ponderous, mullioned window that occupied a large part of the end wall of the room. It must have been getting on towards eleven o'clock, and normally we would all have been asleep. But it was a Friday, and there was a school match the next day. We were now the senior boys in the house, and the Gaffer seemed disinclined to leave us.

'It is odd,' he said, 'because, in the other direction, this territory of which I speak stretches more or less unbroken from here to Japan. Yes, the whole of Asia. Across Europe, down into Greece, Asia Minor, Afghanistan, India, Burma, China,

the nightingale is a migrant visitor. His song has inspired count-
less literatures. Yet here he sings out into the unknown. As far
as he is concerned, it is a wilderness there, across the broad
valley of the Avon and the Severn. Beyond it, apparently, the
land offers him no prospect of finding another nightingale with
which to mate.'

It was only possible, in the dusk, to imagine the expression
with which the Gaffer concluded this further dissertation upon
the ways of the nightingale: a pugnacious, dismissive, flat,
matter-of-fact look at us, in which the revelation of what he
felt was suitable for the hardest and most cynical among us,
without losing the attention and the response of the most
sensitive. Long years as a teacher had taught him how to
embrace all of us within a single and consistent mode of address.

Yet he can hardly have been out of his forties then, a lean,
moody man, slow to anger, slow to praise, judiciously parcelling
out his sympathy among us. He had come to Coppinger after
the war, emerging, as it were, from its shadows. He had become a permanent feature, and his face, set in the lines of
mature resignation that indicated his arrival at a stopping point
in his ambition, represented a form of fixed security to us,
almost as reliable as the buildings of the school themselves.

Perhaps it was this permanence and the atmosphere he
created that had given birth to Mr Forrest's nickname. In
other respects it was not entirely appropriate. But his manner
did suggest a certain bumbling uncertainty, reminiscent of age;
and this was calculated to cloak his perceptions, giving a kindly
and sympathetic slowness of manner to a man who readily
penetrated the odd background from which most of the boys in
his house emerged.

I was in love with Mr Forrest's daughter, Janet, that summer.
I was only half aware of it that particular night; yet it marked
the beginning, and the events which were to follow drew me
forward, faltering and nervous at first, into certain sweet and
heady occasions of desire and fulfilment.

Usually hesitant in conversation, the Gaffer was given to

silences, and unwilling to repeat himself. Early on, one acquired the habit of attention. And it was only in the face of the night's silence, with no song from the dark stillness outside the window, that he had engaged in what was, for him, a flood of words. They ceased; and we waited.

The bird did not oblige us. We lay there in the darkness, in uncertain expectation. For Lytton, Pritchett and myself, the choice of that particular night was unfortunate. But there was nothing we could do. Under the pillow I held the alarm clock, wrapped tightly in a jersey. There was no danger of it going off, although it was set. The timing was well ahead, even of this late hour. But I was nervous of the long, tense pauses as we all lay and listened. And I was conscious of the muffled, thudding tick of the metal clock close to my ear.

After a while he spoke again. 'So you noticed nothing. None of you. I suppose it's not strange. Expectation heightens awareness. At least, I hope it does.' He sighed.

We all listened hard. The night yielded up one or two of its more ordinary sounds, among them the distant barking of a dog from the school farm down the valley. But of birdsong there was none. It was tempting to talk, and at one moment, forgetting for an instant that the Gaffer was there at all, I opened my mouth to say something to Lytton, something that might have been compromising; but stopped myself in time.

The Gaffer spoke again: 'Are you playing tomorrow, Barnwell?'

'Yes, Sir.'

'Will we win?'

'Beat them last year, Sir. But they beat the Stowe second eleven two weeks back, so they seem much better this summer. It's a pity that Hannay's hurt his hand.'

Barnwell was head of the house. He was a slow spin bowler. Hannay was in Kirwan's house, and was head of the school as well as being captain of the first eleven.

'Anyone from Mr Patterson's house on the team?'

'No, Sir.' It was Barnwell who spoke.

9

'That's bad. Must be the first time.'

'Mr Patterson said it was.'

There was a warm friendship between the two masters. They had been at Coppinger about the same number of years, and had come there before Merchant's arrival to take over as head. It gave them a special relationship, both to him and to each other.

'Has he any good younger boys coming on?'

'Yes,' Barnwell said. 'There are some, Sir. Young fellow called Wickham who bowls well. But he's only about thirteen, if that. There are others who could be good if they tried. It seems. . . .' Barnwell tailed off into silence.

'Well?' Gaffer said.

There was a pause.

'It's just that, well, no one seems to try there.'

'They need Hannay in the house.'

Fitful snatches of conversation about cricket had a comfortable familiarity about them. But the Gaffer turned his attention to more practical matters.

'Did you fix the mower, Lytton?'

'Yes, Sir.'

'I meant to ask you earlier.'

'The plug was cracked. It was shorting.'

'Ah.' The Gaffer paused and thought a bit, sucking on his teeth. Lawn-mowers in summer, the central heating and hot water boilers in winter, these seemed to provide him with a satisfactory, even welcome bedrock of practical, mechanical concern. They were also the basis for a relationship with Lytton that was different from the other boys. Lytton, who was neither a prefect nor a monitor, and now would never be either since he was due to leave at the end of the summer, had considerable aptitude where mechanical things were concerned. He was, in fact, going on to an engineering college in the midlands to which a small number of Coppinger boys generally went at the end of each summer term. In a phlegmatic way, he was looking forward to it. Though it had not in any respect jeopardised our friendship for each other, he had already assumed, when he could bring himself to remember it, the vague aloofness of a school-leaver.

We listened in the darkness to the slow, earnest exchanges between the Gaffer and Lytton on the declining merits of the elderly Atco lawnmower which the boy had managed to set going.

'Time's coming when a replacement will be needed. Don't know how we'll afford it but it won't go on for ever.'

'I don't know, Sir,' Lytton said. 'There's nothing else wrong with it. I checked the rest of it and the compression's good. It starts easily enough.'

'Ah.' He paused. 'Maybe you're right. Soldier on.'

It was Lytton whom the Gaffer chose, almost without thinking, for practical house tasks. He had a way with the boiler which provoked unqualified admiration in winter and he seemed to know the electrical system in the house better than anyone. Whenever one found the housemaster engaged in some tedious but necessary task of a practical kind, whether doing it himself or supervising others, it was almost automatic to expect Lytton nearby.

With the disposal of the Atco, silence again descended. It would not have been right for any of us to have spoken, other than to the Gaffer himself. General conversation would seem an impertinence, in view of the collective anticipation of the nightingale. But in the silence we rather hoped for a further exchange of views, and we wondered whose turn would be next.

'Mr Forrest?' Pritchett asked. He then paused. He had what I thought must have been, to the Gaffer, the most irritating habit, quite unique among the boys of our house, of forcing one to acknowledge oneself before asking any question. Other, younger boys might be heard around the house calling out, 'Mr Forrest! Mr Forrest! Please, Sir, can I . . .?' And, among the seniors, our housemaster's even-tempered character had induced a relaxed approach in which few of us even bothered with his name, though all called him 'Sir'. But Pritchett, whose voice was unusually deep, and who was a slow-spoken boy, invariably and even ponderously went out of his way to induce a sort of formal confrontation by pinning down the Gaffer and getting him to indicate that he was ready to hear what Pritchett had to say.

'What is it, Pritchett?'

'I wanted to know the earliest references to the nightingale in literature, Sir. Are they Greek? or does it go back further?'

Inwardly, I sighed. Pritchett and the Gaffer, at the very best of times, did not exactly hit it off. And generally Pritchett, who was aware of this, kept his own counsel. But some demon in him, a tension that was understandable enough on that particular evening, had egged him into speech, and appeared to us all to have thrown a minor spanner into the smoothly ticking mechanism of our collective expectations.

'There is, you know, Pritchett, in Leviticus, a warning about the birds that you shall not eat. The osprey and the cuckoo are there. But not the nightingale. I think if you look in the Encyclopaedia Britannica, downstairs in the library, you will find mention of Aristophanes. But you would know more about that than me, Pritchett,' he added with heavy irony.

The interrogations were clumsily designed to fill in the gaps of time as we waited for the nightingale. Forrest, rather to my dismay, then turned his attention to me.

'Going to win any prizes, this summer?' he demanded.

The question made me wish that I had Lytton's practical skill or Barnwell's ability to spin a cricket ball with an almost ferocious sharpness. I had enjoyed some success, winning form prizes in two, perhaps three previous years. But as a test of my intelligence, and in order to 'stretch to capacity' my abilities, as Merchant had put it, I had been pushed up an extra form, and had spent the year languishing around ninth or tenth in what was known as Lower Fifth, along with boys of Lytton's and Pritchett's vintage, almost all of them a good deal older than myself. I saw no prospect of winning a prize, and wondered why the Gaffer was asking me.

'I don't know, Sir,' I said. 'I'm in for the reading. Mr Parker thinks I've got a chance.'

'Ah,' he said. 'Well, good luck. A bit of literature, nicely spoken, merits reward. Mm.' He sucked again on his teeth. I wondered if he was drawing forth some perverse fragment of meat, caught during his supper. I felt suddenly hungry.

'Philpotts, of course, was our great prize-winner. Managed six in one year. Quite a star turn he was. Quite a star turn. Yes.' There was a long note of regret in the last word.

'What's he doing now, Sir?' It was Danby who asked, from a bed on the other side of the dormitory.

'Oxford. Think he's reading politics. PPE they call it. He'll never take to it. Difficult to know what'll happen with Philpotts. He never came back to see us. Odd, really, after doing so well. He won't make a politician. Too clever. He's too clever by half.'

There was an introspective tone in the Gaffer's voice, coupled with a hint of regret. He had admired Philpotts when he was head of the house, almost as if he had detected in him that fineness of perception, that discretion, which had played so valuable a part in my own friendship with the older boy whom I had not seen since his departure from Coppinger the previous summer.

The night was warm. Through the open windows came the scent of hay, newly cut in the field below the house. And there were traces of headier perfume from the Gaffer's garden, stocks, and climbing roses under the window.

'You are perhaps conditioned by literature,' said the Gaffer, 'to think of the nightingale's song as sad. That fellow Keats, with his attractive but inaccurate observation about the night being tender, has conditioned us all wrongly. It is of himself, not the—' He stopped suddenly. We all listened.

The flood of sound seemed so close. It started with three resonant, deep chirps; it could have been a blackbird, but for the fullness of the sound, a rounded, bell-like tone that gave to the ordinary notes their magic. The short notes gave way to longer sequences. Like the Gaffer, the nightingale favoured pauses to give effect. And in my mind I visualised the bird treating his voice like an instrument, and reading off the difficult phrase of music, going back over it, the notes perfect from

13

the start, but the fullness, the timing, the exact rise and fall of each phrase, open to variations of perfection. I tried to imagine the breast of the bird filled with this flood of music, the note true, the tone golden, the sustaining of it magical. But it did not work. The song was enhanced by the sensation that it was somehow disembodied. It vibrated for us through the night sky, a proud hammering of sound.

'The indefatigable nightingale will sing you all to sleep,' the Gaffer said. He walked slowly down the room between the beds. His task was finished. 'You will not remember his song. But you will recognise it again. He does not sing for long. April, May, and into June; but after the middle of this month he ceases, so you had best make the most of it.'

Under the pillow my hand held the alarm clock, wrapped in my jersey. I was afraid he would hear it ticking and ask awkward questions. But he passed my bed and went on to the door. 'Goodnight, Sir,' someone said, and there was a chorus of 'goodnights'. He grunted and left us.

We lay in the stillness, the thread of notes running in our ears, cut and measured ribbons of sound: three chirps, a run of single notes, then trills, then silence; then a new variation; then the song again. And so it carried us, as the Gaffer had predicted, into oblivion.

II

My hand closed over the button of the alarm clock before it began to ring, and my finger pressed it home. Anticipation, or some subtle change in the noise, had woken me. It was just after one. During the two hours I had been asleep the moon had come up. Its light outlined the solid construction of the single mullioned window at the end of the room. I slipped out of bed, and crossed over to Lytton. He lay on his side, his mouth slightly open, his breathing regular. I put my hand on his shoulder, and the eye that I could see opened. For a moment it looked puzzled. Then it half closed again and he nodded, almost imperceptibly. I moved silently to Pritchett's bed, which was in the corner, beside the window. His head was under the covers. I put my hand on his shoulder and shook it gently. He stirred, stretched, and his dark hair pushed its way out from the bedclothes followed by his somewhat sallow face. He looked up at me, and then sat up, rubbing his eyes.

'O.K.,' he whispered.

I turned away. Beside him lay the sleeping form of Danby, his arm hanging down from the bed as I had seen it so often, when we had been side by side the previous year. We had been friends then, in the same form. But my own double transition had caused us to drift apart. His interest in music had been sustained, and after his voice broke, and he left the choir, he had concentrated on playing the French horn in the school orchestra. The three of us, Lytton, Pritchett and myself, had considered him as a fourth member of our group; but in the end the idea was dropped.

We dressed silently and quickly. As soon as Lytton was ready he went out, closing the dormitory door softly behind him. I did a slow circuit of all the beds, checking that no one was awake. I stood for a while beside Barnwell's bed, listening to his heavy breathing. Pritchett appeared at my side, a dim figure in the moonlight. He nodded once. Looking back down the long room. I could see that our three beds had presentable enough humps inside them to give a poor but passable imitation of our missing bodies. I followed Pritchett to the door, picking up the small satchel of provisions from beside my bed as I went. We let ourselves out.

We had hidden a fire-escape rope in a boxroom used for cases and trunks. We opened the window and gently lowered the rope out. The end of it fell among border plants, dangerously close to the tall stems of the Gaffer's madonna lilies. It would not do to break them.

Pritchett and I waited in the boxroom, the door slightly open, the dead and dusty air in the room faintly disturbed by the soft breeze from the open window. Then Lytton pushed open the door and came in, followed by Janet. She was stifling her laughter with difficulty, and looked at each of us, a faint glimmering of mischief imagined, rather than perceived, in her dark, inviting eyes. Her hand was resting on Lytton's arm, and in the close atmosphere of the small room it was possible to smell a residue of scent from her body; sweet, warm, inviting, it quickened my reaction to her, my uncertain, vague desire. Tempered by respect for Lytton's prior claims, and fearful in my own innocence of what precisely constituted the kind of 'love' that my sense of longing foreshadowed, I was nevertheless instinctively pleased and proud that she was with us, and aware of the physical responses her lightly-clad body and expressive eyes induced. To say I was 'in love' with her is to suggest fulfilment of a predisposition. More truthfully, I was ready to be 'in love' with her, and waiting for the opportunity.

'Who's first, then?' Lytton asked.

'I'll go first,' I said. 'Then Pritchett. Then Janet. You come last.'

'O.K.'

'Is the rope round the central heating pipe?'

'Yes.'

'And hooked properly?'

'Yes.'

'I'm off, then.'

I swung through the lattice window, lowered myself over the sill, and climbed slowly down the rope. Touching the earth very gently I managed to swing my feet out to the edge of the border, in order not to leave footmarks, and stood on the grass looking back up at the window. The boxroom was between two dormitories on the side of the house on which the moonlight fell, and every movement which Pritchett made as he carefully backed out of the window and on to the ledge was clearly visible. He slid down rather too quickly, and I saw his feet settle firmly into the earth beside a clump of flowerless vegetation. He stepped out of the bed and stood beside me.

16

It was Janet's turn. She had mistakenly, or perhaps provocatively, put on a full-skirted summer dress, and it needed some management as she swung down over the window sill, with Lytton's help, and descended the rope. With her predisposition to laughter and what I imagined would be limited athletic experience, I anticipated a clumsy, if not a disastrous descent. But in fact she was lithe and accomplished, barely touching the earth with her toes, and swinging easily across the bed to stand beside us on the lawn, holding both our arms. Lytton also came down easily. He tucked the rope in beside the wall, and looked carefully at the marks on the bed.

'We must check it all before we climb back,' he said.

'Which way?'

'This is the risky bit. It's now we could easily be seen from the house. We'd best go down through the hayfield, from the corner there.'

'There's nothing to worry about,' Janet said. 'The worst bit was getting out.'

The ground immediately around the house was flat, banked up to counteract the slope of the hill. The banking fell away quite steeply. Then there was metal fencing, and the field of cut hay; beyond it loomed the shadowy darkness of the wood which bordered the school, and through which ran a road.

We crossed the field in silence. The hay had been turned once, and the sweet smell rose from it, mingled with the scent of clover. The moon, which was three-quarters full, and was in the sky ahead of us, above the trees, threw a dark line of shadow along the edge of the wood towards which we hurried. Lytton had taken hold of Janet's hand, and their arms swung together. Pritchett and I were slightly ahead of them. No one spoke. Once under the shadow of the trees we could relax. We walked for a while still in the field, and then came to a gate. Through it there was a path, and this led to the road which ran down through the woods and then out into the countryside surrounding the school land.

Our ideas about why we were out at all, or what we were

going to do, were vague. Together, Lytton, Pritchett and I had planned a route that would bring us down through a small village near the school, and into the valley below where a tiny tributary of the River Evenlode followed a winding, weed-filled course among woodlands made up of willow and silver-leafed poplar and hazel. We imagined that we would wander the brief hours of darkness away; talking, eating biscuits and chocolate, drinking beer and taking occasional swigs of Lemon Hart Rum from a small hip-flask which Lytton had recently begun to carry around with him. It was an innocent, unexciting programme for the warm summer night.

Janet had needed no urging to come with us. She seemed excited to be included, and her frequent, barely stifled bursts of laughter, as we moved further away from the house in the still, warm air of that June night, stirred all of us into thinking the adventure more worthwhile for her presence. Out in the open, under the light of the moon, I was captivated by the warmth and vibrancy of her movements; beneath her slim waist the full skirt of her dress swung easily, accentuating her supple hips and the lightness of her step on the moist, cut hay. She had dark hair, and long eyelashes which lay heavily across her eyes. This did not suggest sleepiness or repose; it in fact had quite the opposite effect, emphasising the lively glow, the look of invitation, which derived from a quite marked sparkle in the iris. She was a well-developed sixteen, an indulged only child.

I often wondered how much the Gaffer knew of all the 'goings on'. Before Lytton, she had been for a time Barnwell's girlfriend. Both Barnwell and Hodges, who was the second senior boy in the house, had shown a healthy interest in her the previous year. But, with the pressure of work for exams in their final year, they had relinquished their claims to her and she had become Lytton's girl instead. Just how this had come about was a puzzle to me, and, I suspected, to Pritchett. Tacit understandings, change-overs, took place; we simply accepted them. In due course, and soon enough as it transpired, my own personal involvement would explain things more precisely. The matter was occasionally discussed, even with Lytton. But none of us wanted it to impinge on, or disturb, our friendship, and we simply accepted that his usurpation of Barnwell was natural enough and would last through the summer term until he left at the end of it.

The debate as to whether Janet should be invited to join us on that night's escapade had been brief enough. I had suggested it myself, for Lytton's benefit ostensibly, though really for my own. Pritchett had supported me; and Lytton had shrugged his shoulders and agreed. If anything, he had been the least enthusiastic of the three of us.

From somewhere Pritchett had obtained a soft cloth cap of an appearance and cut that reminded one of old photographs, of strikers during the twenties and thirties, of coal miners idle outside a pit awaiting news of a disaster. He occasionally wore it around the school, watching matches; it had gone unremarked to begin with, even by Merchant, and it was now accepted that Pritchett could use his own discretion about when he should wear it. He wore it now, and it cast his face in even deeper shadow. He was dark, squat, muscular. His hair, which was black, and without the vestige of a curl or twist in it, was nevertheless unruly, and from the top of his head there stuck up a tuft which no amount of brushing or combing, or the application of water, could govern. It was partly to cover this that he wore the cap. He cultivated an unexpressive exterior. It would be wrong to describe him as lofty; but he was intentionally distant much of the time, with a hard stare for most people, imposing on them the need for patience in getting to know him. This attribute, in marked contrast to my own general approach to my schoolfellows, greatly appealed to me. Pritchett was shorter than I was, but physically stronger; broad, dark, silent, I thought of him as my closest friend of all at that time.

We remained quiet until we reached the trees. Under their shadow we turned, briefly, to look back at the house. Lytton had his arm round Janet's waist, and she was leaning her head on his shoulder. He did something with his other hand which we could not see, standing now as we were behind them, and she slapped it away.

'You're not to *do* that,' she said, giggling.

Lytton swung round. 'Turn away your eyes, you young fellows,' he said.

'No,' Janet said, slipping her arm through his. 'They don't have to. How far are we going to walk?'

'About ten miles,' said Pritchett.

'Maybe more,' I added.

'I *couldn't*,' she said.

'It's O.K. We're going as far as the river, then along, and up through the cornfields behind main school. Is that all right?' Lytton looked down into Janet's eyes. He had spoken with unexpected concern, and both Pritchett and I stared at them with curiosity. She nodded silently; then, in front of us, they kissed. I felt a slight shiver of what I suppose was jealousy. I would have liked to have been in Lytton's place.

Pritchett turned away towards the wood. 'Come on, you lot,' he said, and made a move towards the gate, an iron affair that swung in a limited arc inside a separate loop of fencing.

'Hold on a sec,' Lytton said. 'We'll just have a warmer.' He produced his flask and offered it to Janet. She took a small swig, tilting her head back and gasping as the rum ran down her throat. Then he passed it to me. The rum was hot and sweet. Pritchett said he'd have some later. Lytton took a bigger gulp than the rest of us.

We set off again. The silence of the night seemed to palpitate around us, persuading us to keep our voices down.

'I say, what's happened to Gaffer's nightingale?' I asked.

'His what?' said Lytton.

'The nightingale. What he came and told us to listen for.'

'Seems ages ago. Hardly as if it happened at all.'

Pritchett said: 'I thought he'd never leave.'

'Didn't sound all that much, did it?'

'I don't know,' I said. 'There was something good about it. Have you heard it, Janet?'

20

Pritchett and I were still ahead of the other two, and we were moving slowly along a bridle path which in due course led out on to the road. I half turned to look at her.

'He'll sing again before the night's over. Dad heard him at three one morning.'

'Is he often awake then? Your father?'

'Sometimes.'

'We'll have to be careful.'

We reached the road, and then came to the edge of the wood. From shadowy darkness we emerged into a moonlit landscape through which the empty road ahead of us traced its way down the hill between high hedgerows. The hawthorn blossom had gone over, but honeysuckle and dogrose were in bloom, and the airy tracery of several tall ash trees loomed above us as we walked on down into the flat meadowland through which the stream meandered. We passed a small group of houses, used by the workers on the estate.

Pritchett and I were a good deal further ahead of Janet and Lytton now. The natural relationship between us, a relationship in which I fancied, probably quite wrongly, that I played a dominant role, was suspended that night. Lytton and Janet were clearly and increasingly preoccupied with each other, and Pritchett and I were left to ourselves. In age, Pritchett and Lytton were close, and I was younger; they had been form mates for much longer, and I was a newcomer, one who had the temerity to move up to a class-placing close to both of them, in spite of the obvious handicaps surrounding me, as well as the fact that both of them were clever enough to keep within the first eight or so at the top of a class of almost thirty. No, it was more the fact that my advent into their mild, fairly passive friendship had been largely responsible for the heightened, more self-conscious nature of the relationship which then developed between the three of us. It is a long time ago now, and one's pride in such things fades with the years into a gentle self-indulgence, not untinged by occasionally embarrassing re-collections. Among other things I had persuaded them into the

21

formation of one of those schoolboy societies of three—we called ourselves, I think, the Druids—and I had ensured, though with a certain restraint, that we were generally known as such. I had discovered in a shop in the local town a necktie of a particularly startling design, incorporating a large yellow D on a patterned magenta background, and had persuaded the others to agree to the purchase of three of these symbols of our unity as a group. I had also invented and choreographed a brief music hall sequence of dance steps which very occasionally, our arms linked across each other's shoulders, we would perform as a highly secular version of a druidical ritual, and as an outward sign of our close and exclusive fraternity. The other two had been a bit hesitant at first; but the impact, harmlessly noticeable, had encouraged them into acceptance, and then into further embroidery of the fabric of what inevitably was to be a brief friendship, since Lytton was soon to leave.

By that stage, in the early weeks of the summer term, the third in which the Druids had enjoyed an unbroken existence, we already had a sufficient past history for Pritchett and myself, as we dawdled along the road, the air filled with the scent of the hedgerow flowers, of further fields of cut hay, and of the soft, moist smells of meadow grasses all in flower, to reminisce.

'Are we set for tomorrow's expedition?' Pritchett asked.

'Won't we be too tired?'

'If you adopt that attitude we'll never get out,' Pritchett said. He stared at me severely.

I laughed. 'O.K. We'll do the chapel tomorrow. I borrowed a wrench from the blacksmith. He was quite suspicious. Wants it back on Monday. I said we needed it for a scout test. He doesn't know we're not in the scouts.'

We had discovered what, I suppose, would be self-evident about any Victorian institution built late enough to have a form of central heating installed at the time of construction: that the large waterpipes in the main school buildings were routed through a system of underground passages generally large enough to permit the passage of a young boy crawling and squirming on his belly at worst, but much of the time able to move quite freely on hands and knees, and even in places to stand up. We had discovered that, by the discreet removal of certain metal grilles in the library, we could enter this underground world and open up for ourselves a whole network of passages extending throughout the building. Initially, we made it our own territory on Saturday and Sunday afternoons, when it could be explored with little danger of discovery. In due course we became more daring, and more skilful. We managed to perfect tricks of dress and movement that eliminated, more or less completely, the tell-tale knocking of pipes that would have betrayed us. We attended in this way rehearsals in the school hall, staff meetings, occasional classes, even. The expeditions were carefully organised. We were equipped with boiler suits, torches, even tools. We derived our inspiration, our sense of discipline, our persistence, from the prison camp escape literature which flowed fairly freely at that time. But if the risks were comparable, in their fashion, what we tended to derive from the high points of our exploration were humorous or impressive tidbits of information. On one occasion the three of us, meeting Horridge, a rather pompous boy from another house, on the roadway round the rugby fields, were nerved enough to tell him that we felt his grip on work generally was not firm enough, and we were confident he would in due course be hearing from higher powers. Pritchett himself did the talking, his tone flat and without emotion. It was a calculated risk. We had heard general criticism of Horridge at a staff meeting, and Merchant had said he would speak with him. Sure enough, as he told us later, with both suspicion and increased respect, the headmaster had given him a talking-to.

In our general exploration we had come up against a minor problem: the gap leading into the passages which carried the pipes into the chapel had been bricked up too closely for us to get through. For some time we had simply gone in other directions; but for completeness we had at last decided to dismantle some of the obstructive brickwork and finish our underground travel. We had a vague feeling that we should attend a chapel service under the floor. The expedition was planned for the next day, and Pritchett was clearly not in favour of putting it off simply because we were having a night's outing.

We stopped at a gate leading into the grass field through which the stream flowed. We turned. Up the road, perhaps twenty yards away, Lytton and Janet had also stopped and were clasped in each other's arms. She, it seemed, was hungrily kissing him, her hands drawing his head down towards her mouth. He, somewhat taller, had his arms around her, one between her shoulders, the other in the small of her back. If I had felt, up to then, slight surges of jealousy, they had been ameliorated by the excitement of the night's adventure, by the conversation with Pritchett, by the very softness, the unforgettable scented sweetness of the night air. But at that moment desire quickened. I wanted Janet. I wanted the sultry glow of her dark eyes turned upon mine. I wanted to hold her in my arms, her body pressed against me, my hands touching her back, her waist, her shoulders, even her breasts. Beyond that, my imagination became uncertain and afraid. Desire and fear were evenly mixed; but as Pritchett and I leaned pensively on the gate waiting for them to part and come and join us, I knew that I would replace Lytton as surely as Lytton had replaced Barnwell, and that, in some comparable place, more secret and more private than this encounter of which we were witnesses, and in the not too distant future, I would take her in my arms and kiss her, just as Lytton was now kissing her.

III

Dawn light began to show faintly in the east. We ambled along the winding course of the river, all of us together now, and silent as we picked our heedless, erratic course through the thick grass. We had taken off our shoes, and the three of us had rolled up the bottoms of our grey flannel trousers. Janet held her skirt in her left hand, occasionally raising it where the grass was long and catching Lytton's arm to steady herself across the unfamiliar ground. The heavy, pollen-laden grasses swayed as we passed them, and deposited seed on the moist surface of our skin, on hers more than ours, so that she stopped after a time, and made us stop as well.

'I'll have to go into the water,' she said.

We moved closer to the edge of the stream, looking for a safe place. At some time in the past, long before, there had been a damming of the water close to the point we had reached, and the stream, at no time in its course of any great magnitude, widened out a little before dropping over the edge of a wooden construction, and falling a matter of a foot or so. It was all on a very small scale. Two much-weathered wooden posts constituted the centre of the short wall which held back the water, and embraced in some way the gate mechanism by which the flow could be adjusted. Whether it worked at all is questionable. It was a place off the beaten track, rarely visited. As a small boy in the junior house I had known it, because the junior house at Coppinger was well down the hill and not far from where the stream joined the river Evenlode. And there had been occasions when my father had visited myself and my much older brother, Francis, and we had walked to this river bank, even adopting towards it a certain, sentimental possessiveness. There had even been a cold February Sunday when Philpotts and I had trudged through snow to it, and had walked on the thickly frozen ice, marvelling at the encrusted, thick coils as it curved over the edge of the wood, fixed there in the act and motion of falling.

We stood at the edge looking across the smooth surface. In the moonlight it was possible to see the faint flow and ripples in the centre, where the current moved softly and gently toward the equally faint sound of bubbling water falling its short distance to the level beyond the dam. On the far bank stood a mixed group of trees, mainly willow and silver-leafed poplar. Though there was virtually no wind, the unusually mobile

25

leaves of the latter, with their distinctive variation of shade between the two sides of each leaf, twisted and turned sufficiently to create a distracting curtain of movement, a ghostly shimmer heralding the dawn.

'You'll be covered in grass seed again,' Lytton said, 'before we reach the road. The gate's right over there.' He pointed across towards the east, where a line of bluey-green light was showing above the slopes of the hill.

'I just want to,' she said, and she handed him her sandals to hold.

We stood watching, in silence, as she lifted her skirt and stepped into the dark water.

'Is it cold?' I asked. I was tempted to go in as well, but felt inhibited by the others being there. It was as if, at her silent request, we now constituted an audience for her self-indulgence.

She sighed. 'Mm. It's lovely.' She threw back her head and looked upward at the new faint stars that could compete with the moon. Her dark hair hung down her back. The water was not deep, but gathering her skirt tightly up in her hand she was able to move out until it was above her knees. She was perhaps ten feet away from where the three of us, solemn, completely silent, in an absorbed semi-circle, watched her. Not far away from us there was a field pump of some kind, probably connected with the damming of the stream, and its regular, soulless knocking was the only sound to disturb that moment of absorbed silence.

After a while she turned. She did not look at us, but down at the surface of the water, and her steps were infinitely slow and hesitant, as if she wished to delay for as long as possible her return to us. I was reminded suddenly, forcefully, of 'A Woman Bathing in A Stream', a work familiar to me from many visits to the National Gallery during holidays with my father. As she came out of the water, and was able to slacken her hold on her skirt and change the position of her hands, Janet looked just like Rembrandt's model. She had the same fullness of body, strong thighs, practical hands, full breasts;

26

but it was in her face that the closest association lay: the placid lack of expression gave one the conviction that she was seeing, in the dark surface of the water through which she was slowly finding her way, all the mysteries of her life answered.

At that time the Rembrandt painting was no more than a vividly remembered image. Later in the summer I was to go and look at it in the new light of experience, almost as if to remind myself of that night, and perhaps even with a certain sense of guilt. At that time I was also to discover somewhere the suggestion that it might have been a study for a lost or never completed 'Susanna and the Elders', a piece of information that led me to read the romantic and moving story from the Apocrypha in somewhat emotional circumstances. Yet, in the process of recalling it, the different strands that are evoked include the memory of Janet, the image of the painting, the challenging of Susanna's testimony, all rolled together into a confused equation of feelings, the outcome of that particular summer, feelings which now have for me their most permanent form in the deep surface of Rembrandt's canvas.

She stopped now at the edge of the dark pool. She looked at the three of us. For a moment she appeared nonplussed. 'Come on!' she said. 'We're meant to be having fun, aren't we? You're all so solemn!'

She said it playfully, smiling at each of us in turn, confident of her appeal to us, conscious no doubt of her full, rounded thighs rising from the dark water and showing white in the light of the moon.

'You're right,' said Lytton. 'We're a solemn lot!'

'Damp as these water meadows,' Pritchett said. 'We're as gloomy as Horridge.'

'Not that,' I said. 'Anything but that!'

Janet came out of the water and returned to us. She let fall her skirt, and her hands hung down by her side. We were closely grouped, and she seemed slightly vulnerable in the moment of silence that followed our uncertain attempts to respond to her challenge. We stood on the lowest surface of our immediate world, among the windings of the small stream, its course marked by willow and poplar. The gentle outlines of the hills rose around us, the flat valley curved away between them. We began to walk on again towards a gate that gave on to the narrow road which led back, by another route, to the school. There was a pensive lassitude about all of us as we ambled through the lush, wet grass. We climbed the gate out of the meadow in silence and turned back towards the hill, leaving the stream behind us. The sky to the east was growing lighter, its pale, green-tinged whiteness spreading along the edges of fields and hedgerows. Each of us seemed to be absorbed in thought, and conscious of the oppression of fatigue. Somewhere, a long way off, a solitary cow began bellowing; it was a frantic sound, a series of anguished cries which carried through the dawn stillness in quick successive blasts of sound, and then stopped as suddenly. In pockets of ground along the valley floor mist was rising, faint whitish dashes against the darkness which was now briefly accentuated by an emphatic ribbon of light along the horizon. It was a raw moment, as the sweet softness of that summer night gradually gave way to dawn.

'Who'll be going up to the Festival, Janet?' I asked. 'Have you heard anything?'

'No. I've seen no lists. But it seems likely there'll be three coaches at least.'

'That's a lot. Seems like all the seniors.'

'If they want to,' she said.

I knew Lytton wanted to go; I wasn't sure about Pritchett; but I had been fairly certain that the subject was of general interest. It proved not to be the case, at least then, and we relapsed into silence once again. As we turned back towards the school in the growing light of the coming day I was suddenly infused by a Chekovian enthusiasm for work. It was an unprovoked and untimely reaction. In that moment of extreme tiredness I was unexpectedly, almost inexplicably thrilled by a sense of all there was to know and learn. Though enormously eager for knowledge at that time I was hopelessly undisciplined. Facts, theories, experience, were all equally important. When not exploring under its floors, I spent hours in the library pursuing threads of curiosity through the pages of the encyclopaedia. I learned the names and colours of precious and semi-precious stones, the details and developments of army uniform, the flags of the nations (so many now vanished or changed, certainly from that particular edition which belonged to the period between the wars), the history of venereal disease, the outline of prostitution in the world, the development of the firearm, the building of the Panama Canal. I was frightened by the thought of all that I had already forgotten. Wide rich pastures of knowledge lay before me, and there was within me, as the four of us spread out across the metalled road, a thudding sense of relief that I was not at that time pinned down by my future in the way that Lytton and Pritchett appeared to be. Despite the rapidly growing fatigue which was seizing on my limbs and making me worry about whether or not I would be physically able to haul my body back up the rope and through the house window, there was an invigorating sense of freedom and invincibility which secretly thrilled me.

IV

The part of the road along which we were walking had on one side a broad grass verge, planted with horse chestnut trees, and then a thick hedgerow. On the other side the field began without any fencing, and was thick now with corn. Colours were now emerging from the monochrome to which we had become accustomed. In the hedgerow there was a profusion of pale pink dog roses. Dotted through the thick, stately stems of green corn were scarlet poppies, their colours softened by the grey light filtering through the mist. But the red was becoming increasingly vivid as more distant objects were revealed, and the dawn light strengthened. These were the soft prescriptions for the day, which promised to be warm and was already imbued with the fresh newness of early June. Suddenly, from just above our heads, a barn owl flapped vigorously out from the branches of the tree and flew away towards the wood ahead of us.

Janet gasped, stopped, and caught hold of my arm. She already had her other hand through Lytton's arm, and she now drew both of us towards her in a rapid, instinctive huddle. She was trembling with shock. Her gasp, blowing air from her throat in a cry of wonder and surprise, was a warm, thrilling sound, that seemed to relax the tension and the fatigue. She sought out my hand and pressed it to her side. Through the thin cotton of her summer dress I could feel the warmth of her thigh. I felt a choking sense of desire.

'We must get back,' Lytton said. 'It's almost four. We'll be seen.'

'I haven't the strength to climb the rope,' Pritchett said.

'If you haven't, I haven't,' I added.

'What about me?' said Janet.

'You'll all manage. Don't worry. Our main problem is the evidence we might leave behind us.' We had begun to walk on again, and I still held Janet's hand. It seemed impolite to let it go, and her hold was quite firm and natural. She began to swing her arms, so that I felt a twinge of pity for Pritchett, who was not linked to the three of us. Lytton went on: 'With the heavy dew we'll leave tracks on the lawn, and with the gravel we'll make noises on the path which could wake your father.'

Janet nodded. 'He does sometimes wake in the early morning,' she said. 'But not often. It'll be all right.'

We came back by a slightly different route, approaching the house from the other side. For a few moments we stood under the trees looking across the grass at the large stone bulk of what was, at that time, the most permanent home I had ever known. We had done nothing particularly adventurous. With luck, we would remain undetected. The rapidly growing light made us tremble with anxiety about crossing the final stretch of open ground, at the same time there was a tacit agreement to spin out and savour the last few minutes of our adventure. And then as suddenly as the owl had flown out of the tree startling us all, but now with a different kind of shock, one for me of unbelievable joy at the breathtaking timing of nature, the nightingale began to sing again. In the stillness of first light against a much fainter background of pigeons cooing, a long way off, there burst forth the full, flooding sound for which we had waited some five hours earlier. Pritchett began to say something, and then stopped. We looked at one another. From face to face our glances passed, inspecting the pinched evidence of fatigue, the glow of accomplishment, the warmth of love and friendship, the pleasure in this final, magical reward. One by one we smiled; slow, deep, unforgettable, unvoiced acknowledgements of the fact that experience had locked us together. No matter what followed, we had this. Discovery could not take it away, nor silence the song that even then was being locked up, as I imagined, in each of our memories. The rope, the Gaffer's border, the box-room window, our narrow beds, were all equally inviting and presented no hazard nor threat. Nor was there anything more to say. Lytton led us out from the trees; and in my mind's eye today I see us still, carefree revellers of the night, small happy band come home again, across the dew-laden grass, in the misty light of a summer's dawn.

Chapter Two

I

Lytton told us what to do. He lay for a while inspecting the gap with his torch. Then he pushed the torch through and turned it, so that it shone back towards us, into our eyes. He pulled out a measuring tape and checked height and width.

'It still won't do. It's too small. We'll have to dismantle these bricks on the right.'

I looked at Pritchett. He was lying on his side, just behind Lytton, the expression on his face difficult to discern in the harsh and uneven light from the torch. He nodded.

'Do you want the wrench?'

'Yes.'

'Nothing'll fall in?' I asked.

Lytton tapped on the bricks, spanning with his hand two or three of them. 'These back to here are not holding anything. After that you have a floor beam running across there.'

I looked carefully where he pointed. 'O.K.' I said.

'Give me the wrench.'

As Pritchett passed it forward to Lytton the tip of it hit the pipe. Our bodies pressing down on the metal deadened its echo, but the sound was still enough to make us pause.

'Where exactly are we?' I asked.

'We must be at the entrance to the chapel,' Lytton said. 'That bend ahead of us is right under the steps. When we get round it, and if there's no other blockage like these bricks, there should be a straight run under the bronze grating right up to the altar.' He put the wrench behind the brick at the top and levered it out. The mortar was soft, and it came away easily. There was a pattering of dirt falling into the thick dust where he lay and on to the large round pipes. He passed it back to Pritchett who placed it against the wall behind him.

'There could be another cross wall round the corner, couldn't there?'

'It's possible.'

'What are they there for?'

'Well, it's like this: they knew we'd come one day and they thought they'd make it a bit difficult. Not enough to put us off. Just test our enterprise.'

He passed back another brick, and then several more which Pritchett stacked up carefully. I was holding a second torch pointed at the edge of the wall. I could see the sweat on Lytton's face.

'Hot, isn't it?'

'How are we doing?' Pritchett asked. 'It's quarter to two. Match re-starts at three. We should be there in good time, after what Merchant said at assembly. He'll be out scalp-hunting. He'd love to get us, wouldn't he?'

'We'll be there.'

I said: 'This is the last section, isn't it? We'll have done the whole school after this?'

Lytton grunted. He pulled out more bricks and passed them back. 'That's enough now. We'll get through there.'

'It's funny to think that no one's done this before us. All those years since the piping was put down. It must be eighty or ninety years.' Pritchett ran his hands along the floor beside the pipes. 'This is very old dust,' he said. 'You're very old dust. Useless old, old dust. This is antique dust. Victorian dust. Pure dust.'

'God, I'm tired,' I said. 'We're daft to be doing this after last night. I could just go to sleep in the Victorian dust.'

Lytton paused. 'Lucky we had the free morning. Did you sleep?'

'I dozed,' I said.

'We'll sleep in the sun. We've got to get through. We've got to complete our mission.' He spoke through clenched teeth, and I imagined, in the uncertain torchlight, that he was narrowing his eyes down to thin slits of determination and implacable courage.

We laughed, Pritchett and I.

'Come on,' Lytton said. He moved through the gap and slithered his way towards the bend in the tunnel. Pritchett followed. By the time I started going through Lytton had reached the corner.

'It's clear,' he said. 'All the way. I can see patches of light through the grating. It must lead right up to the communion rail and the altar.' He set off.

We were soon breathless. The pulling and slithering was exhausting, and the chapel seemed very long. At regular intervals there were side passages with pipes running to the radiators, and the humpy, cast-iron joints were difficult to negotiate. Eventually we reached the end. Dimly, through the heavy metal grille-work, we could see the glow of coloured light from the stained glass memorial window set in the east wall. It had been put there by the founder's family, the Llewellyns, just before the First World War.

We were bathed in sweat. In front of the altar itself there was an extra though shallow area of space and we were all able to cram into it. Lytton's face was streaked with dust and sweat, mingled together.

He pulled out his hip flask. 'This calls for a drink,' he said. He offered it to Pritchett.

'Just a minute.' Pritchett pulled from his pocket the rather battered log book which he had insisted on keeping. He turned over the pages to the last entry. Sitting hunched against the wall, the torch resting in the crook of his neck and shoulder, pointing down at the page, he entered the date and then began reading out as he wrote the words down: 'Today dismantled the foundations of the chapel. Nothing fell. Must be a miracle. Thanks be to God. Completed final exploration, and reached the east pole. Amundsen's flag not here. Another miracle. Begin homeward journey tomorrow. Signed——.' He added his name, and then passed the notebook to Lytton, taking the flask from his hand as he did so. Lytton also signed and passed it on to me.

'Pity Oates had to go,' I said.

'Yes. The greedy blighter.'

'What'll we do next?' I looked at our three signatures, and then at the other two. In the dusty stillness there was no answer. There was nothing more to explore. It was as if we sat in some trench or dugout, victims finally of the induced quietism of being able to go no further forward; or, indeed, like the fateful explorers whose enterprise we had mocked, crammed within their antarctic tent, waiting for the end.

Suddenly, we heard the clang of the chapel door. We froze in frightened anticipation. The loud echoing noise was followed by the swift footstep of a woman walking up the aisle. We turned off the torches and lay perfectly still. Lytton carefully pressed in the stopper of his flask and gently put it back inside his pocket. I was near to the grating and peered up through it as the footsteps came closer. There was a sudden shadow, and Mrs Patterson crossed over and out of sight towards the altar. She was carrying flowers. I still had the logbook in my hand. I took out a pencil. I looked at my watch and then wrote: '2.17 Mrs Patterson—flowers.' I passed it back to the others.

Lytton and Pritchett both wrote in the book. When it came back to me Lytton's message was: 'We'll be late for the match. Herr Oberleutnant Merchant will put us in the cooler.' Underneath, Pritchett had added: '*Tant pis*. We'll tunnel our way out.'

We listened as she moved about above our heads. Mrs

35

Patterson was much younger than her husband, coolly beautiful, much admired among the boys. She seemed incongruously linked, in our eyes, with the ageing, slow figure of the most senior housemaster in the school. And he, with his obsession about house cricket and winning cups, with his tattered gown and rounded shoulders, seemed more like her father than her husband.

We heard water being poured and the metallic click of the brass vessels on the marble surface of the altar. It was even possible to catch the faint smell of the flowers themselves. Unconscious of our presence, she continued to move about above our heads. Occasionally she seemed to step back towards the communion rail, which was close above the cavity in which we lay. I assumed she was checking the arrangement for balance. Chapel flowers were done by four or five of the wives of staff, and for all we knew the rivalry may well have been intense. Certainly, the display each week was of a high order, and in June particularly, and in July, the pervasive scent of stock and lilies seemed often to fill the whole vaulted space in which we worshipped.

The chapel door opened again. We heard the slow, distinctive squeak of the heavy lever handle, a foot turning on the step, leather working against stone, and then it closed. In the gloom of our sepulchre under the chapel floor, where even our breathing had to be controlled lest we should betray our presence, the new sequence of sounds had a slightly ominous ring. The step of a man approached down the aisle. He walked with just a faint hint of deference. There was no hard tapping of leather heels. He trod on the balls of his feet. It was not for secrecy; his entrance could not have been silent. He stopped above where we lay. Leaning forward I could just see through the grille that it was Bennett, one of the house tutors. He was standing still, his face tense but expressionless. We waited for some sound from above, but there was silence. It was a silence that pressed us all down; we were prisoners under the weight of it.

Then she said: 'I'm doing the flowers.'

And, after a moment, he said: 'I saw you coming in.'

And she went on: 'They're for tomorrow. I picked them in our own garden.' It was as if she had not heard him.

'They look very well. I love the scent of the stock.'

'It's good this year, isn't it? They are beautiful.'

'Yes,' he said. 'Did you grow them yourself?'

'No,' she replied. 'My husband does the gardening. I just do the picking.'

'I see.'

There was a pause. I was perplexed by the slowness of their conversation; little pauses between each sentence; the stilted nature of what they were saying.

Then, as though he were still talking of the flowers, Bennett said: 'You look so lovely, Francesca, standing there, with that strange brass jug in your hand, all battered and dented. I had to see you.'

'Don't,' she said. 'Please don't.'

I could not understand why they were speaking like actors in a play. I wanted Bennett to stop. It had gone far enough. If it stopped now it would still be all right. I put my hand over my mouth in a quite involuntary gesture, as though it might in some way dissuade him from going on. This was the man who described with such passion that love which one found in books, which threaded together Keats and John Donne and Shakespeare. Then, it flowed smoothly and confidently from his lips; now, this talk of how lovely a living person looked, someone else's wife, was all wrong.

'I had to,' he said.

'No.' Her voice was small, plaintive, a feeble dam thrown swiftly across the tide of his feeling, designed to stem the flow of his passion, but lacking the conviction of her heart. 'No. You mustn't.'

He was not dissuaded.

'Yes,' he said. And there was a fine, deep resonance in the word. I could feel it in the pause that followed, and feel also

37

the compulsion that I imagined was in his eyes as he looked at her across the altar rail. 'I love you, Francesca. I love you.'

'Please,' she said. 'Not here. Not now.'

In my own mind I echoed her words. Please stop, I silently implored him. We didn't come here for this.

'Does it matter? Do you want me not to say it?'

She did not answer. For a while they were silent. I had lost all sense of time, and, though still very frightened, my over-riding reaction was one of appalled curiosity. What would they do next? Out of the corner of my eye I was conscious of the other two, staring, staring. The words I heard plummeted down within me finding still deeper corners of reaction. Whatever my feelings were about Janet, whatever the construction I might put upon Lytton's feelings for her, this, of which we were the entrapped witnesses, was different. Into his declaration, into her frail defence, against all the odds that surrounded them, it seemed that the full passion of life itself was flooding with torrential force.

He spoke again. 'I love you, Francesca. I don't think anything else matters. I don't think where we are, or who we are, or what will happen, or how it will happen, is of any great significance. How I feel, and how you feel, that's what matters!'

'But what about . . . what about . . . oh, why do you? Why?'

Again there was a pause. I was captivated and hypnotised. There was an angry fierceness in the demand and the resistance of their words. Up to that moment, it had seemed to me, love was a soft and sentimental encounter involving the folding of arms and the touching of lips. But now it seemed quite different. Above all else, it was frightening. It was so *big*. Their feelings, Bennett's passion and Mrs Patterson's troubled reaction to it, filled the whole chapel, squeezing out God, vibrating up to the roofbeams, penetrating under the floorboards to crush the three of us against the walls of our tiny dugout like the impact of some vast explosion.

'Where can I see you?' he said urgently. 'We must talk.'

It seemed that he paused like a penitent, awaiting her reply.

38

I wondered, if she declined, would he go down on his knees on the shallow, carpeted step where communicants received the Eucharist.

'All right,' she said. 'All right. I will.'

'This afternoon? This evening?'

'Yes,' she said. 'But we must be careful.'

'Where?'

After a moment or two she said: 'I don't know.'

'The quarry road?'

'All right. Is it safe? When?'

'At five. It will be safe. Everyone will be at the match.'

There was silence for a moment. I did not dare look up, but in the space above us, charged as it was with feeling, I imagined him staring at her, and hoped that perhaps a smile was softening the aggression that had dominated his words. Then he said: 'I'll go through this way. To the staff room.' His steps were heavy and determined now, his heels clashing on the metal grille. He passed directly over our heads. The inner chapel door closed quietly. Mrs Patterson seemed to stand for a moment longer, perhaps contemplating the arrangement of flowers which was now so incidental to her afternoon. Then she turned, and walked quickly down the aisle and out of the chapel.

II

In the stillness of our dusty hideout, after the echo of the clanging door had died away and left us alone, we lay for some moments just staring at one another. None of us knew what to say. Nor was there time, anyway. If we were to get to the match early enough to avoid a row with the headmaster, then we were already under pressure, and when Lytton simply set off down the tunnel once again we both followed, saving our breath for the long and difficult journey back to the library.

The coast was clear when he arrived there, and after the usual precautionary measures we emerged, in our dusty boiler suits, our faces streaked with sweat, our hands grimed with dust and roughened with the surface of brick and stone. We washed and changed, and hid our belongings. Then we left the main school just as the clock struck the first quarter after three.

Even then none of us seemed disposed to talk. We walked quickly down towards the cricket field in the June sunlight, a little apprehensive that Merchant would be there, already checking up on latecomers, and disposed to treat them with heavy retribution. But it was not the case, and we were able to settle ourselves in a favourite place, under the edge of the huge shadow spread by a great elm tree. It grew at one end of the cricket pitch above a grassy bank which formed a natural stand from which to watch the game. The tree's large halo of shade spread downwards to the edge of the smoothly mown grass of the pitch itself, and during the course of the match would travel with increasing speed out towards the fielders and batsmen. To begin with we lay fully in the warm sunshine, squinting against it and adjusting to the even, regular progress of the game as the first of the opposing batsmen played themselves in.

Patterson himself was umpiring, and his tall rather stiff figure with its forward stoop, his weather-beaten face and short grey hair, took on for me now a totally different appearance in the light of what we had heard. Next to the Gaffer himself the most familiar figure to all of us in the school, at Coppinger longer than any other member of the staff, something of an institution, a 'character', he had now become, in addition, the object of our curiosity, our concern, perhaps even the beginnings of pity.

I looked at the others. They were all staring at him.

Pritchett said: 'He looks different, doesn't he?'

'It's funny,' I said. 'I've never really looked at him before. I know what he looks like better than almost anyone. I could imitate his movements. But I've never really looked at him.'

'He's not in the zoo,' Lytton said. 'Poor bugger.'

We sat and stared. We could have been taken for enthusiasts, the way the game absorbed our attention.

40

'It's a good thing he has the cricket,' I said. 'He's all wrapped up in it, isn't he?'

Lytton nodded. 'That and his house.'

Pritchett clenched his fist in front of his mouth. 'You realise what we heard is something no one ever hears? That was really *it*! He just said to her, like that, "I love you! I love you!" Amazing. It was really amazing.' He seemed almost to be convincing himself of the extraordinary nature of what we had heard, and his attempt to express it emphasised for me as well how large the impact had been.

Lytton said: 'People must hear that sort of thing. How do you think men and women discover about it?'

'Well, of course they *hear*. But like that! Under the floor of the chapel, and Mrs Patterson arranging flowers, and him coming in to tell her he loved her! That was really something, wasn't it?'

I had never seen Pritchett so excited. My own feelings were more fearful. I felt overwhelmed. I had a sense of dread at what was revolving around me. It was a vortex of knowledge and experience that did not offer power, only a sense of involvement that worried and perplexed me. Yet with Pritchett it was different. He was excited and tense; his eyes gleamed and his clenched hand shook, barely perceptibly, in front of his face. He wanted to relive the intense experience we had just had, the frightened witnessing of a confrontation which had made most of our other experiences of passion or anger insignificant by comparison. It had changed the whole character of our explorations. Never again could we descend beneath the floors of the school without being conscious of the encounter that now outclassed all our other adventures. Pritchett's reaction partially shaped my own. By contrast, Lytton seemed to be taking the whole thing more coolly. Checking, first the one then the other, I settled for something midway between. Sleepily we lay back in the warm sunshine, letting the muted sounds of the game flow over us.

The cricket match was going moderately well. Patterson was

41

umpiring at the elm-tree end, as it was called, and a much younger man from the other school, with a habit of over-doing his scrutiny of the bowler's footwork, as though suspicious of a 'fast one' being pulled on him, was at the other wicket. The game, which had started at half-past ten in the morning, had been fast and exciting. By lunch the visiting school had scored over a hundred for six wickets, but had then been skittled out in the first half-hour of the afternoon for a total of 137. We had lost an early wicket, but Hannay, in spite of his bad hand, was settling in to what promised to be a good innings. Both their bowlers, at that point, were fast, one of them exceptionally so. But already our own captain had managed to turn three balls in a single over for fours, and his score now stood at 28.

It was difficult to concentrate on the game, but necessary after Merchant's harangue on the subject. We all dozed fitfully, surreptitious about the sleep we all craved, aware of the presence of the headmaster, who had arrived and was standing near the pavilion. His recent reminder to the whole school that boys should constitute an intelligent and helpful audience for the school team acted as a restraint on both our freedom of conversation and our freedom to sleep.

'I meant to ask,' Pritchett said. 'Did you fellows take a look at the flower bed?'

'Yes. It's O.K.'

'I half-expected the Gaffer'd be waiting for us last night.'

Lytton laughed. 'Waving a shotgun, I suppose, and shouting, what have you done with my daughter?'

'Yea. Something like that.'

Pritchett rolled over on to his back and covered his eyes. 'God, I wish I could just sleep and sleep,' he said. 'Out of windows, down walls, under floors, over pipes, demolishing foundations, wading in rivers, roaming country roads in the moonlight. You know, we do lead exciting lives. The strain will be too much for us.'

'I want to sleep,' Lytton said. He had sat up, and was looking out at the game. He turned briefly, and I noticed how red his eyes were. My own felt leaden.

After a pause I said to them both: 'It was sacrilege, wasn't it?'

Pritchett, lying on the grass beside me, opened his eyes. 'Them? Or us?'

'Both.'

'Equal?'

'No.'

'Can sacrilege be bad and not so bad? Or is it just what it is?' He was silent.

Lytton said: 'What do you think about the Festival? Will we get to it?'

'I rather agree with what Janet said last night,' Pritchett said. 'There are better ways of spending one's time in London than mooching round the Dome of Discovery. I shan't be pushed if I don't get on the trip.'

The Festival of Britain was much talked of at the time. It had been open for just over a month, and features on it in the picture magazines like *John Bull, Everybody's, Picture Post* and *The Illustrated,* all of which we read avidly, were numerous. At least two school trips were planned, one of them for fifth formers like ourselves, and there was considerable anticipation about it since the general, though, as it turned out, misinformed, view was that numbers would be strictly limited. Lytton wanted to go very much. He had kept a collection of newspaper clippings right from the start, among them a grim and forbidding photograph of the South Bank site in early 1949, when it consisted of mounds of rubble, old warehouses and the shot tower seen through blank mist or smoke. And he had followed the details on every aspect of it. He was a positive mine of information. He knew the internal construction of the Skylon, the quantities of material that had been used for the Dome, and an accumulation of other information that seemed to me excessive, even for a putative engineer.

For me, the interest was much more limited. The Festival symbol now seems thin, unsubtle, self-consciously brave; the

43

whole episode, to many people, in the perspective of time and history, something of a mistake. Yet to me, then, lying under the clear blue sky of that Saturday afternoon in June, a sky in which I had seen massed aircraft towing troop-laden gliders off to Europe to finish the war, a sky which had subsequently held, at great height, the silvery grandeur of the huge American military planes which followed, the Festival represented a point of focus that somehow mattered. The very arbitrary fact of repeating a Victorian event a century later failed to dislodge the sense of occasion. The King's illness in 1949, his death less than a year after the summer events of which I now write, even the Coronation, which was to be intimately tied up with my own last year at Coppinger, the youthful face of Britannia, helmeted head held high, lips parted in anticipation, bravely coloured in blue and red, in white and black, and remembered, by me, above all in the form of a flag, waving and battling in the inclement breezes of Britain's uncertain recovery, all seem to me now a backdrop to the events at that time.

I wanted to go to the Festival. In a sense it was an unnecessary desire. For Lytton, who lived in Manchester, there was some reason. For me, with London at my feet during the holidays, much less.

'I have a proposal to make,' Pritchett said.

'Mm? An adjournment? Swigs of Lytton's excellent rum in the gym?'

'Well, perhaps that also.'

'Only the dregs are left,' Lytton murmured.

'Pay attention, both of you,' Pritchett said. He still lay on his back, squinting up into the sunlight. He had a long piece of timothy-grass in his hand from which he had stripped the seed, and he was twisting it and moving it in front of his eyes. 'I want to say something to you.' He paused and sucked his teeth in a passable imitation of the Gaffer. 'In the light of today's experience I feel that we must face up to the challenge of what we have so far accomplished, and extend our targets for the future a little further still.'

44

Lytton yawned and turned bleary eyes towards him. 'What have you in mind?'

'Well, this. I think that, as another item to be recorded in the annals of the Druids, we should attend chapel on Prize Day underneath the floor.'

He was silent, and went on twisting the stem of grass. Lytton sucked his teeth in imitation of the Gaffer and then said, 'Ah!'

I looked at Pritchett. 'Do you mean it?'

'What do you think?'

'I think you are preposterous. I think the suggestion is quite outrageous. But I rather like it.'

Lytton's response was practical. Looking out over the cricket pitch, he said: 'Have you anyone coming?'

'No,' I said.

'Have you, Pritzer?'

'No.'

'Would we be missed?'

'It's possible.'

'There's never enough room, with parents and visitors. Some boys have to stay outside each year.'

'Suppose we're on duty, meeting people?'

'We'll just skip off.'

I looked across at Lytton. He was staring out over the field. The bowler at the far end had been changed. A left-hander with a good spin was sending down well-paced deliveries which seemed to be worrying Hannay. In the intervals he rested his injured hand on his shoulder. The score was 42, with still only one wicket down.

I asked Lytton: 'What do you think?'

'I quite like it,' he said. 'It's a good scheme.'

'We'd have to plan it carefully, wouldn't we?'

'Would it be worth it?'

'What do you mean, worth it?'

'The risk. The trouble if we got caught.'

I looked at his sleepy profile. I was conscious of my own fatigue, almost numbing now in its effects; and yet I surveyed him carefully, with that intensity, that heightening of speculation or perception that sometimes comes with exhaustion. His jaw was slack, the muscles in his face loose, the lids of his eyes half-covering the irises. His whole visage seemed suddenly unformed, transitional, unfamiliar. Without really taking my eyes off him I could perceive and follow the slow progress of the game. The bowler ran up to the wicket and delivered the last ball of his over, a well-paced leg-break which Hannay played back. The visiting umpire called, 'Over!' Patterson stalked in to the wicket, head forward, hands plunged deeply into the pockets of his white coat searching for the little red barrels with which he counted the balls in the overs. Out of the corner of my eye I could measure these movements; yet Lytton, staring straight at the field, seemed to be responding to none of them. His eyes, fatigued, but also I thought containing hints of regret, were fixed on things much further off. Across the pitch and the figures in white, across the hedgerows and the gently sloping fields of green unripened corn that fell away into the valley and then rose again to the line of the horizon, across that as well, beyond the distant village with its tall church tower set against the blue, his gaze seemed to travel in unrewarded pursuits of certainty and future prospects.

Impulsively I asked him, 'Are you sad to be leaving?'

'In a way.'

'Will you come back?'

'Dunno.'

He lay back suddenly on the grass and covered his eyes. 'I think we'll do it,' he said. 'I think we'll do it.'

'Good,' said Pritchett.

I looked at them both as they lay now, side by side, their eyes closed against the bright sunlight that fell on their faces. Pritchett had stuck the grass into his mouth, and it moved in the air above his face as he chewed the end. I felt a comfortable, reassuring companionship with them. What they decided was enough. I relaxed in the comfort of our preordained agreement and lay back, content, in the drowsy heat of the afternoon.

III

Hannay hit a magnificent six. Then he was bowled. He came out from the wicket in obvious pain, and was hugely applauded, not so much for his score, a modest 38, as for his courage. Then Barnwell was caught out and Hodges went in.

It was Barnwell who came over to me, shortly after he had returned to the pavilion. 'The Head wants you.'

'Me?' I said.

'Yes. You. He's sitting up by the pavilion.'

I looked at the others. Both of them had sat up. They did so rather cautiously, alert to the possibility that Merchant might be watching the three of us, alert also to the hint of danger in the air. I had a feeling of some dread. Why *me*? Someone must have seen us out the previous night. After me, he would cross-examine Lytton and then Pritchett. But to be the *first*? It looked extremely bad.

Lytton stared sternly across at me as I began to get up. 'What have you been up to, then, my boy?' he said. 'A circuit of the cricket pitch for you. Worse than a beating any day. Moral difficulties, perhaps?'

Pritchett, too, was watching me. The grass in his mouth was shorter, and a bit bent. He threw it away. 'I'd come clean about the whole thing. Tell him the difficulties you're having, those unmentionable desires.' He spoke the last two words with exaggerated unction. 'Tell him you need his help. He'll respond magnificently.' He laughed, but both of them were nervous. Barnwell had already turned away and, unwillingly, I prepared to follow him.

Quite quietly Lytton said: 'It'll be something quite different. There was no possibility of our being seen. Remember that.'

I was comforted by his confidence, and by Pritchett nodding agreement, as I turned away from them. Merchant was no longer at the pavilion. He had walked a little away from it, and was standing looking out at the field, though I imagined, in the hunch of his shoulders inside the blue blazer he always wore for sporting functions, a certain degree of impatience that I had not presented myself with greater immediacy.

I ran across the few yards from the pavilion. 'You sent for me, Sir?'

He nodded, but affected to be concentrating on some detail of the game. It seemed to be Hodges' laconic inspection of the field that held Merchant's attention, rather than myself. Abruptly the headmaster turned and walked away on the edge of the field's perimeter. I followed. He had his hands behind his back. My heart sank still further. This was a ritual much favoured by him, intensely disliked by the boys; he contrived the public display of what was essentially a private encounter.

It was invariably the subject of later cross-examination and speculation by the boys, often of a ribald kind, occasionally hurtful, always embarrassing.

He cleared his throat, putting up his left hand towards his mouth. An affected gesture, I thought, eyeing his signet ring.

'How are things at home?' he asked.

'All right, Sir.'

'Your father married again, didn't he?'

'Yes, Sir. Just over a year ago.'

'Do you get on? With your stepmother, I mean?'

I paused before answering. I resented the clinical approach. He assumed a right to information which I did not think was justified, yet had not the courage to challenge. He glanced at me.

'Yes,' I said. 'I do.'

It was a very imperfect approximation to the truth, and I heard in the tone of my own voice the lack of conviction which may have been my subconscious invitation to Merchant to probe deeper.

'You know you can speak quite freely with me. I am used to the difficulties you boys face. I have been through it all many times.' Behind his back he gently raised one hand from the

48

palm of the other, in which it had been clasped, and slapped it back again, several times. It was a familiar if self-conscious gesture. Merchant had fine expressive hands which he kept beautifully, and of which he was sensibly proud. Having seen so many other boys, on other occasions, walking the same circuit, some to be told they were going to be made prefects, some to reprimanded about their work, some to be informed of imminent punishment—a fearful prelude to a painful act—I was relieved that in my case it was, so far, none of these things; nor did it appear that it was the previous night's episode.

After an appropriate pause, denoting a quite unreal self-examination about the extent to which I could reveal the state of my relationship with my stepmother, I said: 'I don't really get on all that well with her, Sir. It's nothing in particular. She just doesn't seem to want me around.'

'Nothing more than that?'

'Well, there do seem to be rows between them when I'm at home.'

'And when you're not?'

'I don't really know.'

We slowly circuited about a quarter of the cricket field, then stopped and turned to watch. In general, spectators tended to stay on the pavilion side. Some episode in the past, perhaps some minor infraction of school rules, had led to this concentration of support, leaving the rest of the grass round the boundary fairly deserted, and we were now in a position to see, beyond the game itself, the figures sitting and lying on the bank which led up to the pavilion. Merchant scanned them with his keen, pale-blue eyes, coming to rest eventually on the green shadows of the elm tree, close to which I could see the prone figures of Lytton and Pritchett, no doubt too tired to maintain any further vigil over Merchant and myself. He seemed about to refer to them, but thought better of it and resumed walking.

'What about your father?' he asked. 'Has his marrying again made things difficult for either of you?'

49

It was one of the curious contradictions at Coppinger that, while the boys avoided discussing their home life with one another unless they were the closest friends, an approach generally followed by members of the Staff, the headmaster felt no such constraint. He believed himself to be the guardian, not only of their moral but of their social, welfare as well. The nature of the school permitted this sharp contrast in attitude, and there were boys who resented it. I did myself. I felt it was an abuse of his position for Merchant to feel that he could so intrude. But I did not have the courage to tell him so. In my experience Philpotts was the only boy ever to have done so. He had, in his last year, recounted to me details of a similar inquisition, and in unemotional phrases had told me that his reply to Merchant had simply been that he did not wish to discuss the matter. 'Do the same yourself, if it ever happens,' he advised.

I could not, however. I lacked the determination, the confidence. I did not wish to answer his questions. They were painful, summoning up recollections that I would have liked to leave dormant. I looked down at the ground.

'I'll tell you why I'm asking these questions,' Merchant said, and his voice took on a more practical, less interrogative tone. 'You are being considered for the Porphyry Scholarship. This is its fourth year. You may know a little about it. Your friend, Philpotts, was awarded it one year, I think it was the first time. Your brother would have received it had he stayed on. Mr Porphyry is one of the newer trustees, in business in London, a City Man.' Merchant pronounced the last phrase on a slight note of triumph, as if it categorised, finally, Porphyry and his like.

I listened attentively, pacing the smooth green grass at Merchant's side, wondering to myself what would come next, relieved at the new direction. I had put on an expression of serious and intelligent concentration. I still felt a bit bewildered at why the choice had fallen on me, but the feeling was accompanied by a pleasurable sense of my own importance.

'What do you know of the scholarship?'

'It's, um, it's given if you have some particular home problem, isn't it?'

'Yes. We don't highlight that aspect. After all, the boys here could all, in a general sense, qualify. But the scholarship, which involves some travel and other help from Mr Porphyry during holiday time, is given to a senior boy, usually older than you, but in any case a fifth or sixth former. We endeavour to choose someone facing difficulties at home who would benefit, during the holidays, from an alternative set of activities.'

I felt what I suppose Merchant would have wanted me to feel, gratitude at the school's capacity to detect, in my life, the needs which would nominate me as a candidate, and these offset the sense of humility induced by his earlier questions. I wondered whether I was making the appropriate responses. Should I speak? Should I remain silent? Did I just continue to pace the edge of the cricket field at Merchant's side, waiting for more information, possibly for more questions? Or would it be better if I expressed my gratitude? The trouble with Merchant was that he never made clear what attitude one was to adopt. He had so many aspects, so many sides, so many different motivations, that a natural response was ruled out, automatically, from the start of one's contact with him. One's face became tired trying out expressions in order to find one that suited.

Does it seem strange, this talk of attitudes and responses? There were others who felt the same as I did. It was a combination of forces acting upon us. It was Merchant himself, it was the school, but above all it was the raw material of our own backgrounds, the secretive beatings of our bruised hearts. We had to protect our uncertain dignity and self-respect from the intrusiveness of an institution that knew a great deal about us, and would not have been able to function otherwise. I confess that I have lived much of my life curiously uncertain just what face to wear, what feelings to have, what meaning and emphasis to give to words. Like an actor defining his way towards the

51

realisation of a difficult and subtle part in a drama, it seemed we were conditioned to see a set of different available presentations of ourselves. Perhaps this is a common state of mind in the young. Perhaps I am hopelessly out of touch with the inner feelings of those around me then, and of the companions of my youth with whom I have had the opportunity to talk since. But uncertainty was a badge we all wore. It came in multiple forms. And as the collector puts away, but never really forgets, the drawers and cabinets of badges, stamps, coins, mementoes of the past, which acquire their indelible quality upon some facet of the mind's surface by virtue of the passion and intensity with which they are acquired, so did we, did I, store up with equal passion and retain as an essential, even a highly prized attribute, what must seem to many people a defect: the instability of emotional response, the desire to feel what was expected, the capacity always to dissimulate.

It was, in part, a response to Merchant's power over us. I may appear to over-dramatise just how tightly drawn were the threads of tension that surrounded encounters with him. The nature of power is understood first by most of us at school, more often in our relationships with other boys, and against a background of judicial restraints exercised by teachers. But at Coppinger its shape was that of a pyramid, with Merchant at the apex, exercising over us all—perhaps over the staff as well— a measure of control that seemed then natural and necessary enough, but appears now, looking back, to have been unnecessarily draconian. It was not, at that time, directed against us. But we were, in time, to be witnesses of its force, and we had experienced enough of it in the past to have developed caution and circumspection.

In a struggle to get back to a reality that would at least mean something to me, I began to thank him.

He stopped me. 'It would be premature to assume the scholarship is yours. It is normal practice to put up three or four names—this year there are three—but the final choice is left, of course, to Mr Porphyry. He does it from the reports which we make on the boys in question, and the winner's first meeting with him is on Prize Day, when the decision has been made and the name, along with other prize-winners, is announced.'

I nodded, but said no more. I felt general relief. There were no misdemeanours which Merchant might hold against me; there were no confidences I was being asked to break; the tenor of our discussion, the first I had had with the headmaster during my lower fifth year, was benevolent.

We were rounding the end of the pitch, and approaching, from the other side, the great bulk of the elm tree which shadowed the bank.

Merchant suddenly said: 'You are much in the company of Lytton and Pritchett, aren't you?'

'They're my best friends, Sir.'

'Bit exclusive, aren't you? The three of you?'

'I don't think so, Sir.'

'Call yourselves something odd? Druids, is it?'

I sniggered in slight embarrassment. 'It's just a name, Sir. A bit of fun.'

'A bit of fun, eh?' He stopped. We were in the shade of the tree. A pathway led away from the cricket field and up towards the school offices, and it was clear that Merchant was going off to deal with administrative matters. 'Well, you can go back to your "bit of fun". Tell it, collectively, and from me, to pay more attention to the game.'

IV

Merchant had opened up the recollections, all too close, of the holidays only recently ended, and of what lay in store for me at the end of that summer term. In spite of all that I have said, in reality I was faced with a form of certainty for the first time in my life, a certainty of place and of people. For years I had enjoyed a nomadic existence with my father. It had been the instability in his life that had qualified me for a place at Coppinger. It had promised to end in a way highly acceptable to myself some two years before when his marriage to Ursula had seemed certain. But then, instead, he had married Laurie. He had been offered the choice of two worlds, and in my eyes had chosen wrongly. After the shock I settled down to Laurie's solid, pragmatic management of his affairs and of himself. In so far as I formed any part of that, it was a small part. Though it is a romantic point of view that fails to take into account the hardships, I looked back nostalgically at the infinite variety of life with my father before his marriage. I suppose there was, against Laurie, a feeling of jealousy, a rivalry between us for his attention, his affection. It replaced the earlier rage and anger, accompanying that deep sense of loss when he had chosen her instead of Ursula, the woman in his life on whom, once, I had foolishly pinned too much expectation of happiness.

With time this had faded. The bruising had healed. I had learnt to live with them. I was, as Ursula had once predicted, growing away from my father; I was older and more independent. Even so, there was a certain tension between us. And I suspected, from the most recent holiday, that he felt it too and had expressed it in his usual violent, passionate way. There had been rows; there had been some heavy drinking; I had found it awkward and unpleasant. And I no longer looked forward with untroubled expectation to holidays which had once seemed the Atlantis of perfection, giving purpose and direction to my life at school. A reversal was taking place. The balance was becoming more even. The lesson was being learnt, that the compass needle has two ends, that its movement is not dictated by the North Pole only, but that it lies in a field of forces in which south and north and all that is gathered between operates upon every swing and shudder of movement.

The Porphyry Scholarship had loomed up out of nowhere, adding itself to the field of forces. It had not once occurred to me that I was in a position to qualify for it. And now it was being held out as a distinct possibility, offering an escape which

I longed for much more firmly than I had suggested to Merchant. The irony was that there was absolutely nothing I could do about it. It was not there to be won. It was Mr Porphyry's gift; and though Merchant had narrowed the choice down to three of us (I would learn, soon enough, the names of my rivals, through school gossip), the final choice lay in other hands.

If one sought to isolate some ultimate barometer of happiness it would derive from the sense in one's life of being watched over. Withdraw that, and the recipe is there for despair, desperation, the final freezing of the heart. It is a sense that fluctuates with time and circumstance. Blissful periods can pass without it. But inescapably it jogs and nudges, pushes, intrudes, interferes, governs. We become what others behold us to be. As a circumstance of life it is to be found in its most concentrated and most obvious form when we are at school. And, if this is generally true, it was given added force at Coppinger by virtue of that element of welfare which surrounded the other forms of concern exercised towards the boys. Merchant, Forrest, Patterson, Parker, other members of the staff, knew us on a variety of different planes, one of which was directly concerned with the most private aspects of our generally troubled lives, and I puzzled afresh at what exchanges there might have been between my housemaster and the Head, between him and my form-master, to lead to the prospect of the Porphyry Scholarship.

I puzzled also at an even more shadowy doubt hanging over me. I tried hard to remember what Philpotts had said about the scholarship two years before. There had been something unsatisfactory about it, some reservation which provoked in him brief words of disdain and then the dismissal of the whole subject into the vacuum of silence. Yet I could not remember the details. What had been wrong with the freedom it seemed to offer? And what about Porphyry himself? I tried, without much success, to remember him from among the trustees whom we saw, really only once during the year, on Prize Day. It was true they came down to Coppinger more frequently than that, and took seriously the governing of the school and the quite extensive estates left in their charge by the Llewellyn family. But they were accessible to staff, boys and parents only at the prize-giving ceremony, which was still some six or seven weeks away. And, even then, as people they occupied a lofty and distant territory.

After Merchant had left me, and with firm decisive steps had stalked away towards the school offices with his hands behind his back, his angular head, which always seemed slightly too large for his body, nodding, though almost imperceptibly, over some new problem, I turned in a mood of bewilderment towards the declining sun, to rejoin the others.

I did not do as Merchant had instructed me. Both Pritchett and Lytton were laid out flat on their backs, and I suspected that they were asleep. I was slightly annoyed, and contemplated waking them. But from a desire to give myself more time to think I decided against it and sat down on the grass higher up the bank, a yard or two from where they lay.

Beyond, further along towards the pavilion, boys were still watching. Because of Merchant's departure and with the generally successful progress of the game, which had us by then within sight of victory, and with at least five wickets in hand, the attitudes were becoming more relaxed. One of the batsmen hit an almighty swipe at the ball, and it climbed up and up. It looked a certain six, but the length was short, and on the far boundary one of the opposing team, running hard into the sun, made a fine catch. Our batsman stood in the middle of the wicket and smiled ruefully for a moment before walking out. The team clapped him; the boys cheered.

Waves of fatigue invaded my senses, and I found it impossible to pursue any constructive thought about anything. Instead, I surrendered to the warmth of the sun and the close succession of images and recollections and possibilities that crowded in upon me from the events of the past night and day. I was overwhelmed by the wealth of experience and opportunity spread out before me. I had prepared in my mind what I would say to Lytton and Pritchett, and was about to nudge them—it would soon be time to go for tea anyway—when I noticed Janet, over towards the pavilion, talking with Mrs Patterson. The afternoon sun was behind them, and through the thin, flower-patterned material of Janet's summer dress it was possible to see the outline of her thighs. It reawakened my desire for her. Through half-closed eyelids I gazed at the two of them. In contrast with Janet, Mrs Patterson was more discreet in her dress; knowingly perhaps—she had been a housemaster's wife for several years—her cream-coloured, pleated skirt was opaque. She wore a blue and cream patterned blouse and brown shoes, and her glossy black hair shone in the sunlight. She looked beautiful, her eyes glowing and darkly lustrous. She was listening to Janet talking, and every so often she glanced across at the game in a way that seemed faintly nervous. Her husband had been umpiring throughout the afternoon. His hair was more ruffled, his step slower, but he would stay to the end, of that there was no doubt. I looked at my watch. It was twenty minutes to five. I suddenly realised she was on her way to meet Bennett, and had come to check on the progress of the game. I felt an uneasy prickle of involvement, nervous, on her behalf, that she might be late for the appointment. I had an absurd and involuntary urge to warn Janet not to delay her.

Reluctant to take my eyes off them I nevertheless looked out at the wicket, and pretended a keen interest in the closing stages of the game. I could not sustain it, however, and surreptitiously looked back at the two women. The youthful vitality of the older one, combined with the rich seasoning of time—she had a child of twelve—gave me an odd and disturbing sense of its passage: from Janet, who was about sixteen, through Mrs Patterson, who must have been in her mid-thirties, to her husband more than twenty years older, there existed a spanning of relationships not unlike the one I had experienced, and lost, in the case of my father, Ursula and her niece Babette. And it made me aware of the barriers which age lays down between

57

us. In our youth they are barriers of longing: we hunger for the knowledge, the experience, and the freedom; in our maturity they are barriers of regret: we hunger for the innocence, the energy, and the lost opportunities.

Janet turned and glanced over towards me. She smiled and waved; and Mrs Patterson smiled also, glancing at her. Did she suspect more than at that time existed between us? I hoped so. Did she secretly revel in the uncomplicated innocence of our feelings? I questioned the innocence, but hoped for that complicity. Then she left, turning away towards the pavilion. I consulted my watch again, and decided that she would be just in time for her appointment. Janet walked up the path towards me. I got up and went over to meet her. I had this sudden wish to be alone with her. She seemed to share it, for when she spoke it was softly.

'How do you feel? I envy those two over there. Are they asleep?'

'I'm all right,' I said. 'It couldn't have been a better night to do it. Merchant's been easy on the whole school, letting us just watch the match. What about you?'

She groaned. 'I had to go to school. It was terrible. I kept dropping off. I can't think what they must have thought of me.'

'It was great fun, wasn't it?'

'Yes. Super.'

'Would you do it again?'

She looked puzzled at first, and then smiled at me, a mischievous gleam in her eyes. 'I don't think I would, like that. Not in a group.'

'How, then?'

'Well,' she laughed and looked down. 'Like, in a group, it's a bit . . . well, a bit uneven.'

'Mm,' I said. 'You're right.' I paused, feeling awkward.

'It's not that I wouldn't—with all of you.' Then she paused again.

'You think, if there were other girls?' I asked. 'Could we go out again?'

'Well. It's a possibility.' She did not seem to view it with a great deal of enthusiasm. Her tone invited me to go on, to explore other possibilities.

'But there aren't any other girls around,' I said.

She looked at me, her eyes serious and direct, her features soft and uncertainly set in an expression that was vaguely one of appeal, possibly doubt. I felt instinctively that she was assessing me, and it emphasised the awkward gap in our conversation, the equally awkward situation of the two of us standing there, face to face, talking. It would not do to stay together too long. Boys, who must anyway have noticed, might even voice, in that peculiar schoolboy tone designed to be overheard, comments of an embarrassing kind. And this provoked the urge to curtail the conversation. Yet at the same time I was mesmerised. I felt a certain hammering of desire, a wish to resolve, by some kind of statement, question, promise, request, the feelings I had for her.

'Perhaps it should just be the two of us,' she said.

'You and me?' I blurted out. Then I felt a flush coming to my cheeks. I was short of breath.

She smiled and nodded. I felt I had been purposely led to this point by her. But I did not mind. 'I must go,' she said. 'Seems we've won. And Hodges did well. He's getting fat, isn't he?' She turned, and then paused. 'See you tonight, then?'

Chapter Three

I

I was drawn to Lytton by my feelings for Janet. He seemed to hold the key to an understanding of her, and this I wanted before I, in my turn, embarked upon an exploration of what lay behind the invitation in her eyes and words, that afternoon. I imagined myself in love with her. It was not difficult, just as it is not difficult now to dismiss those feelings as no more than an adolescent if heady desire.

Nor was it difficult at the time to confide in the very person with whom I was in rivalry. Though it may seem extraordinary it is the truth. I turned to Lytton. He knew what I was about, and seemed partly to welcome it. He was more sophisticated. His concern was for me, rather than for Janet. In retrospect the whole sequence of events has a callousness which can barely be excused by youth's inexperience, a selfishness which our elders tell us is a mark of that age. In reality it is always present; it is dissimulation we learn. And what we remember are the clumsy and awkward events by which the lessons are conveyed. But just then the conjunction of opportunity and feelings pushed aside all else and set in motion the gratification of desire.

We all saw Janet and talked with her that evening. There were veiled references to the previous night's escapade. But we were cautious in the presence of other senior boys in the house.

Being Saturday, we were free to play gramophone records and we indulged in a seemingly endless repetition of what was then popular, the agonising of Frankie Laine or Johnny Ray. At that stage her words, 'See you tonight, then?' took on no greater significance than this collective encounter which the Forrests permitted at the weekend.

It was some days later, walking with Lytton during a school break between classes—Pritchett had been held back for some reason—that I asked him what he felt about her.

'She's great,' he said. 'She's really good fun.'

'She gets on with everyone, doesn't she?'

'Why not? She's lucky. Has us all liking her.'

'But what do *you* feel? I mean, with you, it's . . . it's kind of different.'

He laughed blandly. 'It's good being with her.' He shrugged. 'I don't feel anything special. Except her!'

'But when you kiss her—?' I asked. I wanted the question to carry with it the weight and volume of my other, more extensive queries. Yet having spoken I had the sense of my own words hanging too lightly in the air, and lacking the more intense meaning that lay behind them.

He laughed again. It was friendly and good-natured. He was not in any way attempting to tease or bewilder me. 'When I kiss her . . .' he said. He looked at me, his hands outspread, pausing, and now smiling with an expression in his eyes of fond recollection. 'When I kiss her, I kiss her.'

'And more?' I asked.

'Sometimes,' he said.

'Do you feel she's your girl?' I asked.

'The way Pamela was?'

I had to think who Pamela was. Pausing, I remembered, and the recollection made me wince slightly. Pamela had been a girl at school in Wales with whom Lytton for a time had exchanged letters and photographs. Most of these he had shown to me. Quite early on he had requested, from Pamela, among the photographs and endearments which she seemed ready to supply, another girl, as well, for me. Promptly there had come back a ready-made object for my adolescent affection, Tessa. She was Pamela's best friend. A parallel series of letters, similarly intense, highly charged, and probably quite vapid, were exchanged, together with photographs and descriptive information. We had almost begun the process of finding a third girl who could correspond with Pritchett, when the initial inspiration began to dry up through the difficulty of finding time to write letters, and things to say in them. The intensity lay in the feelings rather than the words, and the feelings did not last.

'No,' he said, shortly. 'It's not like Pamela. That was pretty hopeless, anyway. So was your girl, what was her name? Janet is . . . is just, well, Janet. She likes to snog.'

It was my turn to laugh, partly to conceal the sense of shock at Lytton's rating of Janet, partly to give myself the chance to adjust to a concept of her that was clearly more fleshly than I had considered up to that point. I knew I wanted her; I did not know how. Perhaps I laughed immoderately, because Lytton stared at me.

'Is she good?' I asked, eventually.

'As a matter of fact, yes. But what's so funny?'

I could not say to him that I was shocked. I did not want to indulge in any examination of deeper feelings, which were clearly not there in Lytton's case.

'I dunno.'

We were ambling across the grass playing fields in front of the Main School. Away on the edge was a line of horse chestnut trees, their creamy white cone-shaped flowers in full bloom. The organised physical exercise which took place during breaktime in winter, in order to work up circulation and avoid the generally high level of malingering, was abandoned in the summer, and across the fresh green grass were scattered groups of boys. Lytton and I had turned back towards Main School, and we could see Pritchett in the distance.

Lytton said: 'Janet's keen on you.'

'Is she?'

'As if you didn't know.'

'Do you mind?'

He didn't bother to answer. He just shook his head. We walked side by side towards Pritchett.

'I'm keen on her,' I said. 'I like her a lot.'

'That's good, then, isn't it?'

'Will we go out again at night?'

He shrugged.

I was not fully satisfied with Lytton, which means, I suppose, that I was not fully satisfied with myself. His words made the way towards her easier while at the same time leaving me more firmly on my own, and this brought back again those faint traces of fear that somehow I would prove inadequate or clumsy in my handling of the next stage in the romance. I was undoubtedly nervous about Janet; perhaps afraid of her on top of my other fears about myself, and particularly about the practicalities of resolving our mutual desires.

Pritchett came up to us, a barely concealed look of triumph in his eyes and a smile on his lips which he was endeavouring to conceal. 'I've got a place,' he said. 'I leave at Christmas. It's all arranged.'

We asked him where, and he told us. I had rarely seen him look so pleased. At all times a self-controlled boy, and frequently morose in outward appearances to the point where Lytton and I used to tease laughter out of him, he was clearly delighted with the plans that had been made for him.

'Why Christmas?'

'The course begins in January.'

'And you'll live in London?'

'There's a hostel.'

A prefect had emerged from Main School, and was ringing a handbell. We began to hurry.

'We ought to go over our routes for Prize Day,' Lytton said. 'We'll meet after the athletics practice on Saturday. We'll have an hour before tea, possibly more.'

'O.K.'

63

'You'd better not get that scholarship. We need you with us.'
'I'll do my worst,' I said.

II

Lytton's off-handedness about Janet made some things easier,
others more difficult. It removed any feelings of restraint I
might have had on his account. Our own pursuits were of more
moment to him, and his mind at the time was mainly concerned with our underground planning. We soon became
obsessed with the kernel of our mission, which was that we
should attend the main part of the Prize Day memorial service
immediately underneath Merchant's pew in the school chapel,
and we spent a useful if sticky hour that Saturday, and again
the following week, working out the details of how we would
do it. We timed ourselves, and planned our movements through
the tunnels. Having left behind us the stricter constraints and
less rational fears of childhood, we were free just then to be
obsessive about trivialities.

Merchant did not mention the Porphyry Scholarship again;
nor did Lytton and Pritchett. But it weighed on my mind,
bringing back recollections of the events which had created my
candidacy. At that time letters from my father were few, and,
at my own request, he did not come down at half-term. I told
him I had arranged an outing with friends. He forgot my birth-
day; and when the visit to the Festival of Britain eventually
took place, about a fortnight before Prize Day, I made no
attempt to phone him in London, spending the day with
Lytton and Pritchett, and going with them in the early part of
the evening to the fun fair at Battersea before returning by
coach to Coppinger.

I tried not to care; yet I was really quite disturbed by what
seemed to be happening. Never a good letter-writer, when he
did correspond my father's words were clipped and clichéd.
'Laurie sends her love,' he would always write; and I would

wonder: does she? He would tell me about work, that it was going well, or badly; but I did not even know what job he had or where it was. He receded from me at that time; and I would pick up the occasional envelopes from the hall table in the house, with their unmistakable, firmly written hand, feeling no great urge to read the predictable sentences with their clear, shallow meaning.

I wanted to cry out to him, but no longer knew how. Like the hammer of the water pump in the field at night, heard by the three of us as we watched Janet standing thigh-deep in the waters of the stream, his presence in my life was an increasingly mechanical, repetitive bass note in the background, a regular percussion motif to a series of experiences and actions which were moving with accelerating speed and tension, and inexorably away from him. How he could have been part of all that I did, I simply cannot tell. Perhaps it was an impossibility. But I was increasingly conscious of the gap between us. He, who had once always been at the shoulder or elbow of my endeavours and perceptive about my unformed and vague ambitions, was slipping away.

I could turn to no one about it. I could not raise the question of my father with Merchant, obviously; nor with the Gaffer; and would not with Lytton and Pritchett and decidedly not with Janet. In a sense I suppose I did, subconsciously, with all of them, by throwing myself into school and house affairs, into the secret druidical activities to which we gave so much of our then plentiful supplies of time, and finally into my awkward but consuming desire for Janet. These were not escapes or compensations. A readjustment was taking place. My father, for so long the hub around which much of my life had spun, was becoming a spoke in the wheel, one of many; and, more than other forces, he would in due course spin further, become more distant without disappearing altogether until he represented the element that contained my actions, the surrounding rim or edge of them.

My affair with Janet progressed speedily enough. Emboldened

by the remarks Lytton had made, the indications of affection and interest, we indulged in some clumsy but inflamed grappling and kissing. I was possibly more worried about disparities in our levels or experience in such matters than about anything else.

At that age one's performance in any field is of over-riding importance. Pacing the playing fields, the softened tar of summer roadways, the wooden floors of classrooms with their dusting of chalk, the echoing corridors and the high-vaulted chambers of assembly where we ate our meals, or prayed, or were addressed by one or other of our teachers, there was always a consciousness of how we did, of how we were seen to be doing. And in that most private activity of all, the 'snogging' for which, according to Lytton, and soon according to my own experience, Janet had a liking, I was aware that the subtleties and nuances of our actions, more or less innocent as they became, could be judged, just as everything else was judged, in the same terms.

Did I 'perform' well? It is a long time ago. Memory jumbles together occasions which, at the time, moved in an ordered and disciplined way that made judgment easier. June ended, and July brought a dusting of heat over everything. The nightingale ceased his singing. Gaffer's antirrhinums filled the garden with colour, and the earlier scent of wallflower and stock had given way to the heavier, richer odour of the first of his madonna lilies.

He grew them for Prize Day. Year after year the splendid tall flowers, spread along that side of the house where we had climbed down from the window, were picked the day before, and formed the main arrangement under the platform in School Hall, filling the air completely with the heavy, and to me unforgettable, smell of high summer. I associate it, even now, with chalk and polished floors, books and speeches, large hats and summer dresses, and the endless procession of forgotten boys answering the long recital of forgotten names to a background of discreet, well-tempered applause. I associate it, also, with Janet; with her brown, inviting eyes, her thick hair, her well-formed body.

The occasions on which I could meet her, even for a brief conversation leading to a hurried exchange of kisses, were infrequent. A single house containing about thirty boys and a family runs according to strict rules and allows limited scope for romance. Where she was concerned both her mother and father kept an alert enough watch over her, and the shadow of examinations, both hers and mine, ensured that there was limited fraternising. For their part, the boys collectively did the same, exercising a tacit restraint which was welcome. Without it, harsher rules would have been applied.

And so, within these restraints, Janet and I worked out a romance of sorts. I considered much the question of being 'in love', and was puzzled by the inconclusive nature of the outcome. I also considered the half-formed desires that continually pushed us towards each other: those nameless swoopings of the mind over the territory, the endless wilderness, of sex. How did one relate its brutal, physiological manifestation, to the teasing innuendoes that invaded our conversation? More explicitly, how did one work out the physical limitations within which we encountered each other in odd places in the house?

It had all been so different with Babette. I had loved her with a chaste passion, a narrowness of feelings that had, nevertheless, penetrated deeply into my being. And when it ended, and she had passed out of my life in a sequence of events that had been sudden and painful, the sense of loss had lasted a long time. All of that was some eighteen months back; and at that age it seemed like an eternity. In the interval there had been the pseudo-romance by letter with Tessa. And now I was plunging headlong into something quite different.

And yet . . . and yet . . . where was the unfathomable urge that could justify each act? I search, now, in vain through my memory for the podgy hands that shot the arrow that pierced the heart. Not there. Janet had been Lytton's, and was now becoming mine. Before that she had been Hodges' girl, and before that Barnwell's. And after me there would be others. I was pushed forward by curiosity, desire, the inevitability that I, somehow, had acquired a place in the line of Janet's lovers. I was held back by fear, by innocence of heart, by lack of practical experience. A small voice within me endeavoured to check the heady urge that pushed me forward. It seemed to say: this is not right. But it lacked authority, and I detached myself from its restraints. It was a cool, rational decision, the one to go on. Even as I made it, I was concerned at my own detachment, and yet unable to do anything at all about it. I am puzzled even now, looking back, at the passive way in which I allowed myself to be drawn into what really constituted a love affair. And though, in some respects, it may be regarded as serious, the perspective of time gives to my love for Babette an intensity which Janet could never command.

III

It was the Thursday before Prize Day. Much work had been done to smarten up the school, and heavy penalties threatened against boys who threw down sweet papers. The edges of roadways and paths had been trimmed, gang-mowers drawn by one of the lighter tractors from the farm seemed endlessly to clatter over the acres of grass and there was an edge and a sharpness to everything; trees were statuesque, and slightly artificial in that lush stillness characteristic of July. The weather was fine.

Examinations ended. Final results and places were being worked out, and would be announced the following day, with the names of prize-winners. Because of this, and the staff meeting being held to consider these and related questions, the majority of boys were out on working parties, though in many cases tidying up aspects of the school which could respond no further to their attention. There was an end-of-term atmosphere in the air. It was premature. There was still almost a fortnight left of the summer term into which had to be fitted the finals of athletics, the swimming sports, and the house match which would decide the cricket cup.

I had failed to get the reading prize, coming third in the school. My various examination marks had been respectable; I had held to a placing around ninth in most subjects, but had managed second in the English exam and first in history. When, therefore, among the many summonses that had boys scurrying around the school during that busy but disrupted day, one came for me to go to the headmaster's study, I went with a clear conscience but without optimism.

For the architect of all our endeavour, Merchant was remarkably cool and detached. Clear conscience notwithstanding, I felt nervous standing in front of his desk, my eyes on his hands which were lightly folded on the faded green leather surface, cleared of all papers and writing materials. He kept me standing in silence for a moment or two. Then he raised his hands, resting his elbows on the edge of the desk, and slowly turning the signet ring on the little finger of his left hand. He stared at me, his face without expression.

'You did fairly well in your form marks, didn't you?'

'I think so, Sir.'

'Pity about the reading prize.'

'Yes, Sir.'

'Your housemaster thinks you've had a reasonable term, and a fair year altogether.'

'Thank you, Sir.'

He stopped moving his signet ring, placed his two hands together in an attitude of prayer, and lowered his lips to the tips of his fingers, his eyes looking down for a moment.

'As I told you earlier in the term, you were one of the candidates for the Porphyry Scholarship. Of the three boys whose names were put forward, your claim had really the least to support it. You have a father and step-mother to go to, and a house, which seems to offer not just more than several other boys enjoy, but more than you yourself have had in the past. That's true, isn't it?'

I nodded. 'It's true, Sir.'

'Nevertheless, there do seem to be difficulties.' He paused, and we stared at each other. I hoped that he would not ask any questions. With the matter presumably decided there seemed no point in going into the details all over again.

'As I think I made clear to you, I do not have discretion in the matter. But it is my duty to pass on to you the decision.' Again he paused, and his pale blue eyes stared at me, totally without expression. In seven years, Merchant's inner feelings, as far as I knew, had remained undetected by anyone. He was a chameleon. His eyes could flame with rage or become even more icily blue with the same emotion. But, of all the passions, rage and anger lend themselves most easily to dissimulation, and one was left wondering about Merchant's other capacities and feelings. Questions about him floated before me in the interminable moments that passed as he felt his way towards the phrasing of Mr Porphyry's decision. I was resigned. I saw slipping from me the freedom and independence, the new opportunities, the release from Laurie's leaden hand. They had been held out to me earlier, during our walk round the cricket field, when Merchant had seemed to me positively benevolent. Now, cold and inscrutable, and perversely cruel, he was taking them away. And doing so with a studied and measured care.

'Unexpectedly,' he said, and paused, watching for a reaction in my eyes, 'Mr Porphyry has chosen you.' He placed his hands on the desk, flat this time on its clear surface. 'I cannot tell what helped him to this decision. Your age, your position in the school, the likelihood that you will be here for perhaps two more years, making it rather a different award from the practice previously. I don't mind telling you, I was surprised myself.' A wintry smile flitted across his face.

With great relief I said, 'Thank you, Sir.'

'Don't thank me. I played the smallest part. Your debt is to Mr Porphyry. You will meet him when the trustees have finished their meeting on Saturday. You will show him the school after the presentation of prizes. For the rest, the working out of the scholarship will be between the two of you. That will be all. I hope you get full value from the benefits. Find Archer and send him to me; and tell Hannay that I will see the prefects at noon.'

I nodded twice, dumbly. 'Tha . . . Yes, Sir,' I said. 'I will.' I crossed over to the door of his study.

'One other thing,' he said. 'I don't know whether your father is coming down?'

I turned back and shook my head. 'I don't think so, Sir. I haven't heard.'

'In the circumstances I think it would be better if he did not come. Can you telephone him? It's too late to write.'

'He would write and tell me if he was coming.'

'Can we rely on that?' Merchant trod the ground more delicately than I thought necessary. I was fully aware of the difficulties, but did not relish the idea of spelling them out to my father.

'I think we can,' I said.

I found Archer, and gave him the message. He looked surprised and frightened. I told Hannay as well, and he nodded in an off-hand way. The remoteness he enjoyed, both as head of the school and as a result of his almost legendary capacities, as cricketer, on the rugby field and as an athlete on top of that, had been marginally reduced by my own latest piece of news. He was not disposed to do other than nod, and when I continued to stand in front of him where he had turned from his conversation with two other prefects, he raised his eyebrow in question.

'I got the Porphyry,' I said.

The second eyebrow went up; the expression turned from inquiry into surprise.

'Well done!' he said. He turned to the others. 'Meet this year's Porphyry Scholar!' They, too, looked surprised. I was obviously not the expected choice.

'You're the lucky one,' said Bates, who was head of Patterson's house.

'It's a cushy number, I tell you,' said Marriot. 'Philpotts went to Holland.'

'We'd better get the others together,' Hannay said.

They turned away and I left them. Merchant had said nothing about keeping the matter to myself, and it had seemed a good moment for breaking the news.

Later that evening the group of house prefects, Barnwell, Hodges, Briggs and Chalfont, together with Lytton, Pritchett and myself, sat in the house library talking. Danby was there, as well. The Gaffer had known, of course, and had nodded when I told him, a benign look of understanding on his face. He had been with us for a while, and had then wandered off to inspect, for the last time, his beds of lilies. They would be cut early the next morning.

'It's not as though you win it,' Briggs said. He was a tall, unathletic boy, with a large, angular head, and horn-rimmed glasses. He was clever, and came monotonously top of his class each year. He knew about winning in much the same way as Barnwell and Hodges knew about it on the sports-field.

'It has something to do with trouble at home, doesn't it?' Danby's frankness was disturbing. No one spoke. I nodded. No one else spoke.

'You'll spend some of the time on your knees, you know. There's a bit of that involved.'

'What do you mean?' I asked. It was Hodges who had spoken.

'Oh, didn't you know? It's part of the Porphyry. You have to pray for it. Its donor is the praying kind.'

I looked at them all without pursuing the issue raised. I had not expected this somewhat ominous corollary.

'I think there's travel involved, isn't there?' Danby asked.

I nodded again. Enough had now been said about the Porphyry Scholarship. There were, in addition, reasons for my being chosen which I did not wish to advertise; and beyond that, lingering in the past, were Philpotts's vague reservations from the summer when he had been the recipient. I did not bother to tease out these arguments and questions any further. And later events were to render such activity wasted. What we were all too young to consider at least in the abstract, what took further time to emerge, was the simple fact that Mr Porphyry was a lonely man. Instead of considering that, even as a remote possibility, my mind turned more naturally to the immediate problem: what would now happen to the Druids' Prize Day escapade? It was this that hung over me as I sat there in the fading light of that summer evening in the school library, with Lytton and Pritchett close beside me.

Barnwell got to his feet. 'Bed, you chaps,' he said. It normally took a certain amount of persuasion to clear the room last thing at night. On this occasion the three of us left together with an alacrity that might have excited suspicion. We went through the house and out to the washrooms, lavatories and the communal bathroom with its huge old bathtubs and brass fittings. I was rather sorry not to have seen Janet that evening in order to tell her about the Scholarship. But the doors to the Forrests' part of the house were firmly closed as we passed.

For a while we were alone together. Lytton closed the door. He looked at me. 'I suppose you'll have to pull out?'

'I can't see what else I can do,' I said. 'Merchant says I must meet Mr Porphyry after the trustees' meeting, and stay with him. I have to be a kind of host.'

'Could you not just leave him at the door of the chapel and tell him you'll join him later at a different level?' Pritchett asked. 'Spiritually with him, you could say, but physically apart. No?'

'No. I don't think so. I don't see how I can.'

Lytton was washing. His face all wet, he glanced over at the door. 'We must still do it, Pritzer,' he said. 'There's even more point, now.' He reached for a towel and began rubbing his face. He walked over towards me. He was smiling. 'You'll be standing beside this Mr Porphyry, won't you? Well, we'll come along underneath and poke grass up your trouser-leg. We'll make you laugh. They'll take the scholarship away.'

73

'Don't you dare.'

'I think we'll have to go public,' Pritchett said. 'We'll sing a descant. No, I know. We'll sing "Go Down, Moses" during the memorial prayer.'

He laughed a good deal, but I was beginning to feel nervous. They might easily get out of hand and do something silly.

On our way back through the house, at the turning of the stair, I noticed Janet standing beside the partly open door which led down a passage towards the Forrests' sitting-room. She beckoned to me. The others went on up the stairs.

'I heard,' she said. 'It's very good news. Are you excited?'

'Yes. Very.' I took her hand.

'I can't stay here by the door. I've just finished my homework. Can you come tonight?'

'Where?'

'To my room. About one.'

I felt out of breath. I looked into her eyes. They glowed in the fading light. Her hand was warm in mine, and she squeezed my fingers. 'Yes,' I said. 'I'll be there.'

'Good,' she said. 'Be careful just inside the door. There's a board squeaks.'

She laughed softly, and turned to go in by the partly open door. As I paused at the foot of the stair and looked after her she was standing beyond the narrow opening, looking through. And briefly she waved her hand at me; even more briefly I waved back.

In the dormitory I told Lytton that she had already heard from her father, about the scholarship.

'I expect you'd like to take her with you, wherever you're going?'

'That's not a bad idea,' I said. 'But isn't Porphyry meant to be quite religious? That's what Hodges said.'

'Yes. I heard it from someone else,' Pritchett said. 'You be careful, now. Your soul won't be your own.'

The words did not strike me as odd, but I remembered them. And in due course, long after Pritchett himself had gone from

74

Coppinger, I would recall the oddly prophetic words that had echoed through the dusk. With care and caution, under the bedclothes, I set the alarm, rolled the clock in a jersey leaving the button clear, put it under my pillow, and with remarkable ease fell asleep.

IV

I forgot the board. After opening the door with elaborate efforts to be silent, I stood on it, and its squeak sounded through the house, a wail of protest which I thought would wake everyone up. My heart was thumping madly anyway, and with the sudden noise blank fear for a moment or two over-rode my desire. After the single light of the hallway and land-ing of the house, I could see little in the darkness of Janet's room, and I stood for a while, my back against the door, my bare feet off the offending board, and my eyes adjusting to the shadowy light which came from the window. Then I saw that she was standing in front of it, leaning out, her hair and shoulders dimly outlined against the sky.

'Janet?' My voice was a hoarse whisper.

'Come over.' She said. She did not turn, and her voice sounded vaguely muffled.

It was a clear night. The moon was less than full, sufficient to dim the stars, but revealing only a shadowy outline of trees and fields. I stood slightly behind her, very close, not touching, wanting to touch. I was afraid of the difference between our usual encounters and this one. I rated it more vast a difference than in fact it was. And yet, at the same time as I felt the over-whelming sense of desire and longing and nervousness being with her, alone, at night, in her bedroom, I also felt vulnerable and embarrassed in my striped pyjamas, a little bit ridiculous, and, deep down, I was afraid of the awful catastrophe that would descend upon us if the Gaffer or Mrs Forrest decided to investigate the squeak.

75

'I'm sorry about the noise. I completely forgot.'

'It doesn't matter,' she said. 'Everyone's asleep.'

She spoke softly herself, and though at the time I thought it was a form of easy nonchalance, I imagine in retrospect that, in part, it was her own nervousness that kept her leaning on the window sill, staring out into the night.

My eyes, adjusting to what light there was, could see that she was dressed in one of the then quite fashionable 'Baby Doll' nightdresses, the colour, in as far as it could be ascertained either pale blue or green. Her faint scent was to be detected generally in the room, which I was in for the first time; but it was to some extent overwhelmed by the headier perfume from the lilies below the window.

'It's good about the scholarship, isn't it?'

'You're very lucky. I'd love to go abroad.'

'Have you ever?'

'No.'

I leaned on the window sill beside her. I felt increasingly nervous. I looked at her soft profile, her eyes still fixed on the shadowy trees that grew in a bunch not far distant from the house.

'What's he like? Do you know anything about him?' I paused, then added: 'It's an odd name, isn't it? Porphyry?'

I felt that I was talking in order to postpone some action, even the vague nature of which eluded me, apart from the inevitability of it starting with the still rather clumsy embraces in which Janet and I had already indulged.

She was equally unhurried, but for different reasons, in as far as I could judge. She seemed to be surrounded by that comfortable, warming sense of being desired which, in turn, seemed to plump up, soften, and make large the whole space in which she stood. A vibrant halo surrounded her entire being; it was as if she possessed a magnetic field, into which I was drawn, and to which I had to mould my body and my mind, my feelings and my desires. There even appeared to be a consciousness of it in the way she looked out at the night, her eyelids half covering the soft brown irises, colourless at that moment in the faint moonlight, but remembered for their lustrous invitation. They did not seem to be focused upon the trees or the stars; they dwelt upon inner visions. For a moment I felt afraid. I was the most immediate human part of a world that was on offer to her, just as much as it was on offer to all of us, advancing as we were upon the high points of our youth. And her parted lips, soft and sensuous, through which she breathed the sultry, scented air of that July night, anticipated a natural and an inevitable wonder, an escape, an understanding of beauty, a further exploration of feelings and events, the inexorably advancing contact of hand, body, lips. I yearned to hold the moment where it was. I wanted to suspend the gap between us. Conscious, also, of the maddening desire to clutch her, however clumsily, draw her clothes away from her body, touch her, stroke her, do to her what were still in my innocent and exploring mind nameless acts, I felt at the same time a deeper sensation that was passive and reticent, that seemed to recognise, in the pulsating gap of air, some eighteen inches, I suppose, between our warm bodies, a slower, more subtle magnetism drawing us together in an unhurried, unvoiced, but fully agreed contract of love.

Of course it wasn't love. I felt for her less than I felt for Babette, less than I would feel for others afterwards. She did not fit in with the concepts that Tessier handed to us when, in occasional moments of relaxation during French, he attempted to strike chords from our generally unresponsive hearts by reading what he must have thought of as daring lines from Rimbaud or Baudelaire. She did not fit in with what Keats or Shelley or Byron were beginning to teach. What Bennett had to say about them, and what we had heard him say to Mrs Patterson, were equally remote from what I was feeling at that moment. Neither real passion nor deep commitment stirred me. There was no sense of the future in what I felt, none of the past. The warmth of the present, its immediacy, its overwhelming ability—in later life with tragic consequences—to maim or destroy in a moment the constructions and faiths and affections of a lifetime, were asserting themselves for the first time in my experience; and obediently I was capitulating. Dimly, as I reached out to her, I knew this.

'Janet—' I said.

She turned from the window, her eyelids shadowing her eyes from me, her gaze fixed downward. I touched her breast, tentatively at first with my fingertips, then with my hand closing over the warmth of her flesh. She stepped towards me, brushing my hand aside and putting her own arms round my neck to bring my lips down on to hers. We lay together on her bed. She pulled the nightdress above her breasts but did not take it off. I was bewildered by the size of her. She was neither unduly tall, nor fat. It was just that her well-developed body was so utterly new an experience to me. I was afraid, ignorant, clumsy, just as I had been in earlier encounters, in our fumbling embraces. Yet it did not seem to matter. She kissed and laughed and held me in her arms, and I had the strange sensation that her wisdom about this encounter was infinitely greater than mine, and that, whatever my experiences in life might be, she and her kind would always be tantalisingly ahead of me, by distances which would seem immeasurably great and at the same time infinitely small.

I was precipitate. She was clearly not satisfied. Yet her reaction was sweet and gentle. In the darkness, my hand on her breast, my head buried in the sweet-smelling flesh at her neck and throat, she laughed. It was a sound from deep within her, and I felt her belly move against me with the pleasure.

I suppose that if she had been older she might have spoken then, and so might I. But in our uneven and uncertain, indeed our selfish, fumblings towards satisfaction, the sense we both had of the other was limited by the enormous, overwhelming sense we had of ourselves. I wanted to lie perfectly still mainly because I did not know what movements to make next. She was more practical. Sensing that my inertia was a kind of self-hypnosis she gently disentangled herself, and pulled down

78

her nightdress. She still lay beside me on the bed, smiling into my eyes, her hair massed on the pillow, my hand gently touching it, my lips ready to kiss again.

If I can recollect at all accurately the feelings that I had at that moment it must be confessed that regret was mixed with satisfaction, foreboding with the sense of possession, vague disappointment with relief, and bewilderment with the welcome conviction of loss. Quite what I had lost I did not know. Innocence appears to make its departure so many times, and in so many different fashions, and yet comes back to us again with such sturdy willingness. To tell the truth, I did not fully understand either the physical or emotional climaxes we had shared. This must sound so foolish, so tentative; like a blind man in a strange room, I was feeling for familiar objects where there were none. And, while part of me wanted desperately to come to terms with what surrounded me, the other part questioned, as would the blind man, why I was there at all. Does this suggest a limited or feeble passion? Comparing it, at the time, or a little later, with the thudding force of my father's feelings, which were to be unleashed in so unforgettable a way in the summer months that still lay ahead, or with Mr Bennett's feelings, I was to realise more fully my limitations; and I was then to feel ashamed of what I was dimly coming to understand was my compromised heart. It happened with Janet; it was to happen, differently, with Esther; and after that, on other occasions, it was to baffle me in my desire to lose myself in feeling and emotion. Only looking back, to the clear and simple innocence of my first encounter, with Babette, and forward to the darker counterpoint to that, which lay well in the future, can I find, in childhood and youth, episodes in which it was possible to say that feelings were fully engaged, that passion took complete hold, that the heart commanded totally both mind and body.

Accustomed to the dim light in the room, I traced with my finger the line of her lips, the outline of her face.

'Janet?'

'Yes?'

'I do love you.'

'Um . . . Do you?'

We kissed. The first time the words had been a bit strangled. The lie came more easily now. Convention demanded it, and we were creatures of convention. But even then I knew I did not love her. I had not, from the first. I had followed Lytton as Lytton had followed Barnwell. I would be followed in my turn by others. And a consciousness of this had surrounded all my actions and feelings. That is the truth, burdensome, awkward, inescapable.

'You know something?'

'What?'

'I'll be a house prefect next year.'

'Will you?'

'Your father says.'

'Is that good?'

'I suppose so.' I paused. 'Does he talk to you about things like that?'

'What do you mean, "things like that"?'

'Well, house arrangements, boys being made prefects, things like that.'

'No. Not really.'

'I just wondered.'

'You'll still be here, anyway,' she said. '*That's* good.'

'You mean . . . you and me?'

'Of course I do. You didn't think . . .?'

'Well . . .'

'You *are* silly!' She laughed. She took my hand which was resting gently on her shoulder, and raised it to her lips. She kissed the knuckles, and I felt the determined push of her mouth against my fingers which she held tight for just a moment before letting them fall. We embraced again, then she told me I had better go.

'Mind the board.'

'I will,' I said. I looked down at her. How different everything seemed from the way it had been when I came to her an hour earlier. A net of soft attitudes seemed to cover us. The brief past we had enjoyed together, of kisses and whispered feelings, had been brought to a first conclusion; the uncertain future lay ahead, a mixture of doubts and unspoken promises. I was a little frightened by her conviction about the future. Desire had drawn me to this point, but it had also revealed imperfections in the depth of my feeling for her. And now a strangely voluminous web of different views and obligations had been thrown over the pair of us. To struggle would be foolish. Nevertheless the shock of realising a certain entanglement, imperfectly understood before, came to me just then. Forcefully, Lytton's crude words ran through my mind: 'She likes to snog.' But of what else did she think? What feelings would invade her mind as she prepared herself for sleep? What dreams?

'Goodnight, Janet,' I said.

Her voice was already drowsy. 'Goodnight,' she said. 'Don't forget the board.'

Chapter Four

I

When we are young we prefer absolute evaluations to relative ones. In retrospect they may seem to have been too simple, too obvious, too brittle and unenduring. But then they held us. We were building a road from childhood towards a life. We wanted it to be the hardest, the broadest, the longest, the best. We thought we knew just how it was done. The judgments which decided the superlatives upon which we fixed our eyes may have been shallow. The very choice of them—fastest, biggest, most—was suspect. But they dominated all that we did.

From that particular time I draw no precise recollections concerning myself. If there were absolutes in my own achievements at Coppinger they belonged to a slightly later period, and it was only then that I began working towards them. But I do summon up an image of Lytton, the last and best that I have of him. And it involves an absolute of sorts. No doubt it was destined to fade in the larger world outside, coming to represent for him a past memory, a present regret, a small pocket of faded glory. But it was real enough in those glorious days of high summer, when the warm, limpid climate at the end of that July seemed to bring on, all at the one time, the harvest of youthful ambition.

In two earlier summers he had won comfortably the junior competition in diving. Then, the previous year, he had been ill and had missed the competition altogether. His return to it now was the final chance he had of gaining what was, for him, an ultimate prize, an absolute. His was an accomplishment which far surpassed, in our eyes, the promise he showed in technical drawing, a promise that would presumably come to fruition in due course, as he trained in some branch of engineering. He could dive better than anyone in the school; but it was only this year that he qualified for the senior competition, and it was therefore both his first and last opportunity. The competition itself came in the week after Prize Day, but the days leading up to it were filled with practices; and it seems in retrospect that all of those days, as the summer term drew towards its close, are shadowed, among other things, by the intensely visual recollection I have of Lytton's physique, sleek, lissom, not particularly muscular, yet quite substantial, going through the slow and studied actions that preceded the dive itself. With a fair number of us watching, from places around the swimming pool, he would move with self-conscious deliberation to the diving board, climb to the highest platform, and then step firmly forward to the edge. His toes would grip momentarily, checking that the position of his feet was exactly as he wanted at the wooden edge of the unsprung platform. He would stand perfectly straight, his eyes fixed before him, focusing on nothing. Perhaps once or twice I recall him clenching his fists, an expression of nerves and tension. Then he would be absolutely still. What spring was released in him I cannot tell; what it was he waited for, in the hush of expectation, which seemed to be more intense for him than for others, remained always a mystery; but suddenly he would flex his knees and spring out into the void to make his dive. He must have made many different sorts of dives; but the image that comes down to me over the years is of the simplest kind of jack-knife: his body folding together at the highest point after leaving the board, his hands pointing down and coming together

83

with his feet, a swift concentration of vibrant pointings, and then the whole stretching out again and falling like an arrow into the surface of pale blue. He would puncture the water and disappear into it with a small plop and ripple, quite absurdly small for so much mass and movement. It always seemed to me by far the most impressive aspect of his dive, that precise, economical entry into the pool. Then he would surface, the water streaming from his fair hair which was plastered down over his forehead in a fringe above his crinkled-up eyes. He would come up, his mouth open to take a breath, the general expression in his face one of surprised inquiry. Presumably, until the mark was announced, we had a better idea of how he had done than he himself did. He would turn, and swim to the steps, and climb out, waiting in the sunlight, or often enough shivering in the cold.

Like Hannay on the cricket field, like others in rugby or athletics, he seemed, in that particular sequence of actions, climbing, pausing, diving down through the air, cutting through the surface of the water, supremely without limitation.

As for myself, I was somewhat shamefully conscious that my own achievement in getting the Porphyry Scholarship had been based on need rather than merit. The prize I had tried to win, the only one possible for me that year, had eluded me. And when, at assembly on the morning of Prize Day, Merchant announced all the prize-winners and summoned us to a final rehearsal, I felt detached from the others and anxious to get it all over; rehearsal, Prize Day itself, the term, everything. Merchant also announced the death in Korea of a boy from the school. He did so at the end of all the other announcements, and though his voice was sombre enough, its tone was without emotion, a calm statement of sober fact. The boy's name was Comber. He, also, had been a fine swimmer. Though two or three years older, he had helped and encouraged Lytton as a junior, in his swimming and diving, in the term before he left to join up. He had taken a short service commission in what we liked to think of as the local regiment, the Gloucesters, and

84

had been killed in a shower of bullets on one of the anonymous, numbered hills which made more terrible the distant battlefield in that eastern wilderness. We were dutifully shocked by the news, but did not really know how to react. Lytton was affected most of all. His contained grief, at a time when his most valued accomplishment reminded us all of the dead soldier, made him more firmly the leader of the three of us. For a time he wore a wooden, numbed expression. We felt that the tension in his diving, the perceptible will to triumph, was heightened by the news; that perhaps the anguish, whatever form it took, was exorcised by winning.

School hall was in disarray. The pervasive scent of the madonna lilies made me think again of Janet and recollect, with both pleasure and guilt, our night-time encounter. Staff wives bustled about, Mrs Forrest among them. Looking at her, covertly, in the moments of waiting, as the assistant head-master, who had taken over from Merchant, endeavoured to school us in the simple procedures of accepting what we had been awarded, I saw for the first time in her face the physical qualities she had passed on to her daughter: wide, generous mouth and dark, attractive eyes. She must have then been in her late forties. Other similarities were hard to trace. Then, suddenly, she turned to another woman, someone on the secretarial staff, and said something which caused amusement. Her own laughter rippled out, and I felt a stab of recollection. I became aware also that the other boys had moved away, and I was left staring foolishly in the direction of the stage and the group of women as they moved and arranged the great vases of waxy white flowers around the steps which we would be mounting that afternoon.

Turning away, conscious of my isolation, I noticed that Merchant's deputy had his finger to his lips. A ripple of laughter ran through the prize-winners.

'Perhaps the Porphyry scholar will tell us how we do this?'

I blushed. 'I'm sorry, Sir.'

'Going to take up flower arranging, then?'

85

'No, Sir.'

'Want to be with the ladies?'

I was silent. For a moment he deliberated, casting about in his mind for further witticisms, then he explained once again what we had to do.

'And by the way,' he said, 'if you want to get an autograph, our guest tomorrow is a General and a Lord. But you should call him by the latter title. I understand he wears an eye-glass. But you are not to notice that too obviously. Don't go saying "My Lord" this or "My Lord" that. Just plain speaking.'

After the fairly desultory instructions on how we were to mount up to the platform, receive our prizes, and rejoin the row at the other end, we dispersed. I went in search of Lytton and Pritchett, and eventually found them at the top of the hill road leading down to the farm.

They were standing together both in listless and preoccupied attitudes, leaning on the metal fencing and looking out over the broad valley.

'Are you all set for tomorrow?' I asked, eventually.

'We've decided not to do it,' Pritchett said.

I felt relieved. 'Why?'

They both stared ahead of them.

'It's old Comber, really,' Lytton said. 'Getting himself killed.'

'It wouldn't be right,' Pritchett said.

I had been relatively unaffected by the news of his death apart from the first shock. Someone I had seen moving and talking, and indeed swimming and diving as well, was extinguished into distant nothingness. I had to adjust to a new range of feelings and reactions, where he was concerned; but that was all.

'No,' I said. 'I suppose it wouldn't.'

I stood beside them and leaned on the fencing as well. I glanced surreptitiously at the others. Their eyes were fixed on the sweep of fields which stretched away up the far side of the valley. 'Poor old Comber,' I said. I was beginning to feel quite sad, like them. Through Lytton, Comber seemed that much more special to us, drawing us closer together. Tragedy and grief, descending swiftly, evoked a surprising pleasant reaction. But then I felt guilty, wondering whether it was wrong to draw grains of comfort from an event that, for Lytton at least, must have been painful.

'What will they do?' I asked. 'In the service?'

'Prayers, I suppose,' Pritchett said.

'Buggers, those Chinks,' Lytton said. 'It's a sodding shame.'

We eventually made our way to the chapel, joining the gathering of boys and staff there, the early arrivals among parents and guests adding an unfamiliar leavening and raising curiosity about dress and appearance. The occasion was encompassed by ritual: boys filing in first, the prize-winners sitting in a group together. They were followed by staff, then parents and guests, and finally by Merchant, leading the trustees and the day's speaker to sit together. I had a reasonable view of Mr Porphyry, to whom I would be introduced after the presentation of prizes, and I watched him during the service with new interest and not unmixed feelings about the one-sided way in which we were being drawn together. He was tall, but thin and wiry, his features generally craggy. He had a wide mouth, the ends of it turned down slightly. It gave to the expression on his face a misleading look of disdain, belied by the penetrating directness of his eyes. Disciplined in the way he sat, upright and still, hardly looking around him, he wore in a comfortable and easy manner his well-cut check suit, and silk tie with its small, tidy knot.

I felt a measure of relief that Lytton and Pritchett were not under the floor. I suspected that we had probably made our last trip, and that the subterranean world of adventure was receding into the past. Coupled with the short tribute to Comber, and the prayers, it induced a vaguely chilling presentiment of growing up. I had no feelings of sadness or regret. The robust, even raucous vigour of the singing, and the general speed with which the memorial service was handled, induced an impatience in me. I had done everything I could during the

87

term, during the year, and was ready to move on. Achievements, if limited, were accompanied by the special distinction of being the Porphyry scholar, and I looked forward to the promotion which the Gaffer had indicated earlier in the week. My mind jumped ahead, accelerating some of the aspirations that had been coming to the surface during the weeks of that term. And the hymn which came at the end of the service seemed to fit in with growing confidence and appetite: invincibility was being instilled by its sentiments; a sense of mission by its forceful if misguided ranging over the points of the world's surface, Greenland, Ceylon, and 'Afric's sunny fountains'.

> Can we, whose souls are lighted
> With wisdom from on high,
> Can we to men benighted
> The lamp of life deny?
> Salvation! Oh, Salvation!

I felt vibrant with purpose. Of its nature I was vague; and about the detail, of building brick on brick, the laborious detail of reality, I was dismissive. The broad thrust of my large army of thoughts and ambitions would take care of all that later. Filled with confident if vague anticipations, I sang out the long verses of the hymn. Looking over, just once, at Mr Porphyry, I noticed that he did not sing. His lips seemed to move, but fractionally, a token to the sound that swelled around him, to which he failed to contribute.

II

The high windows in the main hall were open, allowing a slight breeze to blow through the hot and crowded room. The scent of flowers was heavy in the air, and there was the inevitable rustle of papers and clothing, and of feet on the polished pine floorboards. Otherwise, the attention which the speaker was able to command seemed to be complete. He had promised a short speech, and had in fact been speaking for about five minutes. Then he hesitated and laid down his notes on the table in front of him on which stood the impressive rows of books he was shortly to hand out. He had steered his course with some skill through the marshlands of cliché and of accepted wisdom with which the route to the end of a prize day speech is encompassed. Eminent men should permit themselves a strict and meagre handful of such occasions, no more; when the freshness fades they also should fade. I do not know how often he had spoken at such functions before. Probably only at a limited number. His eminence, after all, was of the grey kind associated with War Cabinet work; he had not, at any stage during the Second World War, led an army in the field, though his earlier career, particularly in Somaliland, had been colourful and honourable. He paused now, and looked out at us. Free from the small sheaf of papers which lay on the table top before him, his hands hung awkwardly for a moment. Then he took the single eyeglass from his eye and, producing a red spotted handkerchief from his pocket, began to polish it. Philpotts suddenly came to mind; he would have described it as a piece of heavy theatre. I was not so sure. If the gesture was theatrical it came at a point when, having spoken for a relatively short period, the General had nevertheless gained sufficient command over his very mixed audience to be able to afford this break in what he was saying.

He went on: 'I have been told by your headmaster of the death of one of your boys in Korea, fighting with the Gloucesters. For many of you it must have been a new experience, to know that someone you had seen, talked with, perhaps admired, had met a violent end. We are taught by many things—history, culture, literature—to see such acts in heroic terms. My experience as both soldier and man tells me something different. I have seen many deaths. I have been directly involved in decisions which have resulted in many more. They

89

are not noble, not heroic. In the hardness of my professional heart I have to say this: dead soldiers, however brave, are soldiers who have come to the end of their usefulness.' He stared a bit bleakly out at us all.

'The vast majority of you will go on to do National Service. The country requires your involvement in the protection of something that is large and soft and indeterminate. We call it "democracy" or "the Western way of life". There are lots of things wrong with it. Defending it finds expression in some odd engagements, not the least peculiar of them being the fact that British soldiers are at present fighting in a remote part of Asia against Chinese and Korean troops; and this has brought about this Coppinger boy's death. In order for you to understand this, and to see yourselves having a part in it, I will not speak of patriotism or sacrifice or the greater good . . .' I began to day-dream. I looked across the aisle at the packed rows on the other side. I was close enough to the wall to be able to turn my head without too obviously offending one of the innumerable and detailed warnings we had received about behaviour.

Occasional faces, angular, raw, unformed, perhaps caught with an odd or awkward expression on them, provoked in me the curious and momentary questioning: how much of what we would all become is prefigured in youthful bone and flesh? Is it possible to detect, under the general appearance, which would change fairly marginally from now until death, the more radical currents of ambition and potential achievement? What would they all become, then, my colleagues? And Janet, on whom my eyes came to rest where she sat, more or less opposite the prize-winners' seats, on the other side among the staff, pressed between her mother and father: what of her? And what part would I play—perhaps had already played—in the shaping of her future?

There ran before my mind a series of images that seemed to telescope for me recent events, now detached from the present and the immediate future. Lytton embracing Janet in the moon-light; my own fumbling embraces, in which it had been more a matter of Janet holding me; Pritchett walking on the outside of our group, his hands behind his back, his eyes staring sharply into the soft morning mist, punctured by the red of poppies, as the owl spread its broad wings and flew towards the trees; my two friends lying on the grassy bank in the June sunshine; Merchant and myself treading that fateful course around the cricket field. Did these events foreshadow the future?

'As you know,' the General went on, 'and I am coming to the end of what I have to say, I am on the council of the Festival of Britain. In what we did we sought to express a little of what I have said to you, Britain as it is now. Think about it. There is this country which surrounds you, in which you live. There are all these people. You read about it in newspapers and magazines, you hear about it on the wireless. You are taught about it. I don't invite you to play a part in it, adopt an attitude, be for or against. You have no choice. You cannot really judge it, accept or reject it, or run away from it. You are it, all of you. And the natural expression of yourselves, based on conviction as well as educational achievement, on honesty as well as brilliance, on courage as well as skill, will become the character of the country in which you live in the years ahead. We applaud the prize-winners,' he said, looking down towards us and taking the glass out of his eye, 'but our thoughts are spread more broadly. At the end of a school year, no matter how junior or how lowly, each and every one of you has some kind of account to offer.'

To judge from the applause, he seemed to have caught the mood of his audience. The prize-winners were called out, one by one, and round after round of comparatively muted clapping accompanied the succession of boys, small at first, getting bigger, that mounted the short flight of steps to the stage, shook hands with the General, received one or more books, and descended again into the sea of faces and clapping hands. When my own turn came I was also gratified by the applause. Our guest speaker, perhaps briefed by Merchant, perhaps as a result of an earlier conversation with Porphyry, seemed to understand something of the scholarship, but he smiled quite warmly as he handed me the blue envelope and said quietly, 'I hope you will use the benefits of this well.' Turning, I noticed that Pritchett had raised his hands in the air and was clapping energetically and nodding his head. I smiled at him and Lytton, and managed to turn the tail-end of my glance towards Janet, who also was smiling up at me, before being engulfed once again in the movement of prize-winners round and along the rows in which they were sitting until finally we regained our original places.

III

'That was a useful talk we had with the Bursar,' Sir Joseph Fisher said. 'His ideas are sound on investment.'

Mr Porphyry nodded, but did not speak. He had his back to me. Sir Joseph noticed me where I was waiting. 'Well, Porphyry here's your scholar.' He nodded towards me, a brief and peremptory acknowledgement that overlooked, unconsciously I was sure, that we had met once before.

Mr Porphyry turned slowly and held out his hand. 'Well done,' he said. His gaze was quite remote, his face barely touched by a smile.

'If you're ready, Sir, I'll show you round.'

He and Sir Joseph were part of the larger group of trustees and senior staff, with their wives, who had been sitting on the platform and had come out by a different door. Mr Porphyry looked round at them. He seemed to have no wish to stay any longer.

'Yes,' he said. 'I'll put myself entirely in your hands.'

I was silently grateful that he was not going to keep me waiting on the fringes of the group which attracted a certain degree of shy but widespread curiosity.

Sir Joseph said, 'I'll have a talk with Merchant before tea if I can. I'll insist on a measure of consultation at each stage.'

Mr Porphyry nodded. 'We'll have a word before the end of the afternoon.'

I led him off in the general drift away from the main school building. There was much to be seen, though the thread of interest must have been fairly thin to a man whose broad responsibilities towards Coppinger did not have any localised stab of attachment induced by the work of a given pupil, unless it was my own. I certainly made no conscious effort to point out to him any work of mine, though in the appropriate places he did ask for it and made sensible comments about my capabilities.

'What did you think of the General's speech?'

I countered with a question of my own. 'It was serious, what he said, Sir, wasn't it?'

'Generals are a serious breed of men.'

'I'd never thought of Britain like that.'

'How had you thought of it?'

I was nonplussed at first. 'I suppose I hadn't thought of it at all,' I said. 'Though that's not really true. I'd thought of it in terms of history and geography, and poetry. I mean, a place, and people, stretching back in time. But I hadn't thought of it *now*.'

'And did he give you a sense of the present?' The somewhat gaunt and craggy features of his face, out of which shone the clear, pale-blue penetrating light of his eyes, were softened by the serious interest they expressed.

'Yes, sort of, Sir.'

'It was certainly one of the better speeches we have had. His career as a soldier has been shadowy. He was desk-bound for the war. But he's a considerable figure.' There was a finality in the judgment. We walked on together, heading towards a display of gymnastics on the cricket field.

'I presume you've made no plans for the summer holidays?'

'No, Sir.'

'And you do understand how this works, don't you?'

'Yes, Sir. I'm very grateful . . . I mean, to be chosen. . . .' I avoided looking at him. I felt a vague unease about the territory into which we were being drawn, and yet some impulse made me go on to say, 'But . . . there's not much *winning* about it, is there, Mr Porphyry?'

'That's not altogether true,' he said.

I waited, but he did not go on speaking. In so far as I could judge, his voice lacked conviction. I could not argue the point, but at the same time with what may well have seemed to him a form of delicate persistence, but which in me was more subconscious than premeditated, I waited patiently but expectantly for him to deny the charitable content of what he was doing.

He did precisely that. 'I don't want you to think of your scholarship as a charity. It's not.' He paused again.

'What is it then, Sir?' We had come to the edge of the cricket field, and were watching the tense callisthenics of a group of younger boys. I was reminded of my interrogation by Merchant during our circuit of this same field, and I felt a faint rush of resentment at the whole structuring of the position in which I now found myself. What right had this well-dressed, influential man to patronise me?

'I'm impressed by how well you've done here.' He paused, but I did not respond. 'The main purpose of the little that I can do is to ensure that your future is not handicapped . . .' again he paused; then, gruffly and quickly he went on to say, 'well, by domestic difficulties, problems at home.'

'Thank you, Sir,' I said. I stared woodenly ahead of me.

It seemed he did not detect any resentment in my attitude. 'How are things at home, anyway?' he asked. 'How do you get along with your stepmother?'

'All right, Sir. *Things* are all right.' I still did not turn towards him.

He paused. Then he said. 'I'm sorry. I'm intruding, aren't I? I don't have the right to ask such questions.'

I was conscious of him looking at me, and I did not know how to react. An apology from Mr Porphyry seemed so out of place, and though I knew that a gracious response was called

94

for I just could not find the words. I looked at him, the expression in my eyes perhaps a bit sheepish.

'What would you like to see next, Sir?'

'I don't mind. I'm in your hands.' The warmth of his natural curiosity had been retracted behind the angular features of his face, and his expression was polite and neutral. Looking briefly into his eyes I wondered if, perhaps, he was a lonely person. I knew next to nothing about him, and could recall his previous appearances at Coppinger only vaguely, had never been conscious of him with a wife at his side, yet did not feel I could ask any questions.

We tramped the school premises in a thorough tour. I accompanied it with a full commentary on people and events, to which he listened patiently. The earlier withdrawal of his questions about home, gentle and fulsome, weighed on me. I felt he had a right to know. He did in fact know quite a bit already, from Merchant's report. It made a nonsense of my reserve. Working within the limitations I had imposed by my slightly frozen reaction he kept up a persistent flow of questions and comments. I began to feel easy and relaxed in his company. He talked about the school and about his work; he answered questions, without fuss or pomposity or ceremony. There was a sense of power behind it all. He was sure of himself and free from pretence; and he had the reserve of the businessman. Normal self-interest, in an enterprise some peripheral aspects of which would be divulged to me in due course, had taught him discretion in all things, and though there resided within him at that time beliefs and ambitions which would soon enough change quite substantially my first view of him, these first impressions established a liking and a respect which did not change.

Eventually I said: 'That's about everything, Mr Porphyry.'

'You're an indefatigable guide.'

'Will I show you to the tea tent?'

'Do you take tea with the staff and trustees?'

'Yes, Sir.'

'Well, all right. There's no hurry though.'

We walked more slowly now. Having completed in so thorough a fashion my duties in showing him round, and having accompanied it by an equally comprehensive account of what we had seen, I now felt quite spent.

'I may have to have a word with the Bursar at tea, and also with the headmaster,' Mr Porphyry said, 'so I'm giving you this.' He handed me his card. 'Telephone me when you get home and we'll meet. I'll give you the details of what I've arranged. That gives you the chance to talk with your par . . . well, your father and stepmother, in case they already have things arranged for you.'

'I don't think they will,' I said.

'Perhaps not. But I must allow for it. Just leave things as free as you can.'

It would have been disloyal to explain to him that my father never had things arranged for me, that he was virtually incapable of planning ahead, and forgetful of even major events in my eyes, such as birthdays. I may have betrayed something of this in the look I gave him as I took the card.

He said: 'Tell me about your father.'

This time I felt no reserve. I felt a positive wish to give him an account of myself, and he seemed to welcome it as we slackened pace walking across the mown grass towards the distant marquee. I told him the things he must already have learnt from Merchant. He listened carefully. I found attractive the contrast between his rugged features and the eyes of a dusty blue that seemed always to have a faraway look in them. And then the outdoor appearance of his features, the crisp and vaguely unruly style of his hair, were at odds with the well-cut suit, the gold watch-chain, the plain cream shirt and the blue and gold tie. I was not disconcerted by his attention to what I was saying: quite the reverse. I welcomed it. I told him about Laurie

'And she's . . .' he paused, and seemed to be weighing carefully his choice of words; then he looked at me, his eyes focusing into a question: 'difficult?'

'She's all right,' I said. Inwardly, I smiled to myself. It was an expression used often by my father, almost invariably to mean the opposite. A person so described was thereby identified as not just not 'all right', but positively, even dangerously, wrong. Something of this identification, in the case of Laurie, might have sounded in my voice. But Porphyry did not question me further.

'I understand,' he said.

His words contained a willingness to understand rather than the comprehension itself. How could he grasp, in that moment, what to me, after many months, still contained enigmas? His use of the phrase 'I understand', was like my use of the phrase 'she's all right'. In both cases the meaning behind the words approximated to the opposite of their actual meaning. Laurie was not all right. She had never been all right. Only optimism and hope gave birth to the expression of a belief that *things,* one day, would be all right. And possibly in spite of Laurie, rather than because of her. Just so with Mr Porphyry. He did not understand. I'm not sure that he ever did understand. But in those words he was expressing towards me a commitment of himself, blind perhaps, uncertain, but comprehensive. And I was grateful to him.

We made our way to the tea tent, and for a time he was caught up in discussions with the Bursar and with other trustees. I carried plates of cakes and sandwiches to other guests, mingling among them though feeling oddly aloof. Eventually he returned to me and said that he would have to leave.

'Perhaps you'll come with me to the car.'

Leaving the tea tent in the slanting sunlight and walking back to the place where visitors with cars had parked them, I felt strangely at peace. We all have, I suspect, occasions when we consciously place ourselves in the hands of others; human innocence is sustained by human trust. That July afternoon was one such occasion. It had been brought about by strange and complicated events and judgments. But in itself it had been

D

simple and natural enough. With term drawing to a close, with the accounts to which the General had referred being called in from all of us, with the imminent departure of Lytton weighing somewhat upon Pritchett and myself, with another summer term and another school year over, I had an exhilarating sense of the future. Mr Porphyry offered freedom. He stood on the edge of unmapped but attractive territories into which he was disposed to send me, and for which he seemed prepared to make full and generous provision. What price would be exacted remained to be seen. But I trusted his reserved, contained approach.

The door of his Lagonda closed with a solid crunch. He placed a brown hat of indeterminate style on his head and turned the ignition. Red and yellow lights appeared on the dashboard, and there was a slight ticking sound from the engine. With his fingers clutching the starter he looked out at me.

'I'll hear from you by the beginning of August, then?'

'Yes, Mr Porphyry. I'll telephone.'

'Good.'

The engine sprang into life. The low silvery-grey car moved smoothly out and headed down the hill. Briefly, on the bend, the red brake lights glowed. I watched until the car was out of sight, my anticipation for the future quickening still within me.

IV

'We might meet Bennett and Mrs Patterson.'

'Do you think they're lovers?'

'The beast with two backs, eh?' Lytton laughed.

'It was really something, wasn't it?' Pritchett said.

'Will we do the last staff meeting?'

'I dunno. What's the point? It's all over, really.'

'I suppose.'

We ambled along the quarry road in the warm afternoon

sunshine. The principal guests had all gone, and we had time on our hands before the evening meal. The hedges were profuse, just there, with the creamy greenish flowers of old man's beard; it seemed to run with endless vigour beside us as we walked. The grasses there were thick and tall, and intermingled with cornflower, vetch and clover. At the edge yellow dust from the unmetalled road had discoloured the rich green verge.

'How's the scholar?' Lytton asked.

'O.K.' I said.

'What do you have to do?'

I told them about my afternoon with Mr Porphyry.

'That's a marvellous car he has,' Pritchett said. 'Spect you'll get around in that.'

'Spect so.'

'Did he carry out an examination of your morals, my boy?' Lytton asked. 'They're a matter of constant concern to me.'

'He asked me why I was constantly looking at Janet in the tea tent.'

'Did he?'

'Don't be daft. Course he didn't.'

'You'll have to give it up, though. All the snogging. There'll be no more of that.'

'How do you know I haven't given it up already?'

'I know. That's how.'

Pritchett picked up a stone from the edge of the road and threw it ahead of us. It arched high up in the blue sky and then fell again on the roadway with a little spurt of dust. 'We'd best go back,' he said. 'It'll be tea soon.'

'We have to sit through that concert,' Lytton said. 'Aren't you singing?'

'Yes,' I said. 'I decided to swell the chorus. I think I might go back into the choir.'

'Rash decision. Think of all those tempting trebles.' He paused. 'And Danby?'

'Yes, he's playing some solo.'

'You're too keen. You'll go too far for your own good. The

99

life of the senses will pass you by.' Lytton had stopped, his hand raised, one finger sticking up in the air. His shirt was open, he was wearing no jacket, his hair ruffled. 'I'm afraid Mr Porphyry is pointing upwards. Moved by the spirit of the Lord, of men and of angels, you will have to put the things of this world behind you. I could read it in his eyes.'

'Rot,' I said. 'He's just an ordinary businessman. I like him, too.'

'You're lucky,' Pritchett said. 'You know that?' He raised his eyebrows emphasising the questioning tone in his voice.

We were standing on the rough roadway, ready to start back. Pritchett had picked up another stone to throw and had been testing its weight and suitability with little juggler's throws of it from one hand to the other. Now he stood still, his back to the road ahead, as if barring our way. He was looking directly at me. So was Lytton.

'I know,' I said. 'I am lucky. Is it bad luck to say it?'

It was my turn to look back at them, searching in their faces for their endorsement of my good fortune. Neither spoke. In the perfect stillness of the afternoon, of which we all now formed immobile parts, the occasional distant shout or cry of boys playing carried across to us over the half-mile or so we had walked.

Lytton looked down, and with his foot traced a faint line in the dust of the roadway, then another beside it, then a third. 'Druids,' he said, and left the faint marks on the roadway. Then he turned and started back towards the school.

Pritchett threw the stone. It was less accurate than the first, and came down in the hedge. We fell into step, side by side, and joined with Lytton. Then, linking arms, we performed for the vacant fields and hedgerow shrubs our rudimentary music hall routine. We did it once, and stopped, disengaging our arms. Nothing was said. The distant clocktower bell began to strike, the sullen sound producing a faint, leaden echo from the rising ground behind us. Without hurrying, we walked on back to tea.

Chapter Five

I

It had rained, and the red and black tiles were still wet, though the sun had come out again. It was weather more suited to April than to the end of July. It was uncomfortably cold and damp. The summer seemed to be falling apart. My father sat outside the house among the potted plants on a wooden stool. His legs were spread wide, and he had on a pair of blue overalls, a vest with sleeves and canvas shoes. He wore no socks. He had put on glasses.

'When did you start wearing glasses?' I asked. I stood across from him, my back against the wall, my hands in my pockets.

'A month or so ago,' he said. 'Laurie made me. Told me I was squinting at things. She was right. Makes a big difference. She looks after your father. Takes good care of him. She's a good sort. Make no mistake.' He bent further over the work on which he was engaged, the effort increasing as he did so.

'What are you doing?' I asked.

'Got to . . .' He paused, gritting his teeth. 'Got to . . . make it . . . certain . . . this time.' He spoke in jerky phrases, his jaws clenched together, his strong, broad fingers straining at the particular job in hand. He was repairing his trousers, but up to that moment I had not looked too carefully at what exactly he was doing. The effort, expressed in a series of grunts and puffs, now made me curious.

'But what have you got to make certain?'

'This,' he said, and he pulled the needle through, dragging after it what seemed more like rope than twine. 'Shit!' he said. It twisted and tangled, and he had to tease it out before yanking it through properly. He tugged with enormous strength, the whole trouser jumping on his knee as he did so.

'You really are sewing it for keeps,' I said.

'Do a good job well,' he said, 'and it stays done.' He laughed to himself, looking down at his own handiwork. Then, his face taking on a look of serious determination, he again plunged in the large fisherman's needle, and using a thick steel nut as a thimble pushed it steadily through.

'Is this a running repair job?' I asked. 'Or is it something more durable?'

He looked up at me, peering over the tops of his spectacles. It was the very first time I experienced that particular mannerism, one that became an essential, regular one from then on. At first his gaze was critical, and I felt almost nervous as I lounged, hands in pockets, against the open French window. He hated sloppiness of stance, often told me to take my hands out of my pockets, and particularly liked people to stand up straight and hold their shoulders back and their heads high in the air. But on that first evening home, feeling indulgent perhaps, he overlooked my own attitude and went on to strike another that was new, and yet was to become memorable: he took off the glasses, folded the side pieces in, and, grasping the whole fairly fragile contraption in his huge fist, raised it towards me as if it was a conductor's baton, and began punctuating his words with little sharp strokes in the air.

'It's like this,' he said. 'I won't change my shape. I have these trousers which are comfortable. And they need braces. I like to feel secure. So I have a pair of leather braces and a pair of felt ones. The felt is for comfort, the leather for strength. Sewn together they will last me to my grave.'

'We'll carry you down on them,' I said.

'Maybe you will.'

'Are they hard to sew?'

'I've been at it an hour.' He again put on the glasses and began yanking at the needle to pull it through the layers of felt, leather and beige-coloured twill material out of which his trousers were made.

'Can I help?'

He shook his head, his teeth too tightly clenched together to allow him to speak. I had come home that very afternoon. For some reason he had not been out at work, and I had discovered him sitting there in the sunlight engaged in what seemed like a herculean task. Laurie had let me in, with a smile and a hug, both brief, and had then gone off to the shops. And leaving my case in the downstairs hallway of the house in Chelsea in which they lived I had found my way through to the small, immaculate patio garden which he had created out of the yard at the back.

'Tell me about this scholarship?'

I explained about Mr Porphyry and gave him an account of the various stages, emphasising what Porphyry had said about winning, and playing down, as much as possible, the stress Merchant had laid upon the scholarship as a device by which boys might be rescued from sticky situations at home. My father listened mostly in silence, absorbed in what he was doing, and occasionally grunting or puffing with the effort.

'I got quite a good round of applause when I went up to get the prize.'

'Did you? That's good. Who did you say awarded them?'

I told him.

'Good fellow. Close to Churchill, of course. Man I can't stand. But in spite of that he had a mind of his own. Didn't do a bad job in the war. Did he talk about it?'

'No. He talked a bit about soldiering, National Service, things like that.'

'Your friend, Philcox, he's doing that now, isn't he?'

'It's Philpotts, Dad. And he's at Oxford. He got his call-up deferred.'

'Well, if you never tell me these things, how am I meant to know? Your father's not a fool. Wants to know what's going on.' He paused, looking up at me, his expression one of challenge. Then it softened. 'Why did you tell me not to come?'

I suddenly felt a bit uncomfortable. 'I thought it was better,' I said, 'in view of the scholarship. You have to be with Mr Porphyry if you win. It would look odd, you being there as well. You see, the question of, well, needing help . . .' I tailed off into silence.

'You're not ashamed of me, are you?'

'Of course not.'

Even so, my father looked up at me sharply.

'It's a first-rate school, you know. Make no mistake about it. It's as good as a public school any day. Good as my own school.'

I didn't answer. It was a matter on which he was quite sensitive. Though he had not really been instrumental at all in getting me a place at Coppinger, he had long since recognised its advantages, not the least of which being the extent of the corporate concern for the well-being of the boys, spreading over their holidays as well as over what they did professionally after departing. It would be a long time before I could share his view, seeing Coppinger as he did, and feeling gratitude for the strange accidents which had brought me there. Just at that time the fact of always having to explain the place was a handicap, and I let pass in silence the moment of possible contention between us.

I told him about the term, about Lytton and Pritchett, and about the Gaffer, for whom my father had a certain affection. I felt chilly standing there, but unwilling to move inside.

'I've done what I think is right,' he said. He paused. His expression, as he looked down at the needle and thread, and at the crumpled trousers across his knees, was one of faint bewilderment.

I did not quite understand whether he meant his marriage

to Laurie, or whether the statement referred broadly to everything. I was at a point in my feelings about him that wavered between two extremes: on the one hand, that nothing he had done, in all his life, had really been 'right'; on the other hand, that everything had been more or less right. My childhood had been governed by the latter view, an innocent and uncritical judgment of what was there, and against which there were no alternatives for comparison. But that phase was over. I was now heading in the opposite direction, confirming my doubts and reservations about the 'rightness' of virtually everything. It was an attitude which, as far as he was concerned, had callous aspects. It was governed by selfishness on my part, and by the capacity I now had, through the scholarship, and just through being a bit older, to break away and leave him to his own devices. It never occurred to me that he might want or need me. He had Laurie. She was enough. It was by no means the final state of affairs. It was an interregnum, more brief than I anticipated, and mercifully not coloured, in any serious way, by bitter words or sharp antagonism. In due course I would swing back again, recovering another and softer attitude, that, for all his incapacity, 'rightness' was part of his make up, a spur to his sad ambition, a goad to his wounded heart.

Perhaps he sensed my ambivalence as I stood in idle relaxation against the wall, silent in the face of his claim that he had done the right thing. He looked up at me, pausing in his work. 'We've had good times together.' There was a look of appeal in his face. 'Just you and me, old son. We've been through the mill together, make no mistake. But we've come out smiling. They weren't easy, those days. Trying to make a home for you on my own. Of course there was Alice, and Ursula, and . . .' He raised his hand in a vague movement implying a small and forgotten host of camp followers who had, in some strange way, helped us along in our turbulent passage together. The gesture he made was dramatic, yet quite restrained; it was also, to begin with, totally convincing. The look of appeal on his face had softened into one of recollection.

It was as if, with hypnotic power, he swept me back in time with him, and briefly I recaptured a swift succession of images of those occasions from which we had emerged together, smiling. But the bravery of the smiles seemed now a bit faded, the recollection of happy occasions did not last, and as I looked across at him I found myself wondering at his extraordinary ability to paint a romantic picture of events which had in reality been far from romantic. He was supremely able to obliterate, with his highly selective brand of nostalgia, the drunkenness and dissipation with which I had been familiar since early childhood. But the trick was not working quite as well with me now. There had been a time when I was able simply to banish from my mind, in imitation of him, the dark shadows of hurt, the ominous recollections that provoked in me inescapable feelings of shame, even of disgust.

There had been a time when, as a form of self-protection, I buried in forgetfulness those selected hurts that could not be accommodated in the generally benevolent view I had of him. But now I was more disposed to let them form part of the picture. Laurie, of course, was instrumental in this. She had intruded, and had in part usurped my own position; and my view of her, and necessarily of him as well, had become more objective. One of these buried hurts which I resurrected belonged to the first encounter I had ever had with her. It had been in the doorway of a pub, one summer evening, and they were there together, in the mixture of sunlight and brown shadow. Impatient as always, but curious as well, I had planted myself in front of the door, but had made no real impact on them. Suddenly Laurie seemed to notice me. She smiled, nodded, then turned to him. 'How many have you?' she asked. Then she added, with a throaty laugh, 'Legitimate, of course.' And my father, with typically dramatic evasion, had held his hand out towards me and said: 'He is all that is left to me now.' I had hated her for that, supposing it to be an insult. And when, later, I discovered that it was all far more complicated, I had hated her even more.

It did not last. After the encounter, I buried the memory; after the painful discovery that my father had not been married to my mother, I buried that as well; but it had left a residue of uncertainty about his easy parcelling up of the past into 'good times together'. Laurie had become a permanent obstruction to our mutual journeys back in time. Instead of doing it together I found myself travelling into the territory of the past on my own, re-examining the buried episodes and endeavouring to make fresh judgments about them. The hate which once I had felt toward Laurie had become indifference. She was a fact of life, to be accepted with all the tolerance of my fifteen years. But the same set of attitudes was spilling over into my relationship with him. The vivid, unquestioning love which, for as long as I could remember I had felt for him, had also become diluted by the watery colouring of doubt and disenchantment. I looked on them now as a couple; myself as an individual. I was deriving a certain frail authority from my sense of independence, developing it, protecting it, using it to shape our new relationship.

'Do you ever see Ursula?' I asked. 'And Madge? How is Babette?'

He shook his head. 'They were good days, old son. But they're over. It's a new life now.' He looked at the pile of clothing on his knee, the leathery coils of the braces, and checked out the length of twine still left in the fisherman's needle with which he was working. How many times had I heard him say, 'It's a new life now'? How many small transitions had been accompanied by this large claim? I wanted to see, arrayed before me, all the bedsitting rooms of my childhood, the faded faces of different, unexplained women, the challenges of so many jobs, the muddled geography of small corners of London. I wanted, once again, without the intrusion of reason or judgment, simply to be sure what my feelings were. I wanted the past to possess me again, a past when my command over his affections had been more absolute than now; a past in which the two of us had tramped in and out of other people's lives, but always together, and always having, as it were, a secret territory into which we could withdraw, away from everyone else. But it had gone, just as my love for Babette had gone, just as the rich experience which I associated with her mother, Madge, and with Ursula, had faded, never to return.

He looked up at me and smiled. It was a sad smile, sweet, gentle, apologetic; and then the smiling part of his face straightened out, and all that was left was the bleak, indifferent solitude of his tormented feelings. 'It'll be all right,' he said. He had gritted his teeth. 'Everything's going to be all right. Mark my words.'

'I will,' I said. I tried to sound cheerful. 'I always do.'

He laughed. 'That's true.'

'Shall we have some tea?' I asked.

'You make it.'

I was relieved. I went inside. I needed to escape from him for a while. I felt the importance of this encounter, though not understanding fully that its brevity was a kind of threat. Once Laurie came back I would be contending with the two of them, and they would merge again into the entity which had brought about the certain distancing, the 'hardening off' which I suppose, in a way, had helped to earn me the Porphyry Scholarship. But just now he was mine, and I felt I had recovered, in those few moments of conversation, something of a past that I could never truly have again. In a way I was mistaken; it would come again, though in a different form. But just then echoes, odours, pulsations, the deep instinctive animal tremblings which emerge from far below in our subconscious being, and from far back in time, had surfaced and gripped. As I pottered and fiddled in the small and untidy kitchen, familiarising myself again with things over which I could not feel the legitimate sense of possession which in other circumstances, there might have been, I looked occasionally out from the small window at his preoccupied figure. And so passionately did he appear to be attacking the enormous task of combining braces and trousers that I thought to myself: it is as if he were stitching into the leather and cloth the very substance of his mortal soul.

I took the tea out to him, and we sat together in the sunlight. The weather had warmed up, though it was still cold for the time of year. There was a stone table and a couple of canvas and wood chairs, in one of which I sat.

'You're doing that as if your life depended on it,' I said.

He chuckled. 'You never can tell,' he said. 'Life might depend on it.'

I became more critically interested, leaning over to inspect the general competence with which he had carried out a task of no mean significance. Felt braces were quite common then, so were elastic ones; but the leather contraption had the appearance of something acquired from a harness-maker to hold in check a powerful beast of the field, or even a performing bear. The heavy stitching of leather and felt had made the two loops quite stiff, and they hung down over his knees from the tops of the trousers, which in their turn had been reinforced in order to make certain and secure this basic piece of his working apparel.

He watched me for any sign of disrespect or scepticism. But my inspection was wholly serious and absorbed. He seemed relieved and pleased, a smile of achievement suddenly replacing his preoccupied expression. Then he looked serious again, and stared into my eyes.

'This scholarship,' he said. 'It's a good show. Well done. Your father's proud of you.'

'You know it's . . . partly because of you marrying Laurie. You did know that, didn't you?'

'I had a letter from Mr Merchant, your headmaster, about it. I had to give my consent, of course. He said something about home background being taken into account.'

'And did he say what that meant?'

'No. I have the letter. Straightforward enough. Merchant's a direct enough fellow. At least, always has been with me. What did he say to you?'

'Nothing, really,' I said. 'Just that your remarriage must have made a bit of a difference, and it might be good for me to get away during the summer.'

'And that's all he said?' My father was suddenly alert to the possibility of deeper and more complex aspects to the Porphyry Scholarship. He took off his glasses, folding them.

I thought quickly about how I could sustain the deviation I had made from the facts of the case. I nodded. 'Mr Porphyry said it was on merit I won it. Different things were taken into account. But work mattered, and behaviour. I did well at school the year before, and that was taken into account.'

'You certainly did well then. But what about this year?'

I grinned a bit sheepishly. 'I was a year ahead of my age,' I said.

He looked at me without answering, his expression now thoughtful. Did my age, my progress in the world, my prospects, strike him just then? Or was he thinking of Laurie, and of his marriage, and of the strange, romantic sweetness of our lives that had come to a sudden conclusion then? It provoked another line of inquiry. 'This Por-phy-ry?' he said. 'That how you pronounce it?' He lifted up the folded spectacle frame, pointing it in my direction.

He had given it three, more or less equal syllables. I corrected him. 'Porphyry,' I said. 'Like the horse, a palfrey, but without the l.'

'Ah, Porphyry. Funny name. Well, tell me, what sort of a bloke is he?' He put his glasses back on and inspected once again the job he had done on the braces, which was now complete. Then he laid them aside.

The idea of calling Mr Porphyry a 'bloke' made me laugh. 'What's so funny, then?'

'He's not really a "bloke",' I said. 'He's . . . he's . . .'

'We're all blokes,' my father said.

I was not disposed to argue, but silently disagreed. Quite what I should substitute eluded me. A gentleman? A businessman? 'A city man', as Merchant himself had described him?

'He's in business,' I said. 'He's in the city. He seems to be well-off.' I tried to put into words my observations and feelings, based on the afternoon we had spent together. It was an inadequate picture. I had asked far too little; his had been the interrogation. And I had asked none of the questions which might have been of interest to my father: his school, his war experience, his family. I did not even know if he was married, nor why he was a trustee of Coppinger. But I managed to give some picture of him, and in the end my father gave his endorsement to the unknown programme of events which would colour and shape the long weeks of the summer holiday. He did so a bit reluctantly.

'It's a good thing,' he said. 'Very good. I had thought you might help your father a bit. In his jobs. Good clients. Good money. You'd earn a bit. Come around with me.' He paused, and I saw that in his mind's eye he was travelling through the territory of his clients: jobbing gardening in Belsize Park, in Hyde Park Gate, in the Boltons. And perhaps, coming to the private conclusion that it would not do, he said: 'But I can't stand in the way of an opportunity like this. It's your life.'

He struck an oddly rigid attitude, his hands now resting on his knees, his head turned sharply, even severely towards me, his eyes fixed in a penetrating stare, his final attempt to get me to see things, if only very slightly, in terms of greater involvement in his life. Seeing that there was no progress to be made, he turned towards the tea things and lifted up his cup, now only lukewarm, and drained it, with an 'ah!' at the end.

'Is he . . .? Is he a good sort? This Porphyry? I mean, will I meet him? Would we get on?'

I almost burst out laughing. They might quite possibly meet; but at that early stage in my friendship with Mr Porphyry, after only one encounter, I already knew, even in my father's mystical 'thousand year span' to which all great questions, his own and those belonging to eternity, were submitted, there could never be any true 'meeting' between the two men.

Fortunately, there was no need to answer. Laurie had returned from the shops, and now appeared in the French windows, a cigarette between her red lips, her eyes winking and screwed up against the smoke, the ash hanging, long and perilously curved, from the end. Yes, Porphyry was a good sort, I could have answered. I could not place him here, beside my father; and I certainly could not with my stepmother.

II

'I'll not come between you,' Laurie said. 'You must do things your way.'

'We will, my love, we will.'

'And not so much of the "my love", if you please.'

'Can I help?' I said.

'No. You two just sit here. I'll clear away. I'd prefer to do it on my own.'

She made no move, however. She talked with the cigarette in her mouth, and, though she had perfected certain skills, including that of moving her lips hardly at all as she spoke, there was an inevitable movement up and down of the cigarette. Magically, though the ash on the end seemed occasionally to reach impossible lengths, she managed most of the time to get it over an ashtray before it fell.

'That front room will be free before the end of the month,' she went on, looking at my father. 'You'll have to decorate it.'

'The Colonel's going then?'

'Yes. Off to Brighton, he told me. He's talking about starting a security firm. Run on modern lines. You recruit people, send them out on contract.'

'Sounds interesting.' My father did not sound in the least interested.

She laughed, dryly. 'He'll never do it. He's not the type. He's had it too easy. He's no real drive. Poor man, he'll end up on a small salary, running it for someone else.' She paused, and looked at the table, untidy with empty dishes. 'That's if it happens at all,' she said.

We had finished supper. We sat in the room with the French windows open on the small garden. There was still a residue of evening sunlight outside, but it no longer fell in the garden, which was now in shadow. My father had sown some tobacco plant in a pot, and the scent of it was beginning to penetrate the air in the room.

Laurie got up and took two of the dishes through into the kitchen.

'You don't mind if we go for a drink, do you?' My father asked. He looked at me. He seemed almost nervous.

'Of course not,' I said.

'I think you can't . . .?' The question was also an appeal. He did not want to transfer the uneasy relationship of the three of us to a public house.

'I don't want to, thanks,' I said. 'I'll take a walk, down by the river. Then I'll read.'

'Yes, do that,' he said. 'Much better.'

I stacked up the plates on the table, and then, in spite of her injunction, brought them to the door of the small kitchen.

'Put them over there,' she said. She seemed to have forgotten what she had said earlier.

'It was a very nice supper,' I said.

The remark did not seem to please her. She squinted at me through the cigarette smoke. 'Very simple,' she said. 'He's easily pleased, your father. He likes nothing fancy. Now, sit down again. I've no room for any more.' She managed to make me feel incidental.

My father had left his chair and was standing in the French windows looking out at the flowers. He had put on a shirt and tie before dinner, and was now also wearing a light, loose-fitting summer jacket. His figure was shadowy against the evening light through the open windows, and I watched him as he checked his pockets, a slight rattle coming from the match-box in one of them.

113

'Can I have a key?' I asked.

'Of course. I have one for you on my key-ring.' He felt in his trouser pockets and found a small bunch of keys from which he detached mine.

'Thanks,' I said.

'You won't lose it?'

I shook my head.

'And you'll mind yourself crossing that embankment road? Quite a lot of traffic.'

'I'll mind myself,' I said. 'I'll do nothing stupid. You'd never forgive me if I did!'

He laughed. Then he frowned. 'Your room's all right, isn't it?'

'Yes, it's fine.'

'And you don't mind being at the top of the house?'

'I like it.'

'I try to do what's best.'

'I know,' I said. I passed by him, and went on into the garden, now shadowy in the dusk. The last rays of the sun were disappearing from the walls of buildings.

It was possible to walk no more than ten or twelve paces. One then reached the confines of the area, and came up against a trellised wall on which he had roses and clematis. They were still establishing themselves, but the large white petals of Henryi stood out against the discoloured brick and the dull wood of the trellis up which it climbed. I turned and faced him across what was really no more than a backyard.

'You've done it well.'

'Do you think so?'

I was surprised by his simple reply. He welcomed my approval. A year before he would have taken it for granted.

'I think it's terrific, what you've done.'

'The clematis, of course, wonderful flower. So long as you have the roots right. See here,' and he crossed, and pointed down at my feet, bending over. I saw a round pipe emerging from the ground. 'That goes a good eighteen inches down. Well,

114

fifteen, anyway. Get the water to the roots. Thirsty buggers they are. No mistake.' He seemed suddenly to have come to life. He stood up and looked at me.

At that time I must have been almost the same height as he was. I was a thin, unmuscled boy, but in actual stature our eyes were more or less on a level, and we looked now at each other with a sense of having re-established the unspoken affections of the past. Yet there was a reserve between us, a holding back. The odd conjunction of enthusiasm and love, that force in one's life that makes one seek out a person—parent, child, brother, sister, wife, mistress—in order to make them the spectator of one's deepest endeavour, was there briefly. Once, it would have taken a more directly personal form: an embrace, a gesture, a kiss. Now it was more oblique; it depended on the objective substance of flowers, a more tentative search for contact, approval, the unspoken as well as the spoken expression of the fusion that binds people together. We sensed in each other ancient needs, and responded to them, standing there in the dusk. And I felt a kind of pity for him, that added to my reserve.

Physically, emotionally, in the wake of his growing imperfections, his stature should have been diminished in my eyes. Youthful wisdom, with its rapid and hungry expanse, should have contained him more easily within the confines of his really rather shabby life. Here he stood before me, a jobbing gardener, in his early fifties, married to a woman well past her prime, who kept a London lodging house. A few frail plants marked the limits upon his relaxation; the White Hart, an occasional theatre, books, the Chelsea Flower Show, these constituted his entertainment. Laurie was his security; and I, if I was to believe him, the object of the greater portion of his natural love. Yet, far from bringing him down in size, this all had quite the opposite effect. If anything, he grew in stature. Pity in my heart gave greater depth to the shadow he cast. The appeal which I detected in his eyes was more mute now, and consequently more yearning. Not only did Laurie stand between us; Porphyry did, as well. Marginally, more things were left unsaid. But in the vacuum thus created his slow extension from being just my father into being a man as well gained added force.

I suppose that this is another way of explaining my own growing up. What I was seeing was really something taking place inside myself. Yet its most vivid expression lay within curious visual images associated particularly with that first day home from Coppinger: my father's figure crouched over his trousers, plying his needle as though engaged in a fight to the death; his figure outlined in the dusk; his broad back, as he bent down to point towards the clematis roots; his eyes, close to mine, suddenly afire with enthusiasm over the deep thirst of one of his favourite flowers.

The glow was quenched soon enough. For the second time in a few hours Laurie appeared in the dark opening where the French windows led back into the house. She had put something on her head—it looked like a black beret—and she held under her arm a large, shapeless handbag.

'Are you coming, then?' she asked.

We both went in.

We all left together. But outside the house I turned in the opposite direction, and headed down towards the river. I had no sense of exclusion at not going with them. I felt, indeed, a relief; it was a respite to be alone again, not to witness those aspects of him which really made him something of a stranger. Not with Alice, nor with Ursula, did he behave like this. And though it seemed to suggest to me a less free, a less independent spirit, I had to be careful. After all, this was a chosen situation. I had never witnessed my father before in the binding relationship of marriage; at least, not since I was a small child. Perhaps this was what it did to people? Perhaps the muting, quietening, dampening down was mutual: an outcome of the contract? Perhaps the wild, undisciplined creature who had led me from lodging to lodging through my childhood, who had battened upon women and derided men, was an aberration, and only now, in later youth, was a truer, more homogeneous, more complex figure emerging. Perhaps this was my real father.

Across the river the lights of the Battersea fun fair glowed and winked, their reflection in the lapping water providing a foreground of movement and a barrier of distance that was enticing. Had I been more adventurous I would probably have gone over. But I was content to store that up for a future occasion. There was enjoyment enough, that evening, in the sound of the fairground music which could be clearly heard floating across in the dusk; so could the shouts of people and the laughter, the occasional squeals and shrieks among the lumberings of the machinery. For a while I leaned on the stone parapet which lined the embankment there, trying to identify odd pieces of material where they floated by in the lamplight. Then I turned up river. The air was suffused with a strange, heady perfume, not altogether pleasing. It came from the shrubs which lined the embankment at Cheyne Walk, and as I moved along on the river side, towards the great curving shadow of Albert Bridge, the smell thickened around me, sweet and cloying. I did not know it then, but my nostrils were filled with an odour that had spanned my father's life, from his childhood days in Folkestone until then; an odour which would be associated with his death; an odour that was to cast its richness and its mellow echo of foreboding across the weeks of that summer holiday. For the borders and the beds at the end of Flood Street, where my stepmother had her house, were thickly planted with mature, and in some cases remarkably large, bushes of *ligustrum* and *ligustrum sinense*, the more or less common privet.

III

I came back to the house, and stood for a while in the deserted room in which we had eaten supper. Idly, I scanned the evening paper. It was open at one of the sports pages, and my father had underscored the names of one or two horses. I wondered if he had in fact placed any bets, or whether he was indulging, as he sometimes did, in a form of fantasy wagering. I would ask him.

I was tired, and had no idea when they would be back. For a while I sat in the unlighted room facing towards the French windows and the vague glow in the London sky that never quite permitted night to fall. After a time I decided to go to bed.

It seemed more final, climbing up through the house, with its alien tenants, to the top floor where I had been temporarily allotted an attic room, than it would have been sleeping in the basement with them. This had been the situation before. Though it induced a greater sense of being cut off, I welcomed it. The attic room, though small, was attractive. My father had mentioned that a student was in the one opposite, but had said nothing else. My own looked out on the street. It occurred to me that, judged on the external evidence of my return 'home', I was hardly the needy candidate for the help that was a significant part of the Porphyry Scholarship. The reality of Coppinger was that one knew only as much about the background of other boys as they chose to divulge, and in general it did amount to very little. I did not even know at all well the other two who had been in for the scholarship, but it did occur to me that Porphyry himself might well be a bit perplexed were he to see the house, my father, my stepmother, and the room in which I now vaguely contemplated the summer holiday stretching ahead of me.

I undressed and got into bed. I was reading *Pastoral,* and was absorbed by the romance of it as I lay propped on the pillow turned towards the bedside lamp. I must have fallen asleep without turning out the light, the book open on the bed clothes. For that was how I lay when I was woken again by sounds coming from the street below.

At first it seemed mild enough, a shout, a laugh, and then silence. I looked at my watch. It was twenty minutes to twelve.

Then I felt a prickle of unease. The voice seemed to be that of my father.

I crossed over to the window, which was already open, and looked out. He was below in Flood Street, standing out in the middle of the deserted roadway, pointing at Laurie who was at the top of the steep flight of steps which led down to the basement. She had her back to him, and as far as I could see was bending her head slightly down, as though uncertain of the steps.

'You will do what I say,' he said. 'You fiend! You will do exactly what I say!'

I could not gauge what the tone in his voice meant, but it was far from containing the rage which the words might suggest. It might even have implied a suppressed laughter, or at least a sense of amusement behind the wild and characteristic charge of fiendishness. It was she who laughed, however.

'Come on, George, you old goat. Don't stand there making an exhibition of yourself.' She began to descend the steps.

'I'm not making an exhibition of myself. I'm just telling you, categorically, you will obey me. Do you hear?'

She paused on the steps for a moment. As far as I could see from above she was looking through the railings at him. Then she turned her head down, seemed to shrug her shoulders, and descended out of his sight. From above I could see her, and watched as she fumbled for keys in her bag.

He stood with his hand still outstretched, and seemed for a moment intent on shouting something more after her. But then did not. Instead he crossed to the railings which surrounded the area, and held the thick spikes on the top of them, looking down after her. The altercation had been brief. If it had excited any attention beyond my own then it had been discreet enough to pass without notice. He was not drunk; merry, perhaps.

Wise or not, I decided to go down. Nothing had been said about the next day. I had not been told to go off to bed. No real discussion at all had taken place about the holiday. I had already sensed a new tension between them in the afternoon, after I had arrived, and again at supper time, when the conversation had moved fitfully, with awkward alternations, between the things I had discussed with him and those which she had raised, many of them concerned with mundane responsibilities about the house. But in reality I was curious.

I had no dressing gown. I put trousers and a jersey over my pyjamas and went quickly down. The light was on in their main room. He had closed the French windows and stood in front of them, his legs apart, his hands plunged deep in his jacket pockets, pulling down the lightweight beige material. He was staring at her, and only slowly turned his eyes towards me.

'She's a fiend,' he said. 'Accusing me! Accusing me!'

Laurie sat at the table, an expression of studied lack of interest on her face. She had put on her glasses, and was scanning the evening paper, a cigarette between her lips. She glanced across at me.

'I thought you'd gone to bed.'

'I had,' I said. 'I heard the noise.'

'One of your father's more light-hearted tantrums. It wasn't worth getting up for it.'

'Tantrum?' he said. 'What do you mean, tantrum?'

'He'll calm down,' she said to me. She went on reading.

My father was by no means drunk; but at the same time he was a stage beyond being merry. He was at that indeterminate point at which he was finding it difficult to define for himself exactly what attitude he should adopt to those around him. And, if the confusion had been present in his mind as he stood with his arm outstretched in the middle of Flood Street, it was much more the case now with me there as a sympathetic audience, biased in his favour, pliant to his moods.

'I think I will go to bed now,' I said.

'No you won't,' he said. He raised his eyebrows, looking at me in almost a startled way. 'Sit down.'

I went on standing without answering, but made no move to leave the room.

'He's tired,' Laurie said. 'He's had a long day. You should let him go to bed.'

'Piffle. You don't know what you're talking about. You never know what you're talking about. He's a man now. He's strong. Should be doing a man's job. Should be working alongside his father.'

'You don't know what work is,' Laurie said. 'You're always talking about it. Always telling us how hard you work.'

'Now,' he said. 'Now, steady on. I've worked, and worked. To the bone!' His voice boomed out on the last word. He took a hand out of his pocket and pointed at her, as if he intended saying more. Then he thought better of it. He looked from her to me. Then he fixed his eyes on the carpet in front of him. He was a bit like an animal cornered between two potential tormentors, quite different in what they intended, and not having started any positive action against him. He therefore did not know to which of the two of us he should respond.

'Go to bed,' Laurie said. She did not look up from the paper. It wasn't an order; it was just advice.

'He can decide in his own good time.'

'It's not my worry,' she said.

'She keeps me here a virtual prisoner,' he said, looking up at me, frowning. 'She's cruel. She's a fiend. She'll be the death of me.' He pointed at her, and raised his voice: 'You'll be the death of me!'

I could not really understand anything he was saying. A prisoner? Cruel? How could it be?

'Your father will have to go into an institution,' she said. 'He's getting too difficult for me to handle.'

'You see!' he said. 'It's clear! She's going to lock me up! Oh, Sonny boy, you don't know what goes on here. You've a lot to learn.' He began, in his soft, mellow voice, a snatch from an Al Jolson song, 'When skies are grey, dear, I don't mind the grey skies . . .' He broke off again. 'What does it matter? Where will we be in a thousand years?'

'I'll go to bed, I think.'

'Yes, go to bed. Forget what I've said. She's a good sort. She's a fiend at times, but she's a good sort. She understands George, don't you, luvvy? You understand me. No one else does. Old Laurie does. You're wise, aren't you, duckie? You sit there, pretending you're taking no notice. But really you run the whole show. It's *all* you, damn you! I can't do without you. You fiend!'

He had lost interest in me. He stood in the middle of the carpet, under the light, his half-closed eyes fixed on her, his hands once again bearing down with great weight inside his pockets. He was an uncertain, clumsy, imperfect man, shambling a little in the wilderness of his muddled mind, reaching out to seize upon the almost equally uncertain raft of her stern and, according to him, cruel disposition.

I should have blessed her, I suppose. She was rescuing me from obligations and responsibilities; freeing me for other ventures. But I felt only a cold indifference, and a certain sadness at seeing his dependence turning in a direction other than myself.

'Goodnight,' I said. I turned to the door, half-expecting to be called back. With my hand on the handle I looked from him to her and to my father once again. 'Goodnight,' I repeated. He nodded, but did not speak. He looked slightly drunker than he had earlier, and immeasurably more tired. He took his hand out of his pocket and waved it in the air, half in farewell, half in dismissal. Laurie made no move, and said nothing. I left them.

IV

I can still recover, in my imagination, the scene as I left it. I can still see, in my mind's eye, the room with its single central light, the furniture and the two figures. I can still picture her as she sat, newspaper, cigarette, glasses, and the look of studied unconcern. And I can reconstruct him, almost as though he were some puppet; I place him here, I place him there; by the French windows, or in the middle of the room, underneath the light; and I make him obey what I choose to imagine are the indefatigable resources of memory: when I ask him to gesture towards me, as he did then, he does so again; when I ask him to look towards Laurie, the expression that comes over his face is the same one that came over it then—if that same memory serves me—one of challenge and dependence, mixed. And, if I demand again the speech, the language of that conversation as it pursued its undistinguished course towards my dismissal from their company, I am able to draw its substance back to me.

Laurie was the first who really took him away from me. I had known she would from the time in Oxford when they were first married. Her eyes, her words, the ash on her cigarette, the splash of red round the cork-tip of it, had all been premonitions of alienation.

I was to view it differently later, recognising that it would really have been the same with anyone else, and seeing in it elements that were good and right: the wholesome processes of growing up and away, the welcome gaining of independence. But I had not come to that point on the evening in question. As I walked away from the door, it was not what they did or said, curious as I was about that, but what I felt. Far from being hurt in any way by my father's dismissal, I was relieved at what seemed to be a vague endorsement of the partial understanding of my position that had caused Merchant to put forward my name to Mr Porphyry, and which would now bring me, the following evening, to my second meeting with him. And I began to climb the dusty stairs happy in the sense of release that I felt from a variety of different family duties which had made the few previous holidays with Laurie and my father so unsatisfactory.

Half-way up through the house I became conscious of someone on the stair ahead of me. The step was lighter than mine but slower, and as I turned at the last flight I saw ahead of me the figure of a girl. My father had mentioned that there was a student in the attic room across the landing from me, but an interruption had prevented him from telling me more. I had imagined a man.

She was about eighteen, dressed in a dark full skirt and brown jumper. Her hair was in a pony-tail and she fumbled in her bag for her key as she came to the top of the stairs, looking round, I thought, a bit nervously. She was perhaps relieved to see someone younger than herself, and presumably she had some knowledge of my being in the room opposite.

'You must be George's son,' she said. 'He told me about you. My name's Esther.'

'You're a student, aren't you?' I said.

'Yes.'

'He told me that. What do you study?'

'Music.'

'Do you play the piano?'

'I play the flute. I'm at the Academy.'

I looked at her for a moment or two, thinking how best to explain myself. By comparison, what I did amounted to rather little. She was pretty, the slim elegance of her neck emphasised by the way in which the hair was drawn back and then fell in its full and wavy pony-tail between her shoulders. She wore no make-up, and the youthful lines of her face were clear and determined.

'I've just started my holiday,' I said. 'Home from school.'

'Your father told me. He was looking forward to it. Are you?'

'Yes,' I said. 'I don't know what I'll be doing. Yet.'

'Well, I hope you enjoy it.' She unlocked her door, and paused an instant, looking at me. 'Goodnight.'

Later, in bed, with the light out and the faint glow of the London night sky coming through the open window, I realised that I had not thought much about Janet. I gave my mind, and body, over to the luxuriant recollections of the times I had had with her. It was a pleasing episode of imagination rather than memory. But as I nudged my way towards sleep an odd thing occurred. Her features became confused and uncertain. Instead of Janet's face upon the body that performed the acts I desired, I imposed another. It was so easily done. I made Janet's features, dark and sensual, fade away. In the process I realised how little of her, as a person, I had retained or even understood. With an easy, indifferent exercise of the mind's imagination I summoned a new face in place of the old. Wavering at first in clarity, not remembered in all their detail, but readily recognisable, the emerging features were the youthful and determined ones of Esther.

Chapter Six

I

I asked Laurie about herself and my father, eventually. It was the first time that I ventured towards an interrogation of her. This may seem strange. After all, it was now getting on for two years since their marriage. But she was not easily approached, and the circumstances were difficult. I got on with her more successfully when we were on our own. I never knew what she felt about me. It was almost as if, from the start, she ruled out feelings in that direction altogether. I was an appendage of my father, to be approached, if at all, through him. Even more generally, where feelings were concerned, there was this inscrutable quality about her, this opaqueness.

Unlike him, she did not behave as if the universe itself was latched to all the things that had to be done. When present, he compelled attention, like a child. But, when he was not there, Laurie and I got on in a calm enough way, mixing tolerance with indifference, curiosity with occasional shafts of the jealousy that seemed to warm up and generate itself into action when all three of us were together.

I had hated her to begin with. But that had faded, first into a neutrality of feelings, and then into a calm acceptance that she and my father managed their lives in a fashion that made him marginally more stable than he had been on his own. I really knew little enough about it. I came infrequently, after all; holidays were a small enough part of the year, and, with camps and expeditions of one kind or another, the weeks spent under this new 'family' roof were lessening appreciably with the passage of time.

I judged her partly through his eyes, partly through my own. In seeing a certain stimulation and vigour which she brought to the relationship with my father—'Don't stand there making an exhibition of yourself, you old goat'—I came to accept, what he after all had told me, that perhaps she was the right person for him. In this also, as in so many other things, I was wrong. No one could fulfil the demands that issued from his heart. No one. But just for a time, as I increasingly got on with other things that took me away from them, I believed that all was well.

I even felt myself an intruder. Wobbly and uncertain as I suppose in reality they were, in those shabby basement rooms and that small, shaded yard that served as their scented garden, I felt that the passionate hold which each tried to exercise over the limited gifts the other had to offer was something into which I intruded as a threat. I was therefore relieved at the excuse I now had to be away from them both for parts of the coming holiday.

I asked her about my father and herself that following afternoon. I was to see Mr Porphyry for dinner that evening, and had rung him to confirm the arrangements, speaking only with his secretary. I had gone to the Tate Gallery after that, and had then walked back along the river bank, past Ranelagh Gardens and home to Flood Street.

The morning had been dry, but sticky and overcast; and during lunch it had begun to rain. The French windows out into the yard were again wide open. The water fell steadily on the paving stones, and dripped from the trellis and the leaves of plants. Laurie and I ate in almost total silence, and then she began to clear away. She did so in a desultory fashion, refusing help, and not anxious to complete the work. She even paused once or twice, as if preparing to start a conversation, but then shrugged and carried out a plate or cup from the table. It was during one of these pauses that I spoke to her. I don't know what prompted me. I had been watching her, not with much success, since it was gloomy in the room, and the glow of her cigarette, where she stood by the door, was a solitary point of cheerfulness, certainly not echoed in the fixed lines of her face.

'How did you meet my father?' I said.

She laughed. It was an abrupt, dry sound; quite humourless. 'Why, in a pub, of course. What did you think?'

'But, I mean . . . how?'

'Times I wish I hadn't,' she said. 'It might have been better.' For a moment she stared bleakly at me. Then her face softened. 'He's always telling you not to be like him. Well, don't.'

I thought she wouldn't answer my question. The softness faded from her eyes and lips. She seemed, momentarily, to be chewing the cud of her recollected displeasure; and the taste of bile was bitter in her mouth. She stood, a faint column of smoke rising from her hand, her really quite shapeless figure at rest, with no sense in it of onward movement. Then, again, her eyes came to life, and she smiled rather ruefully at me.

'I remember it so well. It was a summer's day, in the evening. Not like this. It was warm. It had been warm all day, as if the weight of the day's sun bore down in layers upon everything. I was drinking with two friends. You'd call them cronies. It was in the White Hart. He came in. He was with her, that woman, Ursula.' She paused. 'God, I can't stand her. Timid bitch. Never made her mind up. Lost him.' She laughed. It was a brief and hollow interruption: a mark of derision. 'There was a group of them, all together, drinking, laughing. He stood out from them all. There was something fine about him, different.' She paused again. I did not speak. I longed for her to go on. I seemed to be looking inside her heart, and my own ached with the expectation of what I might learn. A minute or more must have passed. Her cigarette, one of her

128

less successful hand-rolled witherings of bent paper and scruffs of tobacco, went out. She did not regard it.

'Oh, yes,' she said, 'he's a fine-looking man. I don't know what he was doing then. Some outdoor work, perhaps. And he'd just come from it. You could tell by the look of triumph in his eyes. Yes, triumph. He was such a baby. Doing any job well raised him up inside himself. Anyway, there really was something splendid about him, that day. Just the way he stood among them, at the bar, laughing and talking. He seemed to dominate the whole lot of them. He was . . . different.' She was puzzled as to what word suited best, and at the same time cautious about overstating his impact on her. Outside, the rain pattered down. It was as if she turned pages of a photograph album, and caught glimpses of golden moments, that pricked the memory with their goodness.

'I wanted him, of course. I think I loved him, then. Love him, hate him, what's the difference? He can do terrible things. He calls me a fiend. He's a fiend. Oh, yes. I shouldn't tell you this. What do you understand of such feelings? You don't understand. With luck, you'll never understand.'

'But how did you actually meet?'

'I was with these two women. Lesbians. You know what that means?'

'Yes.'

'They were just friends of mine. He knew them vaguely. I think he found one of them rather attractive. He was sorry she wasn't interested. He could be a randy old man, your father. So he came over and started talking. It began from there.'

She looked at the cigarette in her hand and picked up the box of matches from the table. She had this infuriating habit: she would wait and wait before lighting a cigarette. Like the ash which she allowed to accumulate on the tip, she left over any action until one had already smoked the cigarette for her, in one's own imagination. She crossed over to the easy chair and sat down. I judged it the right moment for a question.

'What did he say?'

She looked at me, almost blankly, and then, ignoring whatever impression I might have made, almost as if resuming a soliloquy, she went on: 'Oh, I forget. One doesn't remember such things. But I remember knowing, as I looked up at him, that first time, we were right for each other.' She laughed, and struck a match, and put it to the end of the cigarette. It was so thin it required quite hard puffs. Eventually, whiffs of smoke curled upwards. 'I'm not so sure, now.'

'Why not?' What might have been, before Laurie, had faded into the past. Regrets had faded, too. The hint in her remark of the dissatisfaction she felt with the supposed 'rightness' of each for the other sounded a faint note of warning.

Again she laughed. It was a harsh, dry expression of her own dismissal of past judgments. 'He beats me up. He gives me black eyes and bruises. He's a violent man.'

I stared at her. In my heart I found it difficult to believe. I had not lived long enough to know how wrong one can be. He had hardly ever struck me. Deep in the longest furrows of memory there rested episodes of violence shown to my mother, but almost beyond recall; and without familiarity I lacked the conviction that what she said was true.

She may have seen this in my face. She now looked back at me, shrugged her shoulders and stood up. The cigarette between her red lips smoked thinly; it hung, bent and feeble-looking. She spoke without taking it out of her mouth: 'We've had some good times. He's a very charming man. He can be loving and he craves affection. But he's wicked, too.' She turned away towards the table, and passed it on her way to the kitchen door. Just before going through she stopped and looked at me. Her voice was even and quiet in the gloomy room with the rain faintly pattering down on the paving stones outside the window. 'I have to say it. Perhaps you'll understand one day. Your father's a wicked man.'

II

The wicked man came home shortly before I was due to leave. I looked carefully for symptoms of brutality. The simplicity with which I expected, then, an observation about a person to manifest itself in some overt form, and immediately as well, was part of my innocence. Of course I found no such manifestations. He was guilty of no action endorsing her words, and I dismissed with a simple firmness what Laurie had said about him. He seemed in an unusually good mood, jovial, slightly mischievous.

'All set?' he said, coming up to me.

'I think so.' I could smell drink on his breath, and he must have noticed something in the look I gave him.

'Just a couple of pints,' he said. 'Wet the whistle, whet the appetite.' He looked round, and, although Laurie was not in the room, lowered his voice. 'Keeps women happy when you eat well.' He winked.

'Is that the best way?' I asked.

He laughed. 'Where are you meeting your Mr Porphyry?'

'Simpson's. In the Strand.'

'Choose the beef.'

'Do you know it?'

'Ah, in my youth, I used to go there! Those days beyond recall!' He went out into the passage to put away his bag and hang up his coat, which was wet with the rain. He had made the ten-minute walk down from the King's Road, prolonging it somewhere along the way.

I followed him out. 'You don't mind?' I said. 'Whatever arrangements I make . . .?'

'You must do what you think right. It's no life for you here. And as for my work. . . .' He tailed off. He had tugged a pair of overalls out of a canvas bag and was hanging them up on a coathanger.

'Why did you change?' I asked. 'What was wrong with being a salesman?'

'Freedom,' he said. He reached up and hooked the comprehensive garment over a peg. 'That's what was wrong. I didn't have my freedom.'

'And have you it now?' I asked.

'They own you, you see? They own you. And they drive you on. They can't help it. They're being driven as well. And you look upwards, and you don't know where it ends. Everyone is driving someone. And somewhere near the top, high up in the boardroom, it's no longer people. It's ambition, money, competition, public expectation. I don't know what it is, but there comes a moment when it just cracks my nerves. Yes, cracks my nerves.'

He said it in such a way that I could hear the break taking place, the ripping apart of the fibres of patience. I paused.

'And now?' I said. 'Have you your freedom now?'

He stared at me in the darkness of the passage. Then he shook his head. 'She's a slave-driver. An absolute slave-driver.'

'Do you mean Laurie?' I said. It seemed to piece together with what she had said earlier about him.

'Lady Herbert. In Hyde Park Gate. A perfect curse, she is. Always cracking the whip. Always there, wanting to . . .'

'But I thought,' I said. 'In a garden there's just so much you can do. You do it. . . .' I thought of the Gaffer, in the evening light of the summer days of that term which was just past, working beneath the windows where we laboured at our prep, the occasional whiff of pipe smoke filtering in among the scents of summer, as he pottered and enjoyed his flowers and grass.

'They're always chasing, chasing.'

'Why did you change? What was wrong with the Bedding Centre?'

'It was Laurie, really. She needed a man about the house. Rooms to do out. Odd jobs. I've the Colonel's room tonight to look at. We'll go up.' Then he remembered. 'But, of course. You're all dressed up to go out.'

'You don't mind?'

'I told you. You must make your own way. Don't look down on your father. He's made a mess of things. No doubt about it. But he hasn't made a mess of you. Stick to your guns. It's your life. Make the most of it. And good luck to you.'

The benevolent glow with which he had come home, lubricated by the beer, was fading. An irritability was setting in, and I considered the time was ripe for departure. I followed him back into the main room. He called out to Laurie, telling her he would start on the upstairs room after he had eaten. She clattered some pots, but did not reply. With his instructions on how to get to the Strand dutifully absorbed and added to the almost identical information I had already worked out for myself, I left shortly after that, conscious of a faint atmosphere of reproach in the air behind me. I could not fathom quite what he wanted. He seemed dissatisfied. There was a rumble in the air between them, something akin to far distant thunder, crackling and growling on the horizon, many miles off. The affectionate notes of the night before had been slightly false. When he used endearments like 'duckie' and 'luvvy', I had learnt to worry. When she had told me that he was both a violent and a wicked man the disbelief I felt was tempered by a sense of anxiety and foreboding. 'Freedom' he wanted. 'Freedom' he had not got. And as I set out to walk to the underground at Sloane Square, in my own quest for freedom, along the wet pavements in an evening light that glowed a little more hopefully now that the rain had stopped, I thought of him as a caged being, his Lady Herbert cracking her whip at him in Hyde Park Gate, Laurie setting him to do odd jobs in Flood Street, and myself walking away.

III

The burden of sorting out how things stood between my father and Laurie weighed slightly on me as I waited in the hallway of Simpson's that evening. Other people also were waiting, though not many. I had been divested of my mackintosh, I had been downstairs and had managed a sixpenny tip for the elderly retainer who fidgeted with the towels and soap. And I now stood in expectation of Mr Porphyry's arrival. Coming up Villiers Street I had paused briefly in front of one of the bookshop windows there, and the hot recollection of the forbidden delights still slightly tightened within me those feelings of guilt and desire which always occupied a small but important area of my imagination and its curiosity, when on holiday in London.

He was not late. I was early. And when he walked through the doors at just half-past seven, he saw me immediately. He did not smile but nodded briefly. In place of the soft brown hat which had lain on the front seat of his Lagonda when I had said good-bye to him at Coppinger he had a bowler hat on, of a rather flattish style, a tightly rolled umbrella in spite of the wet weather, and no brief-case. Nor did he carry any papers. As I came to know him better I learned to admire the precision and order of his life; and this, I suppose, was part of it.

He was known at Simpson's. He wasted little time in greeting me, and heading straight in to the main downstairs restaurant, with a nod and a word to members of the staff, and a short conversation with the fat but respectful headwaiter who led him to our table against the wall and towards the back. We were beneath the windows, and the evening light from a sky that was clearing up spread across to the cubicle tables on the other side. I followed obediently, and sat down in the seat indicated by Mr Porphyry.

'You'll have beef, I'm sure,' he said, as we sat down.

'My father says that's the thing to have.'

'Your father comes here?'

I reddened slightly. 'A long time ago.'

'There's the mutton, Sir,' said the headwaiter. 'There's a nice saddle of mutton this evening. Very good. But Tom's beef is excellent, too.'

He had handed me a menu, a rather confusing list which began with oysters at ten shillings and sixpence the half dozen, and then jumped to thirty-five shillings for roast pheasant and twenty-six shillings for partridge. I eventually found the entry, 'Roast Beef, Yorkshire Pudding, 7/9'. It seemed rather expensive. 'I'll have the beef, please.'

'And would the young gentleman like soup to start?' He looked first at me, then at Mr Porphyry.

'I think some of the turtle soup. Thick.'

He looked at me for my approval.

I nodded. 'Thank you, Sir.'

'And for yourself, Mr Porphyry?'

'I'll have the thick giblet.'

'We've fresh carrots, Sir. With the beef.'

'Good. And roast potatoes.'

'And, er . . . will you have a little wine, Sir? A half carafe of the red?'

Mr Porphyry shook his head. 'A jug of water, please.'

He looked at me. He seemed entirely at his ease, and yet at the same time alert the way one is in anticipation of an encounter, perhaps of some importance. I could see myself only as having small impact upon his affairs and was faintly puzzled, and perhaps a little frightened of what lay ahead.

'So you came back last Thursday?'

I nodded.

'And how is everything? At home, I mean?'

'It's all right.'

'Room of your own?'

'It's at the top of the house. It's really an attic. But I like it rather.'

It was clear that he had no real conception of what it was like, life in Flood Street, and I sensed a reticence in his approach. He did not want to get involved in a discussion that would really cover again the territory we had talked over, and he had read about in Merchant's report. No written words by my headmaster could capture the life itself as I lived it; and my own descriptions and explanations, both to Mr Porphyry, and earlier to Mr Merchant during our circuit of the cricket field, had been governed in their texture and their motivation by considerations which affected my objectivity. It would be some time before I could feel able to unravel to this man my real life, even if I could be said, then or later, to have understood it.

Perhaps he sensed this. 'I have arranged for you to go to Germany in ten days' time,' he said.

'That's absolutely terrific, Sir!' I smiled. I felt a flush of gratitude. What had been plotted and planned, and endlessly discussed since winning the scholarship, was now coming to life.

He seemed pleased by my reaction. 'You'll go to Hanover. Stay with friends of mine there. I had hoped to send you on down to Munich, but it can't be arranged at this time. They live outside Hanover, of course. The city was badly bombed but they're building it up. It will be an experience for you.'

He talked about the family with whom I would be staying. The soup came, and the water. I noticed that he bowed his head briefly over his plate before beginning to eat. After that, 'Tom' trundled up a side of beef and carved off generous portions. Mr Porphyry asked after his children, and I saw the gleam of a half-crown tip changing hands. I thought at the time it was personal between them, not knowing the Simpson's tradition, and I was perplexed by the lack of awkwardness in the action of taking and receiving. He went over in greater detail the visit he had arranged. Without referring to notes he knew all the travel arrangements. He had already, through the school, made arrangements for my passport, and he now handed me a blue envelope.

'The money for your ticket's in there, and for your passport, and some extra for the time you're away.'

I took it and thanked him.

'When you come back, later in the month, there's a camp I wanted you to go on. That's if you're free?'

I thought swiftly, and nodded. The uncertain spectres of

Flood Street lurked in the grey mist of my foreboding. Escape, they seemed to say.

'Have you been to the Festival yet?' he asked.

'We came on a visit from Coppinger.'

'Oh, you were on that, were you?'

I said I was.

'And did you get to the fun fair?'

'Yes.'

'I seem to be organising your life quite fully enough for one evening, but I wondered if you would also like to earn some extra money in the next few days. I have the two sons of one of my business colleagues coming over, and thought you might like to guide them round London.' I agreed, with a pleasurable sense of relief that my time would be taken up at Mr Porphyry's beck and call rather than my father's. Again, with precision and without making any notes, he dealt with the details and instructed me on how to get to his office.

'It will be some help to you?' he asked. 'To have a holiday job?'

I wondered how much he knew, or guessed.

'Oh, yes,' I said. 'It will make a great difference.'

'Is it sometimes difficult? Getting away?'

I nodded. He said no more about that. He seemed, visibly, to be absorbing and storing away the implications of everything I said. He was a prudent but in no sense a devious man; that I had already learnt in my dealings with him. As far as I could judge, his was a sensitive, rounded appreciation of what mattered. But it also seemed that he had something else that faintly hovered like a shadow in the background: a sense of purpose and direction, this conviction all the time embraced me.

I do not know what made me say it. I was still nervous in his company. We had come to no easy or relaxed compromise over names. We had settled a wealth of practical matters which seemed to have filled up much of my holiday. And it may have been this, with the concurrent sense it produced of my life being absorbed quite extensively into his life, that forced me to seek a reason.

I said to him: 'Mr Porphyry?' My tone, like Pritchett's with the Gaffer, was one of preamble to enquiry; I was in a classroom, drawing attention to a point that I wanted to discuss and understand more fully.

He looked at me expectantly. 'Yes?'

I hesitated, looking down at my empty plate. I felt rather full. 'Why do you do this?' I asked. 'Why do you give the scholarship?'

The corners of his mouth seemed to turn down more firmly, as if to aid the concentration of his mind. He gave me a rather clipped, controlled smile. He paused. The smile then faded. I waited politely. His was a slow reaction, cautious, as if he felt relief at the question, but was worried at the same time that he might handle the answer wrongly. 'I thought you might ask that,' he said.

I felt myself blushing slightly, but had no feeling that I had said anything wrong. 'Should I not ask?'

'You should, of course. I'll try and explain.'

I waited politely.

'The trustees are there to benefit Coppinger,' he said. 'I felt it was hard to do so without understanding the boys better. And yet there was no easy way to do that. On Memorial Day you're all so much on your best behaviour. *You* certainly were; telling me all the good things! What you thought I wanted to hear!' His smile was engaging, even boyish. Then he was serious again. 'It is hard to bridge the gap between what most Coppinger boys have known and the kind of childhood and youth that I experienced. I felt that, however much I knew generally about you all, there would be no real understanding. The particular problems of an individual boy would make sense of the kinds of things we had to judge as trustees.'

I did not fully understand. His tone had changed dramatically, distancing him from me, emphasising his trustee status, and I suddenly wished that I had asked Philpotts how he had

138

found it all, winning the scholarship, meeting Porphyry, going abroad. One question did still obtrude: why Porphyry? None of the other trustees did what he had done. Why?

He was looking at me calmly, without expression. Until my question, he had made all the running; it was quite understandable that he would now reverse this situation.

'But you're the only trustee that does it?' I said.

'We all have different ways,' he said. 'I'm a practical man. I run a business. If I want to understand an enterprise I look to the people in it. Even knowing well just one man among many involved in something can help you to understand it.'

'You must give up a lot of time to it,' I said.

'It would not be worth doing at all if I could not make my time available. You see—' He hesitated, looking round the large room in the light of that summer evening. 'You see, I have had the security which you boys have lacked. Parents, brothers and sisters in a comfortable home with nurses and so on; then public school; then family business; then the war. It was never very difficult in the human sense. One always knew where one stood.'

I listened carefully, drinking in the words with which he touched upon a life so utterly different from my own. Looking back, I must have been a very solemn, even a disturbing audience: inquisitorial, deeply retentive of the sense of what he was saying, increasingly aware of *his* shyness in *my* presence. Is privilege normal, or the lack of privilege? Was he apologising to some greater being for the fact that he had power, certain influence, the capacity to devote time and money to others, and to pluck out occasional individuals, transforming what they were able to do and be; perhaps transforming their lives?

Did it go deeper than that? I still did not understand why, and I did not have the courage to ask. Instead, I said to him: 'What about Philpotts? Do you still see him? I mean, what happens to scholarship boys afterwards?'

'Is he a friend of yours?' The question was rather sharp.

'Yes, Sir. He is. He was head of our house before he left.'

'A very intelligent boy.' It was said with slight severity, as though Philpotts had somehow offended Porphyry by being too clever.

'He's up at Oxford,' I said. 'I think he's doing politics.'

'Yes. He'll do well.' He paused. 'I keep up with scholarship boys if I can. It's not always easy. Philpotts is no doubt very busy at University.'

We did not pursue the subject of Philpotts. A junior waiter came and took away our plates. Mr Porphyry insisted on a pudding, and I crumbled and crunched my way through a meringue glacé. After I had finished I ventured to ask him about Tom, the carver. A faint look of diffidence came into Mr Porphyry's eyes; across the table they seemed suddenly to become pale and remote. He looked away from me, and across the room, not in search of Tom himself, who was relaxing beside his trolley at the other end with no demands for beef waiting on him, but at some more distant, less temporal object, summoned up for him by my question.

'He was an able seaman on my first posting. Quite by chance he turned up as a petty officer when I got my first command. Nothing more than that.'

'What did you—?'

He cut me short. 'I will give you my war reminiscences on another occasion,' he said, with a brief smile. 'I think now it's time you went home. We will see a good deal of each other in the days to come, I hope.'

I nodded, and sat in obedient silence while he dealt with the bill. We left Simpson's at about nine o'clock. I thanked him for the dinner, and promised to report to his office to undertake my guiding service. I also gave him assurances about collecting my passport, and buying my ticket. We were back in the safe realms of fact and action. Under his bowler hat, and with his umbrella firmly grasped in his hand, he had suddenly become more remote from me. I was one in a sequence of boys; Philpotts had gone before, others would follow after; he would understand Coppinger better as a result of this encounter, and he would feel that he had extended his service to the school. That was how I saw it, vaguely, perhaps with a measure of disappointment, as we parted company on the pavement of the Strand that August evening. He had his eyes alert for a taxi, and could only give me part of his attention. It emphasised my general feeling of awkwardness. I did not feel that it was quite correct to move away, and return down Villiers Street to catch my train back to Sloane Square, until he had first departed. Yet there was nothing more to be said, and the evening, with its watery but clear light after the day-long rain, was cool enough for August. I shivered momentarily. Dressed in his blue city suit, with waistcoat, he was better fitted for the weather than I was.

'Cold, isn't it?' he said. 'You'd better cut along. I look forward to seeing you on Friday.'

I hesitated for a moment longer, but then saw a taxi approaching down the Strand with its 'for hire' flag up. I pointed, all set to 'cut along', as he had instructed me. 'Thanks for the dinner, Mr Porphyry. And . . . and for everything else.'

Rather gruffly he said 'Cheerio', and stepped forward as the cab pulled into the side, his umbrella held like a sword at rest, ready for further battles. From the corner where the narrow street joined the Strand, with a glimpse of the river in the distance, I watched the vehicle join the comparatively thin movement of traffic in front of Charing Cross Station.

IV

There are momentary flashes of experience that have often brought back to me that August evening: odd conjunctions of traffic in a street, the reflection in a puddle of a sky clearing after rain, the flashes of sunlight on a group of windows along the side of a building. To call them 'involuntary', and yet to assert their specific power of reawakening the same occasion, the same set of feelings, may seem contradictory. Certainly, as a reconstruction of the past, it is not a method that fits into that category of spontaneous intrusion of an intense, even magical force, which so obsessed Proust. It is almost the reverse; the event exists, in its physical sense and also with its psychological and temporal implications, and periodically one is jolted into vivid recall by the senses. It is as if the event—in this case the simple parting on a corner in the Strand of Mr Porphyry and myself—has become the controlling force behind the action of memory. On a roadway, in a field, on a crowded street, very occasionally one is made completely captive by the past; years are shed, and a younger self, briefly, takes over. The mind, in demanding from memory a justification for the invasion, breaks the spell. But just in that brief span of time the transportation into the past, vivid, unstructured, total, seeks and finds an anchorage where the already-fading impressions can be protected and re-assimilated before they have gone completely. For years after reading Proust I could not fully understand the difference between the two kinds of memory; growing up with my father I had been overwhelmed by his sense of the past, much less by my own. And his avowed devotion to the apparently obedient exercise of nostalgia, a weapon that is held in reserve in the armoury of those who are unhappy, shielded me from other forms of memory until a relatively late stage.

Can we say that the slightest is also the most true? Can one really assert that those stabs of experience, when a fragment of the past is flashed momentarily but completely before us only to be withdrawn again, and no specific detail filled in around, are more important, more complete, than the slow recollections and recreations of the past that inspire our many different perceptions of the present? I have no answer. I am confused by the multiplicity of voices from the past. But, when they speak, the whiff of authenticity, the unchallengeable feeling of being transported back and forth over the years without knowing when or why, is a convincing encouragement to the slower and more tedious engine of recollection.

That parting in the street began for me a new liberty and the imposition of a new set of restraints. Like so many second meetings it was far more important than the first. And, though such things can never be proved, I believe that, staring down the Strand long after his taxi had vanished from sight, the feelings I then had, in their confused but intense way, seeded themselves in my subconscious in order to germinate and grow many years later, not in vague terms, but in the precise recollections of that occasion.

If what I understood from Mr Porphyry's slightly archaic, schoolboy phrase implied a certain lateness, and an urgency to meet a domestic curfew, then I had no urge to 'cut along' any more. Quite the reverse. The washed light of the early dusk, the residual streaks of colouring from the vanished sun which still left traces and reflections on the buildings towards the west, uncertain promises for a better tomorrow, and the soft enticements of the narrow streets down by the river in which the first lamps were already lit, diffused and muddled my endeavour. Mr Porphyry's sequestrations of my time and duty opened rather than closed my ambition, freed rather than enchained my prospects. I wanted to dwell on the unlimited sense of opportunity which I now felt.

To me at that time London was always a holiday city. Until my father's marriage to Laurie the sense of impermanence had been emphasised by the fact of so many different places of habitation, shifting of roots each time I came home from school, opening up to me, often only marginally, different parts of Notting Hill Gate, Kensington, Chelsea. This, combined with the limited time, a few weeks at Christmas, and Easter, and the long summer break, interrupted, on occasion, by school events of one kind or another, still further intensified the transience of my reactions to the city. There was one further burden of expectation, quaint, and not entirely credible: a threat my father uttered in his cups that he would return one day to rural England, where he had once worked before, leaving behind him the 'rat race', the 'meannesses and the limitations' of the city I had come to regard more or less as 'home', and that he would strike out into England. This promise, accompanied not only by strangely incoherent gestures which he often failed, in his inebriated state, to complete, but also by even more vague and puzzling references to the fact that his 'real and ancient roots' lay out there, did not convince me that he would ever leave the city. Yet at the same time, and perhaps more subconsciously than otherwise, they did further encourage a feeling that nothing at all was fixed. Neither he, nor Laurie, nor the house, nor any other woman, nor work, was finally and immovably anchored in reality. It made London many things to me. It made it a dream kingdom of the imagination, pulsing all the time with so many attractions, demanding attention, inviting use, never boring, never to be taken for granted. Like some marvellously rich and diverse courtesan, it demanded that one should attempt to devour it greedily, only to become hopelessly exhausted in that attempt.

The abrupt parting from Mr Porphyry left me in possession once again. To say that it induced a certain light-headedness may sound a slightly eccentric claim. Yet I felt deeply the possession, and it induced a yearning, an ill-defined, vaguely absurd, hopelessly impossible desire to fix in the chambers of the mind, the only true repositories for all material possessions, the pavement stones, the glint of light on the river, the faded evening colouring of the buildings along the lower Strand, the indifferent glances of people passing.

Chapter Seven

I

I came down the following morning with a light step, looking forward to the day. It was cool, and cloudy. The hot, even thundery days of July seemed to have given way fairly permanently to the indifferent and tepid weather that eventually persisted for the greater part of August. But it had no impact on my spirits. I was ready to depart, and take up my first practical task for Mr Porphyry. My father also was ready, in working clothes, and eating his breakfast. I gave him a brief account of the events of the previous night. He listened carefully, without interrupting me. When he did eventually speak it was simply to ask:

'So it went well?'

'Very well.'

'And what's this job? I want to know more about it.'

I gave him the details, as far as I knew them.

He adopted a truculent pose. 'Well, you take good care of yourself, understand? Watch the buses. Remember what I say: when you're looking after somebody else you can find yourself in trouble. So pay attention to traffic, and think before you move!' He ended on a forceful note.

'I'll be careful,' I said.

He spread butter across the slice of toast on his plate. He did so with a single sweep of the knife, leaving the distribution uneven over the golden brown surface. It was the same with the marmalade; a generous helping lumped towards one end. It did not matter: into his cavernous mouth it was all engulfed with accomplished ease.

'What are you doing?' I asked.

He drank some tea. 'Swiss Cottage. Rheinhardts. All day.'

'Not Lady Herbert?'

'No.'

'Slave-drivers?' I ventured.

He smiled. 'Jews!'

Though my father, generally speaking, could never think long enough about anything to hate it, he did pretend a hatred of Jews, and in his more outrageous moments would revert to an anti-semitism that must have been, I suppose, a relic of the thirties, a period in his life that was particularly difficult, uncertain and basically unhappy. Whether he blamed the Jews for this, I shall never know; they were certainly blamed by him for most things at that time. By the early fifties all that was left was an admiration for Hitler, and the occasional outburst in which he claimed that the German dictator had been right.

Like so many of his stances, this one was idiotic in the most immediate and personal way. Jews were among his best employers, and the Rheinhardts had always been particularly kind to him. And there were to be further and even closer unions between himself and the Chosen People. But that lay in the future. Just now he seemed intent on a racial dissertation.

I headed him off with news about Germany. It particularly pleased him that I was going there, and by an association of ideas in his own mind he seemed, on reflection, to be prepared to leave over, for the time being, the examination of certain racial prejudices which had seemed uppermost in his mind. But it was with a faint reluctance.

Part of this, I felt, was due to a diffidence about Mr Porphyry, almost a feeling of rivalry. It did not, at that stage, manifest itself at all clearly. Almost the reverse, he seemed at pains to

146

conceal it behind the discussion of facts and of practical issues.

'And he gave you the money for the ticket? The right amount?'

I agreed that he had.

'And it's safe?'

I nodded, putting on a somewhat pitying smile.

'All right, you can smile. But you can't be too careful about these things. When do you get the ticket?'

I told him the different tasks that faced me, one of which was to meet Mr Porphyry's aunt at the railway station from which I would eventually leave. 'I'll buy it then,' I said to him, 'but that's in two days' time. It's these two German boys today.'

He nodded, approvingly. 'You like him, don't you?' His voice had softened.

I didn't answer straightaway. I thought back over the two encounters we had had, remembering the occasional flashes of remote sadness that seemed to come into Mr Porphyry's eyes. 'He's a lonely person,' I said. 'And at the same time he seems very busy.'

'Not married?'

'No.'

'Lives alone?'

'Don't know. He talks about "the flat".'

'And he was in the Navy?'

I nodded. 'That's really all I know.' I paused. 'I do like him,' I said.

I could not interpret the pinched look in my father's face. I, who was curious about Mr Porphyry's wartime career, was even more curious at my father's lack of interest. His expression became grumpy.

'Seems we'll see little of you,' he said.

I had to admit that the programme was a full one. 'I'll be earning some money,' I added, in amelioration of what seemed like a parting of the ways.

'You'll be getting too important for us.' The inclusion of

147

Laurie who had, I think, returned to bed with the newspaper and a cup of tea, lent weight to his indication of a grievance.

'There's a girl in that room opposite yours. Name of Esther.' He seemed to be talking more to himself than to me. The tone was perfunctory.

'Yes.' I said. 'You told me.'

He looked up. 'Have you met her?'

I nodded. 'Just once. On the stairs.'

'Pretty, isn't she?'

'Very.'

'Bit old for you.'

I didn't answer. The womaniser in my father assumed certain echoes in myself. His simplicity usually imagined relationships into being as soon as an occasion like this one—the proximity of a pretty girl—presented an opportunity for friendship or love with myself. Yet he was curiously old-fashioned in his approach to sexual attraction where it might affect me. And now, dutifully obedient to the shackles of fidelity, those thin but surviving fibres of convention in his character which imposed an added patina of restraint, he adopted a guarded line on Esther.

'Do you like her?'

I smiled. 'I hardly know her.'

He laughed at that. 'You know straightaway. You always do.'

'I like her,' I admitted. Then, to tease him, I added, 'She has lovely feet.'

'Splendid! You're not your father's son for nothing.' His look was triumphant, then tender, as though recalling an event from the past. When he spoke again it was with a solemnity that he seemed able to summon up on the instant. 'I have kissed Esther's feet; it is right you should admire them.'

I was not surprised. It was a characteristically flamboyant claim for him to make. I did not feel inclined, at that early hour, to pursue the circumstances. I felt sure that they would recur, and I guessed they had been both innocent and memorable. My own inner emotional upheavals would not be helped by his interrogation. The thick sense of desire which had driven me towards Janet was now redirecting itself towards Esther. I gave the easy substitution of the one for the other a legitimacy in my mind by arguing a greater degree of purity in my feelings for Esther. Janet was of the earth; Esther of the air. With Janet I had tasted forbidden fruit; Esther was probably unattainable, and her desirability therefore much greater. I was feeding on dreams, of course, and echoing in my easy switches of affection both my father's past life and also Janet's own taste for 'snogging' and for a variety of partners. Her soft, willing flesh was there to go back to; and an adventure now, in Chelsea, seemed in keeping with the flood tide of my undisciplined desires.

My father's thoughts had obviously pursued a quite different channel. He got to his feet. 'Don't look down on your father,' he said. He gathered up his things ready to leave. Then the stern look softened. 'And mind how you cross the road!'

Fathers are not ridiculous. They just seem so at times. Why can they not grasp or penetrate the seriousness of youth? I looked up and smiled, my shining face hiding a welter of mixed and incomplete reactions.

II

It was what might be termed 'a brave day', more suited to April than August. It was cloudy though not overcast, with sufficient wind to change often the look of the sky, to intersperse bright patches with grey threatening ones, and yet to bring no rain. We spent the morning at the Festival and had lunch at the Skylark, a jolly enough place overlooking the Nelson Pier. Privately, I thought it expensive, and suffused with a certain artificiality. My two 'charges' thought otherwise. To call them that seems odd. They were both older than me, one of them quite a bit older. They spoke good English. They were resourceful and determined in their approach to London, wanting to see as much as possible, and they had certainly given a clear enough indication that my remuneration, as their guide, would be earned. This was to be no sinecure.

Klaus, the elder, was thin and tall. His lank hair, brown in colour, fell across his eyes, and with quick and frequent movements of his head he would toss it back. He wore clothes of a dreariness that was remarkable even in London in the summer of 1951. And the dark grey shirt, of rough texture, which was buttoned at the neck without any tie, emphasised the scrawny physique and the bony, protuberant Adam's apple. He must have been nineteen then, and was studying in some kind of technical school on lines similar, I imagined, to those which Lytton would follow. He had large expressive hands, and while he was speaking he held them poised in front of him over the table, his forearms balancing against the edge, and his fingers and palms shaping a space in the air as if they were filled by an invisible bowl.

Werner was altogether softer, more relaxed. Though in no sense plump, he had none of his brother's drawn, intense, even deprived appearance. He was close to me in age, though a bit older. He left most of the talking to Klaus.

'So you are going to be with the Grönings, are you? In Hanover? That is excellent. A very good family.'

'You know them?'

'Oh, yes. We both know them. We have stayed with them. Not together, of course. That would not be possible. Their apartment is very small. I think they can manage only one guest at a time. Is that not so, Werner?'

'Yes, Klaus.'

'They are not in the centre of Hanover.' He paused. 'Of course, there is still not much centre of Hanover. It was badly damaged. They are rebuilding.'

'Did you just go because they are friends?' I asked.

'Well, of course we would not have gone if they were not our friends.' The size of the invisible bowl in his hands became greater, and flatter.

'No, what I meant,' I said, 'was whether it was because of Mr Porphyry.'

'Mr Porphyry is a friend of ours and of the Grönings.'

Werner spoke a few words to his brother in German. Klaus put down the invisible bowl for a moment, and placing his hands flat on his knees, rubbed them backwards and forwards, rocking slightly on the uncomfortable and clumsy restaurant chair which, if I remember correctly, had a rather nautical design, appropriate in its way to the establishment.

'We have good fellowship with the Grönings,' he said.

'Later in the summer, when we return from our expedition to the Lake District, we will have Peter Gröning's mother to stay with us in Düsseldorf. I am really sorry indeed that you will not be able to visit us. We would like to have shown you that part of Germany, wouldn't we, Werner?'

'Absolutely,' Werner said. Then he smiled at me. 'Is that O.K.? To say that?'

I said it was.

'You must tell us, you see, all the time if we say things wrong.'

'Where are you going, in the Lake District?' I asked. 'I'm going there as well.'

'Ambleside Hall. But we go from there to camp, among the small lakes, I forget the word for them. . . .'

'Tarns,' I said.

He was holding the bowl again. 'Ah, yes, tarns! I am looking forward to it very much.'

I felt that the three of us seemed to belong to a hidden fellowship that also, in some way, embraced the Grönings. And I assumed, from the little I had gleaned at Coppinger, that it was part of the religious force that motivated Mr Porphyry. But I was at an age when to conceal ignorance was less disadvantageous than to glean information, and I avoided direct questions about Ambleside, indicating, by look and gesture, a familiarity that I did not possess. They were both encompassed by some hidden force, as though time pressed on them and they had to hurry through.

'You know about the Lakes, I suppose?' I looked at Klaus.
'Glacial de—'

'We have read up about them. Yes. Most interesting. My father was once there.'

'And Amble—'

'That was where he stayed. It was a couple of years ago.'

I felt that I was obliging them by prompting their knowledge. This was more with Klaus than Werner.

He asked me: 'What does your father do?'

I looked at him for a moment in the noisy atmosphere of the restaurant. 'He's retired,' I said. 'Lives in Chelsea.'

'Retired? And does nothing?'

'He looks after the house we have there. He's interested in gardening.' A strangely impressive picture hovered in my mind of an absorbed and relaxed old gentleman, minding a house in Chelsea and pottering over geraniums and fuchsias.

I asked them whether they had seen enough of the Festival, and we should go on. We were planning a visit to the Victoria and Albert Museum in the afternoon, and I was trying to remember whether or not it was South Kensington Underground that we needed, and if I would know the way from there without asking. I looked forward to the museum with greater curiosity than the Festival had inspired. From the start, I had found it difficult to suppress a certain boredom with the South Bank.

I paid with money which Mr Porphyry had given me. The three of us walked through the crowds in the sunshine, under the shadow of the Skylon, and took the footbridge across the Thames and back to Charing Cross. It was windy, and the surface of the river was choppy. A boat packed with people was pulling into the Nelson Pier with more Festival visitors.

Klaus had only partly satisfied my curiosity about Hanover and the Grönings. When he talked of 'good fellowship' he was extending the linkages of a faith I did not share, and forcing me, beforehand, into certain commitments. And though I said little directly in response, and though in part my silence and expression of 'knowing' was deception, all the time I felt that the web was drawing me in.

I was a willing victim. The process itself was welcome. And through those crowded, busy days it was not the events that mattered, nor the people. It was the sense of form that was given to my life. It was a strange process by which my own identity and relevance were created out of errands and transient encounters. Vaguely at first, then with my dutiful and at the same time willing involvement with Mr Porphyry, it all took on more purpose; a dim design became gradually more clear; and at the heart of it I felt there was a hand reaching out towards my mortal soul.

As in detective fiction, or in spy stories, my account of these somewhat disconnected episodes, therefore, has a purpose beyond the people involved. They were like bell buoys or light ships to the mariner, bringing him across well-charted and previously much travelled seas. Some of them I met again; others only once. And even Mr Porphyry's aunt belonged to a shadowy cast of extras giving background to the story. She did, however, bring up the subject of Philpotts; and, in a more direct way than the various other people who represented to me holiday 'tasks', she gave me a firmer sense of Porphyry's background and family.

She stood on the platform at Liverpool Street, holding her handbag, a suitcase at her feet, the porter beside her. It had been Mr Porphyry's idea that, since most people move away from a train when it reaches the station, if she simply stood and waited I would find her. This was so. No one else was standing in such obvious expectation of being claimed. But even without the arrangement I would have known she was Mr Porphyry's aunt. She was dressed in a summer coat of a pale, faded pink colour. Round her shoulders was a fox fur, and on her head a hat, pale grey matching her gloves and handbag, and with a small spray of artificial flowers at the side.

'Excuse me,' I said. 'Are you Miss Porphyry?'

'Yes. I am.'

She looked at me for a moment, checking, it seemed, whether I would do.

'You are the boy sent by my nephew. Take that case. We shall find a taxi on our own,' she added, turning to the porter beside her who had removed the case from the compartment. 'Thank you.' She gave him what I thought was the rather generous tip of a shilling, since he had done so little. But perhaps she was taking into account what he might otherwise have gained.

We walked together down the platform. The case was quite light, so much so that I wondered to myself if I had been necessary at all.

'You're a Coppinger boy,' she said.

The question seemed odd, as though other boys from other establishments also featured in her experience of her nephew.

I agreed that I was.

'And what is your house?'

I told her.

'That used to be Cartwright's. Before the war. He was there a long time.'

'Do you know Coppinger?' I said.

'A little. Yes.'

'You know about the scholarship then?'

She turned her face towards me as we walked. Her eyes were pale blue like those of her nephew and with some of the same penetrating directness. Like him, she seemed to assemble around the words she spoke a certain range of ideas and considerations with which she weighed quite carefully the sentence before it came out.

'You are this year's scholar, then?'

I nodded.

'And my nephew is sending you to Germany?'

I smiled at her. It was the quite natural expression of pleasure, even excitement, at the prospect of going abroad for the first time.

'Yes,' I said. 'I'm going to Hanover.'

She did not answer. We found a taxi without difficulty. She got in, and left me to give the instructions.

'Brown's Hotel, please.'

We drove through the city streets in the indifferent, chilly weather. I asked her polite questions about her journey and about how often she came to London. I consciously avoided mentioning Coppinger for the moment because I did not want to waste such an important conversation inside a taxi, moving through the streets, where at any moment we might be distracted. It had been arranged by Mr Porphyry that we would wait for him, at Brown's Hotel. I did not know what we were waiting for, but he had told me to keep the evening free and I had dressed as smartly as I could. I had borrowed from my father one of his neckties. It was a piece of rich-looking, silken apparel: shades of red in an ornate pattern given to him by Ursula, and of almost all his possessions at that time most clearly evocative of the summer of that year. And I went on wearing it for a long time, until the edges where it was knotted began to fray, and it was noticeably past its best. Still I kept it. And in a curiously concentrated way the flat surface of patterned cloth, hanging in my locker at school, or folded for packing, then becoming an unworn burden and finally a memento, remained charged with the atmosphere of those events.

In the hotel Miss Porphyry asked me to order tea, which I did. She had instructed me to leave the case with the hall porter, and we then sat together to wait.

'I think I have met the Grönings' son, Peter,' Miss Porphyry said, reverting to the mainspring of my purpose, in her eyes, that of having been chosen by her nephew for the scholarship. 'He came to London last summer, when I was on a visit. A clever enough boy,' she added. It was an afterthought. She poured out the tea.

'How do you know the school?' I asked.

She seemed to be considering what she should tell me. When she did speak it was in a collected, almost a compressed way.

'My father was a trustee for many years. My mother was related to your founder. The Porphyrys and the Llewellyns—that's my mother's family—have long been associated with Coppinger. When my father died, just before the war, he wanted my nephew on the board of trustees. But Samuel went off to fight, and it wasn't until 1947, I think, that he actually became a trustee.'

The perspective was sudden, and large. Mr Porphyry, who up until that moment had loomed within the compass of my perception substantially enough on his own, and in part to the exclusion of others, was now reduced in size, and placed in a certain balance and restraint with this elderly lady, with her father, her mother, even with the founder, whose stern features stared down at us from his portrait on the walls of main school. With an almost effortless ease, a kind of conversational indifference, she had laid out a tapestry of something like eighty years. My mind tried to struggle backwards into it. Miss Porphyry, I knew from her nephew, to be about seventy. This meant she had been born in about 1880, and must have known at least something of the school at the turn of the century. She must certainly have known the founder.

I was overwhelmed by the sense of all that I did not know. I was also overwhelmed by the *importance* of it. I needed to know. My identity, which to some extent depended on Coppinger, had become casually enmeshed with this woman whom I hardly knew at all. The iron, ineradicable fact of her life, lived in Norfolk, but reaching out, in a past that soared back beyond my own birth, to that corner of England which more than any other, even more than London, was home to me, was of infinite and exacting relevance as we sat together in the airless warmth of Brown's Hotel. So oppressed did I feel at the urgency of my questions that I did not know where to begin

'And used you to visit?' I asked.

'Sometimes,' she said.

'And what was it like?'

Her smile was resigned.

156

'I am a little tired,' she said. 'Are we not dining together this evening? We must delay that investigation into the past until then.'

She was reticent to a purpose. She wanted Mr Porphyry's endorsement of what she might tell me about herself and Coppinger. And it was not until we were sitting down to dinner in his flat that she turned to her nephew and said to him: 'Samuel, I am being asked about Coppinger and the Porphyrys. I don't know where to begin, or how much to tell.'

He glanced briefly at me. 'Everything,' he said.

'In that case it would be better if you helped me.'

'I will, Aunt. Just let me get the rest of dinner.'

I followed him from the room, having excused myself, and helped bring in plates and dishes. He lived in a flat in a block of apartments on the corner of Great Peter Street and Millbank. It was a large Edwardian structure, with an open-cage lift that worked on air compression and was necessary since the rooms he had were high up. This was my first visit, and I inspected each room, the furniture and the pictures on the walls, with an unconcealed curiosity. He had referred already to a 'Mrs Staples', plainly a housekeeper figure who had prepared and left dinner, and this we now conveyed into a dining-room which looked out on the trees in Victoria Tower Gardens.

'I don't know that there's a great deal to tell, is there? Your father was involved in the school, and your mother, in a sense. It doesn't really go back beyond that.'

'I've told him all that.'

'Then there's great uncle Damien. He had certain responsibilities in the school for quite a time. Managed the securities remarkably well through the Slump. And old uncle Pentecost. Do you remember the visits he used to talk about, Aunt? He was most odd, wasn't he?' Mr Porphyry laughed.

'And your cousin, Philip. He used to love Pentecost's stories.'

They laughed together now. I felt none of the sense of exclusion that family chatter can occasionally impose upon the outsider. On the contrary I was warmed by it, and felt myself gathered in on the fringes of their discussion. It was not for my benefit; but the general drift of their talk had sufficient reference to Coppinger to keep me interested, while at the same time it led me on into what struck me, even at that time, as a vast multitude of Porphyrys, Llewellyns, Powyses and Plunketts; Norfolk, Cumberland and the Lakes, the Cotswolds, Wales, even Ireland, seemed to be encompassed by their discussion.

I saw Mr Porphyry in a different light. Up to then he had loomed, tall and spare and important before me, and essentially solitary. There had been no attenuations. There had been the faint impression of loneliness. But it was loneliness easily contained within his self-assurance. His aunt diluted him a little. Watching him watching her made me think of him as much younger. Up to that point in my knowledge of him the question of his age had not arisen, still less the much more subtle question of the 'meaning' of his age. He had featured too importantly for it to arise. It had therefore remained indeterminate; and any guessing was severely handicapped by the relative difficulties one faces at the age of fifteen in guessing anyone's age. It gets easier as one grows older; consciousness becomes more important as we steadily accumulate years and bind down our energies to the confines of the main action of what we do. He had passed that point, perhaps long since. Quite what its meaning was had yet to be revealed; so had my part in it; but that I had a part was given greater conviction simply by virtue of the fact that I sat at his dinner table that night on the fringes of his conversation with his aunt.

I was occasionally included directly. She mentioned the Grönings; also Ambleside; it seemed to me, from the soft smile that accompanied her remarks, which themselves were designed to get a reaction from her nephew almost more than from me, that she had been along the same course before. And it provoked a question.

'Did you ever meet Philpotts?' I asked her.

She and Mr Porphyry exchanged a glance. More to him, she

replied with a question of her own: 'He was two years ago, wasn't he?'

'Three.'

'I did meet him. Yes. Tall, dark, curly hair. I remember.' She did not wish to pursue the discussion. Mr Porphyry got up and began clearing the plates. I helped him.

In the kitchen he said to me: 'If you're free tomorrow you could perhaps take Aunt Amelia to the Festival. She would like the company.'

I wanted to ask him what it was Philpotts had done. But the firmness with which they had locked him up inside the glance that passed between them at table dissuaded me. And when, shortly afterwards, he offered to take me back to Chelsea, I felt a certain relief at the end of the evening with both of them.

III

He drove me home in the Lagonda. It was a short enough distance, and I could have taken the Underground. But he said he wanted to get out, and we went quite slowly along the embankment in the dusk. Though the traffic was light, and the road broad, he looked ahead with a single-minded concentration that was faintly disturbing. He seemed to have something on his mind. The evening was still unsettled, but as we swung more to the west at Pimlico Pier the light up the river from the broken cloud was tinged with soft shades of pink.

'You don't mind this work?' he asked. 'Meeting my relations and friends, guiding them round London?'

'No,' I said. 'I like it. Very much.'

'And it doesn't provoke problems for you?'

I frowned. I was not really sure. Nothing had been said; nevertheless, I felt that it might, and I was conscious of faint echoes of resentment, too faint to pin down, and far too faint to register with Mr Porphyry.

He laughed. It was a shy, almost an embarrassed prelude to

a repeat of the question in a different form: 'Why don't you answer?'

'I can't,' I said. 'I don't know, Mr Porphyry. My father seems to think I should help him a bit.'

'And do you want to?'

It was my turn to laugh, also with a certain measure of embarrassment. 'No. Not really. But it makes me feel guilty.'

He pulled the car in to the side of the road at the beginning of Cheyne Walk. I began to open the door.

'And how is everything else?'

'Oh, everything else's all right, Sir.'

'Do you . . .' he said it quickly, in order to prevent me from pushing wide the car door; but then he paused. I still held the handle, but waited politely, conscious that he was still looking ahead of him. 'Do you go to church when you're on holiday?'

It was my turn to pause. It was the first direct reference to that area of faith and belief which, by popular consent among other senior boys at Coppinger, was the mainspring of Porphyry's purpose in awarding his annual scholarship.

'Sometimes,' I said. It was a compromise answer, and I was not happy with the truthfulness of it.

'Regularly?'

'Not regularly, Sir.'

'Do you read the Bible at all?'

'You mean, on holiday?'

'At any time.'

'Not much.' I looked out at the trees across the river, feeling trapped and uncomfortable. I could recall surges of faith in the past, oddly motivated, mainly by events or people at school, but unsustained.

'I'm only mentioning this,' he said, his hands quite tight on the steering wheel, 'because you will find with the Grönings a Christian fellowship, possibly of a kind unfamiliar to you.' He tapped the steering wheel with his left hand. For a moment I thought there would be more questions; instead, he turned and smiled. 'Have a good time there. Ring me when you get back.'

'Goodnight,' I said. 'Thank you very much.'

The road was wide enough for him to turn in a single sweep, and the powerful, well-kept car sped away eastward, back to his flat.

On the corner of Flood Street I met Esther. She had got off the bus in Oakley Street in order to come round by the river, and she asked me in to have coffee. My father and Laurie appeared to be out, so I accepted, and followed her up the stairs.

'What have you been doing with yourself?' she said.

'I have a job,' I said. 'This firm in the city.'

'And what do you do?' She moved about her room, putting on the kettle, tidying away her things.

'I'm a courier,' I said. 'I show people round, meet them from trains, take them to places.'

'It sounds most impressive.' She smiled, looking at me.

I felt a bit ashamed of the exaggerated title I had claimed for myself.

'And when you are not hurrying from place to place? What then?'

'That's all I do.'

'So it's not full-time?'

'Oh, no.'

She made the coffee and brought it to the window where I was standing in the fading light. We sat on the floor.

'What does your father think about all this?'

'Has he said anything?'

'I haven't seen him recently. But before you came home he was looking forward to it, hoping to have you with him.'

I sighed. 'I'm going to Germany the day after tomorrow.'

'He's a sweet man.'

'He says you have beautiful feet, Esther. He told me he kissed them once.'

She laughed. 'He's dreadful! What a thing to say!'

'He's always admired beautiful feet.' I paused. 'Do you think everything's all right between them?'

F   161

'What do you mean?'

'My father and her. Laurie.' I said her name emphatically, suddenly conscious of having raised a question which might make Esther draw back.

'Why do you ask?' she said, her voice gentle. 'Has anything happened? Are you worried?' There was a tenderness in her words that seemed specially directed at me. I wanted the moment of twilight to last for ever.

'No,' I said. 'Nothing's happened. It's just they're always bickering.'

'Just bickering?' she said. She got to her feet and picked up the empty cups. 'That's all right. You don't have to worry. Bickering's normal.'

Her words made the bickering between my father and Laurie a desirable state in marriage, one that I should seek out and encourage. I felt better, and got to my feet. She did not discourage me when I said that I ought to go.

'We'll go out together when you get back from Germany. I get tickets to things. You like music?'

I nodded. 'Goodnight, Esther. Thanks for the coffee.'

Chapter Eight

I

'You've got your passport?'

I nodded.

'Where is it?'

'Here.' I pointed to my inside pocket.

'Show me.'

'Oh, Dad.' I took it out and showed it to him. 'And the money, and the ticket. I've got everything.'

'You can't be too careful going abroad.' He stared up and down the platform. People were still arriving, and it looked as though the train would be full. I had secured a window seat and had then stepped out again to say good-bye to him.

His face was stern as he surveyed the crowd. Eventually he turned back to me. 'Now remember everything I've said. Roads, traffic, strangers, keeping your wits about you, not making a fool of yourself, and above all don't panic.'

'I'll be all right,' I said. 'Just don't worry.' I gritted my teeth.

One or two of the doors were closed. Latecomers were beginning to hurry.

'You'd better get in,' he said.

I looked at him. He seemed tense. I wanted to say something that would soften the occasion, bring us closer together.

He had left work earlier that day to see me off, and had fussed over the details of where I would change and who would meet me, what I would do if I lost my money or became ill. I had now grown impatient.

'Good-bye, then,' I said.

"Bye old son. And send a postcard. As soon as you arrive. Don't forget.'

We shook hands and I got in and sat down in my place. Still he stood on the other side of the glass, his florid and hooded countenance fixing upon me a look of stern injunction. I wished he would just go away.

At last the train moved, and with a modest enough gesture, a hand raised by each of us, we parted company. I watched as he was obscured by other people. He had made me feel resentful, and now, as he vanished, I was sorry. There had been a time when concern of this kind had served as an adequate enough expression of his love for me. I had bathed in it, and then in the laughter which the long and repetitive catalogue of injunctions usually induced. It would speed me on my way and at the same time leave him satisfied. It was an odd mixture: love, mockery, impatience. The balance was a delicate one, and now it seemed to have gone wrong.

It had been going wrong before. What had happened now was a proving of the inadequacy of this level of exchange between us. I was slipping away while he was trying to resurrect, from an unsatisfactory but less perceptive past, the insubstantial chains of material concern with which to bind me to him once again.

As the train moved on eastwards, gathering speed, I felt a stab of reciprocal concern for him. The enlargement of my perceptions should not diminish the quality of my love for him. Perhaps it should change it, altering the flow and pattern, but not make it less. How, then, was it that my mind dwelt increasingly at that time upon the unsatisfactory nature of all that surrounded him?

I leaned my head on the glass and stared out at the untidy,

164

sprawling urban mess through which we were passing. Bright sunlight fell upon the ribbons of little, mean, back gardens, rampant with repetitive rows of summer beans, lettuce, onions. I was impatient for the placid, even spread of woodland and cornfield, the larger canvas of the countryside, more organised and at the same time more natural.

I was not satisfied with who I was. I tried to visualise my father, sitting now in a tube train and rocking his way back to Sloane Square, and the image of him in my mind was remote and unsympathetic: the easy, relaxed posture; the stern, hard look in his grey eyes; the set, weather-beaten features. He, who loved freedom, was governed by the routine of his marriage. I, who wanted freedom, was so small a part of the routine, and could throw it off when I wanted.

I thought of Mr Porphyry: what would it have been like to have been born his son instead? The shift in thought made me smile out at the shabby uncertainties where London fringed into Essex. What sort of person would I have been had I inherited those complex woven textures of family? Uncle Pentecost? Great Uncle Damien? Aunt Amelia herself? It was an absurd, attractive daydream. It stirred both pleasure and regret within me. Already, even then, I regarded Mr Porphyry as a permanent fixture in my affairs. If there was a shift in my loyalties it did not really make me feel guilty. I just felt privileged that I had both; that I could look back to one life, forward to another, balancing inheritance and gift.

The journey was long, and every moment of it made vital by the excitement of my anticipation. I ate sandwiches on the deck as we thudded our way out across calm sea in the summer evening light. And I stayed on deck to watch the flat East Anglia coastline fade below the horizon; then the sunset; then the gathering darkness of night ahead of us as we steamed monotonously forward.

I suppose in reality I concealed my excitement at my first trip abroad well enough, insulating myself inside my belted mackintosh and rather battered suitcase, and assuming various romantic or adventurous roles out of fiction to alleviate the monotony of the journey. I slept fitfully in the small hours, watched in fatigued amazement the seemingly endless manifestations of industry in the valley of the Rhine, and was awake again as dawn spread its grey light over everything.

I was red-eyed, and it was light, as we drew into Hanover Station. Peter Gröning identified me quickly enough, and carried my case to the bus. He must have risen very early to meet me. And yet we were two among many at six o'clock in the morning. Determined men, in leather coats, with bulging briefcases, and the short stubs of fat cigars grimly clamped in their mouths, seemed to be moving in every direction, obedient, as I conceived them at the time, not to ambition or purpose, but to some clockwork intent, as if a huge film, of endless length, and unlimited budget, had been started just as we left the station, and for my express benefit, entitled 'German Recovery'.

The Grönings' flat was small, dark and rather uncomfortable. It was on the third floor of an apartment block on the outskirts of the city. In the tiny hallway I stood for a moment listening; nearby, in one of the rooms, a man was singing scales. The deep bass voice, carefully precise and controlled, was moving up through the register. I looked inquiringly at Peter.

'That is my father,' he said. 'He will practise for ten minutes more. Then we shall have breakfast. After that you will wish to rest?'

'Does he sing every morning?'

'Yes. He is with a choir in Hanover. We shall be going to a performance.'

His mother appeared and welcomed me. She was a plain woman, dark and heavy-looking, her muted colouring enlivened a little by her kindly eyes and expressive mouth.

'You must be tired,' she said. 'You will have a good sleep this morning.'

I had imagined otherwise, but realised that my head was leaden with fatigue. We went into the small dining-room against one wall of which was a narrow bed that turned out to be my own. Above it was a window, and I noticed that an English bible had been placed on the sill. The singing stopped and Herr Gröning appeared. The four of us sat down to a breakfast of pumpernickel, cheese, jam and slices of salami. Herr Gröning did not speak English as well as his wife or son, and relied on them to express his sentiments, which on that morning were brief and welcoming. Then he left and I was invited to rest until lunch-time. With the shutters down, and the faint careful noises coming to me from the kitchen, I turned over in my mind the events of the journey, and then slept.

Four or five hours of untroubled sleep distanced me from the night's journey. I awoke in the stillness of the darkened room, not knowing how to raise the shutters through which filtered only the faintest evidence of daylight. But I could see enough to open the wooden doors which led into the larger living-room, with its piano, where Herr Gröning did his practice. I dressed and walked quietly in to the larger room, looking carefully at the furniture and pictures, curious about the smallest detail, determined to absorb it all as a physical inventory of my excitement.

In the early afternoon Peter and I went for a walk. The sun was warm and, as we strode along, he told me about the district, the people, his friends, the vague plans for my stay.

'And I suppose you are going to Ambleside?'

'Yes,' I said. 'Have you been?'

'Last year I was there.'

'What was it like?'

He shrugged his shoulders and pursed up his mouth. It was a dismissive expression that stopped me from pursuing the line of inquiry which might otherwise have satisfied my curiosity about the visit I was to make there later in the holiday. We walked on in silence.

I asked him: 'Did Philpotts stay with you? A couple of years ago?'

167

Peter's face brightened. He seemed relieved not to be asked any more about Ambleside. 'You know him?'

'He was a friend of mine. At school with me.' I paused. 'He's left now. I haven't seen him for a while. He's at university.'

'He came. He was great fun. We went often that summer to the opera. There was a season here. He used to make me go. We had no seats. We used to queue up for standing room. It was only one mark fifty. He was crazy about it. Every day he would say, "We go now to the theatre. See if we can get behind the scenes." He was very good fun. Oh, yes. Your Philpotts. He was very English.' He laughed.

I could imagine the irreverent intensity with which Philpotts would have pursued his interest, and I smiled as well. Peter, in age, would have been somewhere between Philpotts and myself, perhaps no more than a year older than me. I felt a certain trepidation that I would not be able to provide a comparable stimulus during my stay.

We entered a civic park of some sort, and Peter led me across to a small knot of boys of his own age. He introduced me. Though one or two spoke a little English they were preoccupied with what seemed to be a fairly lacklustre argument in which there were quite long pauses. I stood politely on the fringes of the group, and eventually we parted company, walking on through the dry and dusty pathways, among stern laurel hedging and occasional magnolias.

I was treated in a kind and considerate way by the Grönings and the days I spent with them were crowded, the simplest of expeditions taking on excitement because of the strangeness of every detail. The burden of entertaining me shifted quite early from Peter to his mother. Sometimes I went out with him and his friends, and tried, not very successfully, to involve myself in what they were doing. But inevitably, for most of the time, I was a spectator rather than a companion, and when the opportunities were presented to me I chose rather to go out with Mrs Gröning, whose sense of obligation, and possibly her affectionate nature as well, caused her to devote all her attention to me.

There was more, besides. It was clear to me, on the first day, that whatever Peter had experienced staying with Mr Porphyry and then in Ambleside, had faded into residual feelings of guilt. He avoided my questions, and to some extent, I felt, he avoided me. Frau Gröning referred to it, obliquely. It was the day we visited Herrenhausen. She had wanted to take me, and had encouraged Peter, though he needed little enough encouragement, to go off with his friends. The weather was warm, the sky clear, the bright sunlight played on the broad green avenues that criss-crossed the extensive parklands with their lovely pavilions and their varied views back towards the main palace. We walked slowly among the trees, beside the stretches of water, along the well-kept pathways.

She spoke little at first, just letting fall occasional remarks about the city and its history. She had already asked me a good deal about myself, and when alone with her I had found it comparatively easy to talk about my father and stepmother, and the disparity that existed between Coppinger and Mr Porphyry on the one hand, and Chelsea on the other. Her detachment from it all made her a suitable recipient for confidences about the current tensions in my life; her sympathy did the rest. At times it seemed shadowed by a sadness of her own, and to this also I responded.

She mentioned Ambleside. I told her I was yet to go there, referring to the place as though it were one of life's proving grounds.

'Conviction does not have to be sudden,' she said.

I looked at her and frowned. Had her otherwise excellent English gone awry? What did she mean? She seemed to be speaking more to herself than to me. 'Belief can be gradual,' she went on. 'It can grow in you, be part of you.'

'I am sure that is so, Frau Gröning.'

'I am afraid of the sudden leap.'

'So am I,' I said, quite fervently. I had no real grasp of what she meant. Sudden leaps seemed totally incompatible with the ordered existence of the Gröning household.

'The danger is that one falls back. The conviction is lost. And starting over again is more difficult. Have you not found that?'

'I think it is true. Yes.' I spoke without understanding what she really meant. In a loose and undisciplined way I had allowed the presumption of my living faith to prevail in the Gröning family since my arrival, joining in with them in prayer and admitting myself to a spiritual fellowship any doubts or uncertainties about which were partly cloaked by language differences. From the start I had been aware of a certain measure of uninterest on Peter's part, and on one occasion had observed his mother looking at him, her face troubled by doubt and concern.

By the time we went together to Herrenhausen sufficient had been left unsaid by me, or had been assumed by her and tacitly agreed by me, to make difficult and embarrassing anything as fundamental as a plea of ignorance now about the dangers of falling back from faith. And it added to my embarrassment that I was covertly aware that all was not right.

'I think it has happened with Peter,' she said.

She waited to see if I would answer.

'He does not talk to you about it?'

I shook my head.

'Perhaps he is shy.' She paused. 'I want to be wrong. I think it would have been better if it had been different. Slower. Not forced.' She looked at me. We were standing in front of a small baroque pavilion, its windows and plasterwork painted in soft shades of green. It was open to the public, and we were about to go in. She smiled at me, the gentle sad expression in her eyes compelling me to take seriously the words she was uttering, even if I failed, as I did then, to understand their purpose.

I felt her regret spreading out towards me. In my mind I associated the circumstances of it with Mr Porphyry, seeing him as a powerful spiritual engine in the commitments that had been made around me at that time, and possibly were to be made in the future.

'Was it Ambleside?' I said.

'Partly.'

'And Mr Porphyry?'

'I cannot explain easily to you the way a mother feels,' she said. 'The chances that one has in life, the opportunities. . . .'

'Do you mean that Peter might have made a mistake?'

She looked at me without direct comprehension, as if my words were uttered on a different plane and were no more than an interruption to her troubled thoughts. 'It has not come right,' she said. Then, resignedly, her voice flat and conclusive: 'He has lost his faith, I think.' She paused for several moments, then her face cleared. 'When did your mother die?'

I told her.

'How old were you?'

'I was seven.'

'And now? This woman your father has married?'

I shrugged my shoulders.

'It will be all right,' she said.

I smiled at her. Almost, I laughed. Her use of the phrase, oblivious of its ironic impact, conjured up for me the shabby spectacle of Laurie, the remote prospect of it being in any sense 'all right'. She took my smile at face value, and responded with one of encouragement. We prepared to go in. Vaguely, in reaching out to me, I felt conscious, in her, of an approach to life that was the opposite of the greedy, passionate striving and fumbling I witnessed in my father, and felt I was inheriting in myself. Away from home, and sceptical anyway of how far the term 'home' had any meaning, I was probably vulnerable to feelings which I only half understood. She had sought in me someone in whom to confide about her son. I responded by finding in her words and sympathies perhaps more than was really there. My father's many women had conditioned me to take what I could from them, just as he did. My needs were different, but the emotional flexibility was the same. Only in this way can I explain the ease with which I responded to her. Standing in the sunlight, the ground in front of us dappled by the lime trees' foliage, I felt she embraced so much with her affection. Her eyes questioned me for reassurance. Had she been my mother, I would have responded. I would have shown wisdom, and persistence, and resourcefulness; in return she would have imparted to me softness and strength, a certain detachment, a reserve of patience. We looked at each other. I did not known what to say. My feelings were so shallow. We were surrounded by people moving towards the entrance door of the small ornate pavilion in the palace grounds. It offered new experience, new interest. It was time to set aside the taxing examination of faith and feeling. I remained silent.

'Be careful,' she said. 'Life is very long.'

We were never as close again, and yet we seemed to share a secret for the rest of my visit which acted as a subtle bond between us. It counteracted the tension induced by Peter's really very modest form of rebellion against his parents, the brunt of which was borne by Frau Gröning. Though she did not turn to me again, those moments of confiding in the dappled sunlight of the palace grounds exercised a stabilising influence upon my quite volatile thoughts while on holiday there. I think the limits of our friendship were reached on that afternoon and, in a negative sense, confined by what had not been said as much as by what had.

My holiday in Hanover was an intense interlude from which remembered images tumble in profusion. I can still feel the moist pumpernickel crumbling between my fingers; I can still hear the incipient groan of the tramcars starting up from the palace gates and climbing through their scale of notes to the high, wavering whine they made at full speed; I can still smell the *bratwurst* at the street stalls. Though Herr Gröning remained the most shadowy figure of the family he yet provided the deepest and most lasting memory of all: the early-morning practice wrenching me from my dreams.

I would lie in the darkness, my eyes following the thin sliver of light from the shutters as they penetrated across the surface of wallpaper and paint. His routine was always the same

172

scales first, then some work at the end, a brief indulgence before finishing.

One morning he sang Schumann's '*Schöne Wiege meiner Leiden*'. I did not know it, of course. Not then. I could not have identified the composer, even; and would have said Schubert, in the belief at the time that any classical song sung in German must be by him. Nor could I have made any real judgment of the quality of Herr Gröning's voice. It was powerful, but firmly controlled; the words and notes flowed over me in their sad splendour. To my uncomprehending ears only the flow of notes had any meaning: the quick and passionate pulse of the first phrase; the note of doubt in that subtle change by which it is almost, but not quite, repeated; and then the sighing hesitation at the end: '*Schöne Stadt, wir müssen scheiden, lebe wohl.*'

I have been many times to Germany since that first visit. Part of my life was spent there, and a wealth of recollections, easily summoned up, is woven deeply within me. Yet none prevails with quite the force that stirred my heart in the darkened room; that sad, unrecognised farewell.

II

Ambleside is inescapably interwoven, in my memory, with Commander Wilfred Cochrane, RN; and Commander Wilfred Cochrane is inescapably remembered, as he used to stand, in the evenings, before us, with his loins so clearly girded up to the herculean task of bringing our souls to the throne of God. It is easy, from the dark forest of later life, when we have become subtly enmeshed in the secondary colourings, the cross-hatchings of many human obligations, to look back a little indulgently upon the blaze of glorious light that illumined the open country of our youth. Bathed in the sunlight of his fervour, conviction glowing from his eyes, salvation tingling like lightning flashes from the tips of his fingers as he stabbed the air in

173

front of him, he was an emblem of goodness, a cipher for the saving grace of Jesus Christ, a symbol for God's forgiveness in a world that had not really begun to impose upon us the deeper need to be forgiven. Far ahead of us lay the dry plains of doubt, the thickets of iniquity, the slow, meandering, sluggish brown waters of cowardice and betrayal. He did not tell us that. Perhaps, in the blinding glow of his own zeal he had not encountered too much of the accumulated dross of the middle years, and to him our present doubts and imperfections were faults in us large enough to be hunted out and washed clean.

Ambleside Hall had lawns which ran down to the lakeside, and on our first evening, after supper, when the rain had cleared and the slanting light of an invisible sun was colouring water and hillside in shades of pink and mauve and tinted greys and blues, we walked there in small groups or alone. I was on my own to begin with, and content to breathe the air and feel the mild wind from the lake without associating with anyone else. There seemed no one remotely like the Coppinger boys with whom I might have felt at ease. We were a group of thirty or so. Ostensibly we were there to walk among the lakes, and explore. For this purpose we had been divided into groups of five or six and a programme had been devised which daily set us different starting points aimed at bringing about an evening rendezvous from which we returned to the hall for supper. On the noticeboard were details, with the names of group leaders. After a fairly superficial discussion with the others in my group, immediately after supper, I had wandered away faintly resentful of the school-like atmosphere that prevailed. Most of the boys came from public schools, and the universal question had been, 'Which?' With me, it was, 'Where?' It could have made me recalcitrant. But there was a tall boy in our small group called Christopher Akenside, who was at Fettes College in Edinburgh, and who followed me after a few minutes and came and stood a few yards from me along the lakeside, gently lobbing small pebbles into the water.

'I think it'll be a hard slog, all this walking. Have you done much of it?'

'I've never hiked in mountains,' I said. 'I've gone hiking, but it's not like this on the Cotswolds. I mean, here it's thousands of feet.'

'Well, not many thousands.'

'I look forward to that part of it, the hiking, if it's not too wet,' I said.

'It'll be wet.' He laughed briefly. 'It's wet everywhere. And, even when it's dry everywhere, it's wet here.' He paused, and lobbed more stones into the brownish water where it lapped in the shallows. 'What about the other part?' he asked. 'The fellowship? Are you a "Crusader"?'

'What's that?'

'I thought everyone was, here.' He stared out across the lake. A few lights in Windermere had come on and winked at us, reflected uncertainly in the water, and still faintly superfluous in the intermittent radiance of the fading light of evening.

'It's a Christian fellowship.'

'Oh.'

'I wouldn't worry too much about it.'

'I won't, then,' I said.

We both laughed.

It was not until the following evening that we experienced Commander Cochrane in action. Again, it was after supper. We had walked and chatted for about twenty minutes, and then reassembled. From the windows of what had formerly been the library of Ambleside Hall it was possible to look down over the lawns in front of the house to the lake itself and the clusters of dark green rhododendron bushes that edged the garden at one side. And as he joked about our day, and the state of our feet, and the stretching of our muscles which we would feel in the morning if we did not feel it now, I was lulled into a sense of easy relaxation and false security. He would not intrude upon my idle fancy too much; daydreams, in which Janet or Esther or some other object of rampant desire might feature,

175

would hardly be disturbed by this not particularly distinguished-looking retired naval officer, with his hair thinning on top, and his enthusiastic smile which could so effortlessly evolve into laughter. And even after he had picked up from behind him the black Bible which fell open and hung like a limp dead animal across his broad palm, the pages curved over like a seagull in flight, and had offered for all of us the first elusive thread of his argument, moving from his own words into those of greater authority, words that tell us 'because iniquity shall abound, the love of many shall wax cold', and had allowed to flicker in his eyes the light of exhortation, I still lingered in the arbours of pleasure, my eyes roaming the dew-laden lawns that stretched down to the gleaming waters of the lake, my mind reaching out towards unattainable desires.

Talk of love has its own compulsion. 'That love of God is yours and mine,' he said. 'It is here in this room. It is abundantly available to us. From the Father, through the Son, manifest in the Holy Spirit. It is ours if we want to take it.' He paused. His hand, which had pointed at us, and at himself, and at the floor of the room, and upward at the shadowy grey of the unlighted ceiling, now descended upon the book in his hand, and set the leaves flying over and over in a tempest of familiar investigation. 'Let us see what Jesus said. His last prayer, before he went out across the brook Cedron. Who can tell me?' He looked round the silent room. 'The Spirit does not yet speak in you. I will tell you.' His short, stubby forefinger stabbed out in the air towards us all. 'He spoke unto God and he said: "And I have declared unto them thy name, and will declare it; that the love wherewith thou hast loved me may be in them, and I in them." God's love, that is, through his Son, Jesus Christ, penetrating the hearts of all that believe.' Again he paused, and looked at us, his hand raised, and gently traversing the room, so that his clutched fist, out of which rose the index finger like a pointer upward to a higher realm where belief, perhaps in a day or two, might descend upon us as we walked among the misted fells and still tarns, embraced us all and drew us in. Then the hand descended again, an eagle in search of prey, and the pages flew, and he was among the Ephesians: ' "for his great love wherewith he loved us, even when we were dead in sins, hath quickened us together with Christ, (by Grace ye are saved;)" by His grace truly do we come to salvation. But remember the starting point; remember it is God's love. If we go back to Isaiah, we find it there.'

He flung back the pages, and his finger descended with instantaneous, lightning perception. He hardly needed the reference, still less the words themselves. He stared out at us all as he spoke: ' "he hath poured out his soul unto death: and he was numbered with the transgressors; and he bare the sins of many, and made intercession for the transgressors." He did that for us in the absolute infinity of his love. And the authority for what I say is here beneath my hand.' He laid his hand flat upon the book, he seemed to press down hard upon its spread pages, breathing into them a miraculous sense of purpose. 'It is all here. Listen.' He turned just one page, glanced down, pointed, and again, hardly needing to read at all, he spoke with love and compassion in his voice: ' "For as the rain cometh down, and the snow from heaven, and returneth not thither, but watereth the earth, and maketh it bring forth and bud, that it may give seed to the sower and bread to the eater: so shall my word be that goeth forth out of my mouth: it shall not return unto me void, but it shall accomplish that which I please, and it shall prosper in the thing whereto I sent it." '

I felt moved. His words, and the intensity with which he spoke them, gathered me up into an invisible bower of comfort and peace. I felt that I mattered to him, and that behind him there stood a greater presence that cared also for me. I had heard these words before, or some of them; but they had sounded unimportant, distant from all my guilts and indecisions. Now they drove straight and true, arrows of conviction launched from a mighty bow of passion. Coming from the lips of this quite diminutive man, a figure to be passed by, almost shadowy among the other older people who helped to run Ambleside Hall, until that moment when he had turned and taken up the black seagull and set it in flight among us, the words—I suppose I should say the Word—brought him suddenly to life. He was almost threatening; he was telling us, plainly enough, that the words from his lips 'shall accomplish that which I please', and we were moving into the territory of belief, obedient to his will and the will of God which so palpably spoke through him.

He shook truth out of his Bible. The pages were bent at the corners, discoloured by endless turning, marked with pen and pencil and crayon, wrenched and pummelled and bruised in the service of the covenant which Wilfred Cochrane had made with us all. If we imagined that the general panoply of love which he cast over us like a net was the sole work of the evening, we were much mistaken. He was determined, there and then, to ensure that his word would not return void, Indefatigable, he pressed on. Love was a frame of reference. By it, he established a form of government over our hearts. We could not deny him the claims he made on our other instincts once he had established that they were being made in the name of God's love manifesting itself through his Son. There is a logic in faith. There is an absolute logic in the workings of love. And it developed into a tussle in which the reality of betrayal was real; even the reality of a devil called Satan.

Wilfred Cochrane had a boundless appetite for that particular fight, as we would learn in due course. But his purpose on that first evening as far as he was concerned, the beginning of his mission among us, was the assembly of a host: 'Who is on my side? Who?' Having spent twenty minutes or so in establishing the pervasiveness of love, the forceful catalyst to which he would endlessly return, he embarked upon a second foray in the familiar pages of the book which lay like a symbol of his power across his open hand.

It had the formal pattern of a piece of music: gently, softly, with 'comfortable words', he embarked upon the second movement of his symphony of salvation. Dealing with profound

178

things he chose simple words, and uttered them softly and without stress. It was the larghetto from Elgar's second symphony, in which the very quality of his personal impulse towards us assumed large and general immediacy. ' "Who is the greatest in the Kingdom of heaven?" That was the question Jesus was asked. And how did he answer? "Except ye be converted, and become as little children, ye shall not enter." From the eighteenth chapter of St Matthew's gospel, to the first chapter of St John's, verse twelve, and the third, verses three and five and six, and fifteen, and seventeen.' In the gathering dusk that turned the light in that long room, filled with warmth and stillness and expectation, into a shadowy filter through which his words reached out to us, the spiritual act of becoming 'the sons of God' was presented as a possibility, there and then. He leaped, like the pentecostal fire itself, from proof to proof, in faith. The pages flew under his hand, salvation, conversion, being born again, it was an act, a decision, a commitment. St Paul joined with St Peter, in this at least; the gospels found common ground; even the Revelation of St John the Divine was brought to bear upon the question.

And if all these emanations from the word of God, powerful and quick and sharper than any two-edged sword, able to dismember joints and marrow, 'a discerner of the thoughts and intents of the heart', were to fail, what then? Having given us the closely-woven web of abundant goodness, the alternative questions had to be asked.

The next movement was a scherzo: short and brilliant, it had but one argument—'this is the condemnation, that one light is come into the world, and men loved darkness rather than light, because their deeds were evil.' The precision of his anger was great. The wrath of God spoke through his mouth. It was firmly controlled. It was briefly identified. It was not designed to frighten us, but to suggest a certain anguish in Heaven at our wilful and wayward lives.

He concluded with an andante in which all the arguments were folded back into the net of love. Whatever we wanted to do, or be—and it seemed that out through the window and across the dull gleam on the surface of the lake in the fading dusk of that August evening all one's opportunities and ambitions stretched away into an infinity that was more absolute than it could possibly be again in one's life—whatever it was, the accomplishment of it needed this pervasive force, hammered out by the shadowy figure of Commander Cochrane as he stood at the end of the room, preparing to fold the wings of his bird of salvation in a final act of prayer.

III

Blea Tarn was small and remote. It had the perfect shape of a tear. It was cradled in a simple loop of steep mountain wall, regular, and at times forbidding. On the afternoon we hiked there the end of the valley was overshadowed by heavy grey cloud giving it this close, sombre, threatening appearance. The light of day, which came stronger from behind us as we passed over the lip, at the tear's apex, and stared ahead over the impenetrable, shadowy waters, emphasised the still, dark gloom that faced us. When I think of 'the valley of the shadow of death', through which the psalmist supposed that we might all, at some point in our lives, be obliged to walk, it is always Blea Tarn, on that particular afternoon, that rises before me, filling my imagination with the same doubts and hesitations I felt then. It was a still, dark sepulchre, and I think we must all have shivered a little at the sudden contrast. We had walked up the steep valley, in intermittent sunshine, clouds gathering, to step over the rim and be faced by the limpid waters, dark reflecting dark, the sky an angry, heavy grey mass high ahead of us, where the even, steep edge of the fell rimmed us round, leaving only the broken gap through which we entered, and out of which tumbled the stream we had followed in order to bring us there.

What did they know that brought us there? We were all

together for this day's outing, the last before the holiday ended. And the leaders, after a brief pause to allow us to gather and feed our eyes on what was an entirely natural phenomenon, with no house or byre visible at all, set off along the shores of the small lake to begin the long circuit.

I had made casual friendship with some of the group, but nothing that looked like lasting. Perhaps it would be fair to say that a certain tension existed, imposed upon us by the Commander himself, who saw all of us in spiritual communion with himself or with one or other of the group leaders, and treated as a form of disaffection any serious attempt at friendship that might challenge the deeper bonds that were to be forged between us and the Lord Jesus. Perhaps I malign him and them; perhaps I am over-sensitive about the state of mind in which I found myself after a week of prayer and witness and exhortation. I did not consciously stand out against it. I was not unduly wracked with guilt. No one sought from me any confession that might bring to the surface the vague and irritating conviction that I loved darkness rather than light, simply because my deeds were evil. They *were* evil. My selfishness was evil; so were my lusts and their satisfaction; so was my pride; so was the easy indifference with which I turned away from my father and his chosen bride, and sought escape from his world, a world that offended my sense of dignity and my own destiny.

It was beneath this that a deeper force stirred. In the Lake District, given tradition and fable, combined with the great depths to which many of the lakes go, a certain expectation of monsters is alerted. Even Blea Tarn, in its stillness, seemed just possibly a repository for deep movements of threatening life. So much was this so that one almost hoped for it. And the same was the case with one's anticipation of a deeper force than guilt stirring in the bowels of uncertainty created by Wilfred Cochrane's emblems of love and faith and salvation. It would not do to be forced by fear into calling on the name of Jesus Christ.

I had formed with Christopher Akenside rather more of an attachment than I had with anyone else during the week, and we were side by side that afternoon as the long file of our party headed forth into the gloomy valley. He had 'found Christ', he told me, the previous night, and diffidently he spelt out for me the implications of the step he had taken. Though at school in Scotland, he came from Yorkshire, and his accent had within it some of the slow echoes that I remembered in Kessner's voice, and which took me back to the time when he and I were trebles in the choir, and when Christian beliefs of a much muddier colouring had failed me in their credited purposes. I told this to Akenside.

His reply was abrupt and slightly censorious.

'It is not what it can do for you that matters. The demand is His, and is inescapable.'

'But how, since I have so far escaped?'

'The eye of the Lord is resting on you.'

It seemed that a dark and angry eye was resting on all of us as we trudged forward into the gloom. There was no mist; not even the threat of it. And it was warm, and still. But the heavy cloud gathered beyond the fell's edge seemed to thicken still more, and bear down with added force upon the distinct possibility, itself reinforced by a long week of tangling with what seemed then to be the deepest questions that ever would face us, that the Lord indeed had his eye upon me. I had the urge to laugh. It did seem faintly absurd, the imposition of a physical state of observation on God.

I asked Akenside: 'Do you not think we should relate our faith to our lives?'

'Of course.'

'But if there seems no way in which Christ can be brought into the family . . . just suppose, Christopher, you had problems at home. Just suppose you and your father—?' I left the inquiry hanging there.

'He would find a way.'

He was so sure, and after so little a time. Looking at his

strangely intent face, the narrow, high head, the faint expression of perplexity, embodying concern for me rather than himself, I was drawn closer to a feeling of conviction.

I probed him further. I tried to fault his certainty. But I was inhibited. There was the need to conceal from him much of what weighed most heavily upon me: guilt, shame, a sense of the bizarre and unacceptable nature of my situation. If he was right, what could I *not* do? I was young enough, conscious enough of my imperfections and of my own perfectibility, hungry for the strength that faith might give me, aware enough of my nakedness in the world to long for the clothing of belief. I sought the breastplate of righteousness; I believed in the helmet of salvation; I had seen on the backs of others that week the garments of vengeance, and, like them, I wished to throw across my own shoulders—and not without a certain flourish, a certain incipient pride at being able to become, at one and the same time, a little child and one of the sons of God—to throw across my shoulders the cloak of zeal.

How easy Wilf made it! How fine and high and proud would one's steps be, once the decision had been made, the promise given, the Gift received! The dark, silent waters of life, like the limpid, monochrome, oily texture of Blea Tarn round the banks of which we steadily trudged, would hold no further threats. The half-expected monster, whose terrifying head might rear up at any time from the still, dark, mirror-like depths, would be so easily vanquished. My father's rages would be subdued, a balm of infinite capacity, easing, healing, making well again, would be always there to soften the anxieties of life. Nameless desires would be set aside; purity would prevail.

We had spread ourselves out, figures rising up and sinking down again as we traversed the small hillocks, glacial deposits, along the side of the tarn. Then, at the end, where the full, heavy, round curve at the bottom of the tear seemed to come in closest to the smooth, steeply-curved sweep of the fell above us, the ground flattened out and became marshy where the water drained into the upper end of the small lake. The leaders

183

picked a way, and led the line onward. We followed the splashes of colour, the determined movement, heightened by the lonely stillness of the place and the thickening darkness above us. We had stopped talking, more or less. The going had become rougher, and we were all a bit stretched, both in terms of energy and in the lengthening gaps between people.

I was ever one to dramatise, and it may well be that I remember it wrongly, but the belief materialised in me that this really was the valley of the shadow of death, the death of an old life, and that as I crossed through the sodden rushes at the furthest point into the mountain side, beneath its darkest shadow, and with the grey mass of still unbroken raincloud moving over the edge of the fell, I decided for Him. The heavens did not open. No gladsome shout came down. I was out of breath, and the heel of one foot was beginning to hurt. But instead of facing into the gloom one now had, on the right hand, the still swathes of light across the water, reflections of a clearer sky, broken by distant sunlight beaming down onto the lower fells and valleys towards Ambleside and Windermere. And though there was no shout to salute my sudden sense of conviction, thinly, uncertainly, from far ahead up the line of diminutive figures trudging now towards the mouth of the valley, there came faintly the words of Charles Wesley's hymn, 'Rejoice, the Lord is King'. Gradually, they were taken up and re-echoed back at us from the high enclosed space in which we tramped. Far distant from us, as we climbed to the tops of the rounded hillocks, and occasionally paused before descending, we could see, more firmly cutting their way through the banks of clouds, the strong straight beams of gold from the sun.

> His kingdom cannot fail;
> He rules o'er earth and heaven;
> The keys of death and hell
> Are to our Jesus given.

IV

'Our Jesus' became mine that night. I forget the precise form in which I framed my invitation. Perhaps it is better that it remain buried in the folded tents of the past. But I believed that the flame of the spirit of the incarnate God settled then upon my lips and wrote there a guarantee of salvation. And, if I believed it then, what, subsequently, can take that belief away? The doubt about this deepens with the passage of time. I could not then conceive of prayer having a relevance that would outlast normal mortality. I could not think, then, that the image of 'bread upon the waters' might have a meaning involving not just months and years, but decades, even centuries, with one life folding into another. How could I know, then, as I stumbled forward with urgent and passionate steps, that the real force, the real perceptions, might lie many years in the future among events and experiences that could in no sense be foreseen.

'Mr Porphyry will rejoice at this,' Wilf told me.

I nodded, too shy to venture any observation about my new state of grace. He talked of God's grace. He outlined for me swift and invincible arguments that were personal to me. And, though I never again saw him, never revisited that place, never followed his particular work, the sense of him, that close, breathless atmosphere of dedication, is as real as if it had happened yesterday. I see his shadowy figure in the dusk. I see the great black bird spread across his hand. I see its white spirit fly out over us all.

Wilf was a good deal more outspokenly enthusiastic about our new state of grace than we were, and the last evening was one of zealous exhortation to those who had found salvation. The dark shadows of the world outside that room, made stuffy and close by the uncertain, threatening storms of the day, which had failed to break, and had failed to dissipate, were enumerated for us in an effort to clothe rapidly our fledgling souls against the perversities of reality. There was always an answer; there would always be an answer; and the immediate need was to assemble an armoury and appoint some place where new ammunition might be obtained. When tolerance is adumbrated as an answer to strife it overlooks the warlike imagery of conviction. We were soldiers of Christ; we were being sent out to fight; it was a particular insignia we had chosen to wear, a particular army to which we had been recruited, and the nature of the war would govern our actions.

The nature of the war! All the way back to London, on the long train journey, when conversation with those whom I would almost certainly never see again had petered out, I went over the particulars of my own situation, warmly confident that the new strength I had acquired would make me a quite invincible force in the places to which I was returning. They would all respond, for surely the Lord was now on my side? 'Be strong and of a good courage; be not afraid.' Wilfred Cochrane had written these words on the fly-leaf of a New Testament which was even now in my pocket, already marked, as he had marked the familiar pages of his great black limp Bible. And I was strong; and I was not afraid. And all things seemed possible as the train came into King's Cross. And London, familiar and enveloping, was yet new; it represented an invigorating challenge to the armoury of words and convictions by which I was now possessed.

Yet how short a time was that sense of invincibility to last! How soon was I to be dashed down by realities which were simply not amenable to the myriad answers that filled booklets, leaflets and scriptural guides! I had suffered rude awakenings before. My childhood had been peppered with ups and downs. But I think my vulnerability on that summer's evening, coming back into London after a long, indeed hypnotic train journey, was very great. So was the shock prepared for me. So was the fall.

I said good-bye to the others. Christopher Akenside had left the train early on, and now the rest of us dispersed. I felt both a release and a measure of faint spiritual uncertainty as I made the long journey by underground back to Chelsea. The impact was of a multitude of lives, disconnected, faint in purpose and meaning, just going on. Like that first dawn in Hanover, the opening and closing of the carriage doors, the entry and departure of people, had an unreal, clockwork quality. There was the wound-up mechanism of automatic repetition, and there was an endless supply of people.

As I turned into Flood Street, and headed down towards the river, I felt doubt tracking behind. But it was to be far worse than that. In the basement of the house was Laurie. With her, standing in the middle of the room, frowning, with her hands to her side, was Esther. And my father was nowhere to be seen.

'We don't know where your father is,' Laurie said. 'He's just gone off. Two nights ago.'

I moved into the room, looking at Esther, and then more closely at my stepmother, whose back was towards the French windows. I perceived in the uncertain light that she had a black eye and that her lip was bruised. My first instinct concerned him; what reciprocal damage had she inflicted? But I suppressed that, and asked her what had happened.

She was quite off-hand. 'He had a few drinks. He beat me up. It's not the first time. Then he went off. I don't care if he never comes back. Never.'

'Don't say that,' Esther said. She turned to me. 'I came down because George told me you'd be back. He was worried about you.'

'Not worried enough to be here himself though,' Laurie said. 'Leaves it all to children.'

'I wondered if you would like to come out,' Esther said to me. 'We have a first rehearsal this evening. We're doing "Messiah". I think I could bring you. We'd have supper after.'

I stood bewildered by the turn of events. I hardly knew Esther, and here she was, extricating me from a baleful aura

187

of hate for which I had no equipment whatever. I looked at Laurie.

'You go,' she said. 'You'll do no good staying here. And if you find him. . . .' She tailed off into a shrug of her shoulders. She was fiddling with her cigarette-rolling machine. Suddenly she clenched it in her hand, and then hurled it into the corner of the room. For a moment there was no sound, no movement. I crossed over and picked it up and brought it back to her. No one spoke. We were all isolated from each other. Laurie just sat, staring ahead of her, ignoring me, so that I could only lay the offending object on the arm of her chair. Esther looked at me and raised her eyebrows. I looked down at Laurie, at her crumpled, shapeless, and now battered form. I wondered if she would cry, or if she had already. I felt a brief stab of pity, but it did not last. There was nothing I wanted to say to her. Esther left the room, turning at the door, and questioning me with her eyes. Slowly, I followed.

Chapter Nine

I

I was worried about him, but in that tired and gnawing sense of being dragged back into a pattern of behaviour that I believed belonged to the past. Standing on the pavement outside the house, being urged by Esther to go with her to the Messiah recital she had to attend, I was swept again by the doubt, the uncertainty, the shame, all feelings that had so often flowed through me in childhood. Now they made me angry. What right had he to do this to me?

It was a selfish attitude. It obscured my perception of him, what he might have been going through, what he felt, and to what despairing refuge he had run. Aware of things only on the surface I had seen no need for agony or despair, and therefore no need for flight. I had seen only the humiliation to which I was being subjected. This, I suppose, is a mark of the stature he still retained in my eyes. I revolved in my own blind uncertainty around him, and his sudden, violent departure, without a word to me or a message, was cruelly insulting.

Yet I did care. Hidden within the folds of my bruised sensibilities was a deeper feeling of emptiness. It did not manifest itself immediately. My first instinct was simply to get away. And I accepted Esther's suggestion that I should accompany her to the rehearsal. For a while I lost myself in the music,

189

watching her taut, attentive face with an absorbed affection for her. The choir sang five or six choruses from the first part of 'Messiah', and ended with a noisy and scrappy rendering of 'His Yoke is Easy, His Burden is Light'.

Before the end, from the rehearsal hall, I telephoned Mr Porphyry. In the ordered way he had, some arrangement had already been made between us for meeting and talking over my ten-day visit to Ambleside Hall, and there had been no plan for me to telephone. He was at first politely surprised, then puzzled. He could not grasp what had happened.

'You mean your father has gone away?'

It was an over-polite way of putting it.

'Yes. He's gone. He was drinking. He hit her.'

'Oh, dear. What can I do? This is really too bad of him. And on the very night of your return from the Lake District. I hope it all went well?'

'I have to find him.'

'Do you need money? Will you be all right at home?'

'I'll be all right,' I said. Suddenly I wished I had not telephoned. Mr Porphyry seemed incidental to the tide of feelings that was carrying me along. Yet I could not be short or dismissive. In any case I did not know how; but even more significant was the fact of that high value I placed on him as a friend, and a source of my freedom. He did not fit at all into a world where men struck women, and were reviled, and drank, and ran away. And in a curious way I realised that I should protect him from the events at which I had only hinted in my brief conversation.

'I shouldn't have rung you,' I said. 'It'll be all right. I'll ring again tomorrow.'

'You must always tell me if you're in trouble. You will do that?'

I said I would. I was hardly listening to him any more. My mind had cleared as we talked. I felt suddenly sure of myself. I knew where my father had gone. He had gone to Alice. I had been wrong to ring up my benefactor. All I had done was to make him annoyed at my father for so swiftly overtaking the benign aspects of Ambleside Hall.

'Is there anything I can do?' he asked.

'I don't think so,' I said. 'I'll see you on Sunday.'

Drinking coffee in the King's Road afterwards, I told Esther what I thought.

'Who's Alice?' she asked.

'Alice?' I looked back at her, bewildered by the problem of making Alice intelligible. 'She's just a friend,' I said.

'Why are you sure he's gone to Alice?'

'She always helps him.'

'Always?'

'He's gone to her before.'

'You know where she lives?'

'Yes,' I said.

'Does your stepmother want him back?'

'*I* want him back,' I said. 'At least, I want to know where he is, and how he is.'

'Do you want me to come with you?'

I shook my head. 'It's better I go alone.'

'I'd come if you wanted me to. I'd do it for George. Poor George.'

I stared at her. I could understand the impact of his charm, the response to his gallantry. But this was different; a deeper concern, from a girl no more than two or three years older than myself. It made me feel ashamed.

'I'll come to you if I need help,' I said.

We parted in the King's Road, and I walked up towards Sloane Square. The night was soft, the air still, the pavements uncrowded.

And he was with Alice. He was sleeping in her bedroom.

After she had answered the door, and had acknowledged his presence, she led me into the flat, and took up a position on the other side of the table from me, the bedroom door behind her. From it there droned the persistent sound of his snoring. I looked at the details of her room, so familiar to me, so much a reproach in that I had not been to see her—and they reminded me of this—and so disposed as to make me want to laugh: the small assembly of food on the table, clutched together there for him; the Ronson lighter and the cigarettes, the brand he chose when he had money; the order, the limitations, the careful frame for her self-sacrifice.

Her appearance had a rocklike quality. My familiarity with it, as with her room and her possessions, was a familiarity with a childhood from which I had only recently departed. Though it was probably less than a year since I had called on her last, the occasion seemed remote. So much had happened, so much had changed. The very sameness of her own position emphasised this, making me want to apologise. In my memory, uncertain at the time, she had been part of my father's life for many years. In reality it was about four years, always somehow present at moments of crisis, leaned upon, rejected, used, ignored. And I might have smiled at the irony of it did I not at the same time feel the weight of purpose there between us, the dignified consistency of her love.

Other women could be said to have passed through my father's life; about some one might even use the phrase 'flitted through', though in general the encounters, whether brief or not so brief, were intense and passionate. But with Alice it was different; her life was the constant against which other variables of behaviour were measured, including the greatest variable of all, my father himself. This was even so at that time, during his marriage to Laurie.

Her face, as she stood there looking at me, was devoid of expression: no reproach, no resignation, no anger; dogged purpose might be said to have lain behind the look in her eyes, but nothing more. She was in defence of a position about which she had no choice whatever, and what I might feel played little part in what she did. Neither her past actions, nor those that lay in the future, could really be related to any other force than her abiding love for him. Though often, then and later, he derided her for her woodenness, her lack of natural ease, her

192

inability to respond with instinctive force and emotion to the world around her, there was never, in my experience, a woman with quite the same profoundly animal reaction to the man she loved as Alice had towards him. Morality, convention, social propriety, the law, his marriage, even myself, were as nothing beside the protective instincts she felt; and, no matter what he did to her, often cruel, often humiliating, that force in her survived it all.

She looked down at the table. 'He had better go back,' she said.

'Yes,' I said.

'I don't want to wake him.'

I could hear the sonorous rumble of his snore, from the partly open door behind her. 'Is he drunk?' I asked.

She nodded, still looking down. 'Very,' she said.

'What has gone wrong?'

She looked up at me. Then I noticed there were tears in her eyes. They were the isolated evidence of feeling in an otherwise expressionless, immobile face. My own heart, wise by instinct to the baleful reality which was facing her, went out to this small woman, with her stoic disposition, clutching at what she could from the frenzied catastrophe of his existence, and finding always that it was too late.

We stood for what seemed like ages on either side of the table, looking at each other. The tears that had welled up in her eyes stayed there. They did not trickle down her plump cheeks; they glistened for a little while on the lower lids of her reddened eyes, and then she managed to blink them away.

After a time she spoke. 'It's not the first time,' she said.

'You mean he's walked out before?'

'Yes. More than once.'

'How many times?'

'Three, my dear. Perhaps four.' She shrugged. 'It depends what you mean. He comes to me when he can stand it no longer. Usually he wants money. Then he goes and drinks. Then she turns him away.' She paused. 'He comes here to me.' In that

G 193

last phrase there was just the faintest hint of satisfaction.

'What's wrong? Why does he do it?'

'I don't know. Nobody knows.' She looked round at the carefully chosen possessions that had surrounded her in her different habitations. It was as if among them might reside an answer, since they had been silent witnesses of part of his agony. But they seemed not to inspire her with new perception. She looked slowly back towards me. 'Your father is tormented by something. If all of us helped him all the time it would still go wrong. It's inside himself. It's incurable. It's a host of demons. I know it sounds silly, but that's how it seems to me.'

The biblical expression, at that moment, was singularly out of place. Wilfred Cochrane and Ambleside Hall, and the capacity 'to mount up with wings as eagles', when confronted with his snoring, drunken body, and the soft tears held in Alice's eyes but flooding through her heart, seemed particularly ineffectual. Could I offer her the comforts of the gospel? Would Jesus lighten her load? Could the Holy Spirit banish from him the myriad demons who had tormented him and had gone on tormenting him in all the years I had known him?

'Is it Laurie?' I asked.

She placed her hands, with the fingers extended, on either side of the small array of Marmite and cheese and sandwich spread. 'I don't know how to answer that,' she said. She paused for quite a while, staring at me. 'He . . . perhaps I should not tell you. I don't know any more. I just don't know. But you're growing up. He tells me you've been to Germany, and up to the Lakes. There's this trustee and the scholarship. You've done well, my dear, at Coppinger. He's told me about it, all muddled up, when he was drunk. He needs you. You mustn't desert him. You see. . . .' Again she paused, and looking down at her right hand she traced with her fingernails in the pink damask which covered her table, the slightest of parabolas. Then, as though clearing her mind from any further sense of restraint, she looked up at me quite calmly. 'You see, he tried to commit suicide.'

I gaped at her. 'Suicide?'

'Yes. He took some pills. But he bungled it, thank God. He rang me to tell me so I rang the police and the ambulance.

'He was brought to St Luke's. There was a policeman at the foot of the bed. I think it's better that you should know. It's not for me to judge, but . . . he thinks he's lost you. He thinks you've gone from him, like your brother.'

I was close to tears. I shook my head, stupidly, endlessly, a sustained negation of what she said. I moved away from the table, and sat down. I was still vaguely shaking my head, in disbelief now, and in bewilderment. More to myself than to her I said, 'Why didn't he tell me? Alice, *why* didn't he tell me?'

She looked at me without answering for a moment. Behind my own questions I knew why. I had known why for a long time, seen the drifting apart, acknowledged it, in a curious way welcomed it.

Her answer seemed, in part, to be a reading of my own mind. 'You couldn't have done anything,' she said. 'He was thinking of you. Why should he drag you in any further?'

'But *suicide*?'

She looked down at the table. There was defeat in the rounded curve of her shoulders, the way she withdrew her hands from the table and folded them together. 'You'll want to see him.' It was a statement of fact, foreshadowing other thoughts.

'It's quite early. Only ten.'

'Will you have some tea?'

'I think he should go home,' I said. I looked across at her. She had moved towards her kitchenette, and her hand was on the little curtain that covered the door of it, but she had then turned. She looked at me, a faint smile of resignation on her lips, sad emblem of another temporary defeat.

'He *should* go back,' I said. The word 'Home' seemed just a little out of place, since in certain respects this small flat had been his 'home' for longer than Flood Street.

She nodded. 'Yes,' she said. 'He must go back.'

II

'You!' he said. He stood in the doorway, red-eyed, angry, his braces hanging down below his hips, his collarless and crumpled shirt open at the neck, his sleeves rolled up, emphasising the slack, powerful muscles of his arms, the broad reserved strength of his hands. 'How did you get here? Did she phone you?'

He was surrounded by the anger of bewilderment. His gaze was concentrated on me. His mention of Alice had produced a shrug in her direction, no more.

I stood up as he shuffled further into the room. 'No,' I said. 'Alice didn't phone. I guessed you'd be here.'

'But have you been to Flood Street?'

'Yes.'

'And you saw her?' Just the faintest hint of fear attached to his mention of Laurie.

I nodded. 'Esther was there as well.'

A brief smile touched his lips. 'Sweet child.' He seemed, for a moment or two, to be enjoying a secret reverie. Then he shook his head and rubbed his face. 'She's a good sort, Esther. She's a soft spot for George.' The gentle smile faded. 'Oh, God,' he said, 'this awful, awful life. How much longer do I have to bear it?'

'It's not as bad as all that, George dear,' Alice said. She had a way of standing in frozen attitudes, oddly awkward, but often sustained throughout a conversation. She was in one now, beside the curtained doorway into her kitchenette, clutching a drying-up cloth in one hand, a milk jug in the other. With her appeal to him to look on the brighter side, she slightly shifted her arms, turning towards him, and adding, 'I'll make you a nice cup of tea.'

'I don't want anything.'

'I'll make it anyway.' She pushed back the curtain and went in to put on the kettle.

He still stood there looking at me. He seemed unsure of me. The expression in his eyes was as if I would depart again; perhaps that I would simply vanish. 'So you came to find your father, did you?'

I nodded. 'I went out with Esther. She took me to a rehearsal. She's singing in "Messiah".'

'Did she tell you what happened?'

I shook my head. 'Not really.'

'Oh, she's a fiend. A fiend.' It was said sadly, with regret. It was an unwilling judgment. 'It's better you don't know. You're striking out on your own. You're breaking away. It's the only thing.' He hooked the powerfully stitched braces up over his shoulders, and moved towards the chair opposite the one I had been sitting in. Then he slowly lowered himself into it, stretching out his legs, one after the other, as though they ached. His movements were slow and tired; he had the appearance of a man heavily weighed down by age.

I should have felt sanctified by Christ's blood at that moment, and ready to witness on his behalf. The words of the Lord to Joshua, after the death of Moses, were still fresh in my ears from the final morning's prayers at Ambleside Hall. Three times: 'Be strong and of a good courage.' Three times! And yet it shrivelled within me, my courage, my strength. What withering scorn would he turn upon me if I offered prayer!

I felt that I was wrestling with Satan himself, and that he was winning, first time out. I tried to offer up a simple prayer; I wanted guidance, strength, support; I wanted his peace of mind; I wanted to know what to do.

'You don't say anything?' he said. He was looking at me where I stood beside the other chair.

'I . . . I was praying.'

'Oh. Do you think it will help?' His tone was one of polite inquiry. Suddenly, I wanted to laugh. Suddenly, I loved him again more than anything else in the world. Laughter, in human terms, seemed more valuable than prayer. 'I think I'm gone beyond all that,' he said.

I crossed over to his chair, sat on the arm, and put my hand on his shoulder. 'It's never too late,' I said. 'We'll patch things up. We have to go back to Flood Street. You can't smash it all up.'

'You're right,' he said. 'Have to go back. I can't live without her. You know that.'

I don't know what Alice heard of all this. She felt as I did, anyway. And he would not have concealed from her, in other conversations, the general sense of compulsion induced in him by Laurie's peculiar emotional strengths and her powerful, if vaguely distorted personality. She was strong in a way I had never encountered in any of my father's women. Perhaps, in the end, Alice was the strongest of them all. She, at the very end, was to bear by far the hardest burden. But the time was not yet.

Alice came in with tea. He drank it thirstily. He said little. After he had finished he went off to wash, and then to struggle into his collar and tie, and slip on a blue blazer. While he was out of the room Alice gave me a blue envelope. 'That's money,' she said. 'It's in case anything happens and I'm not here. It's for him. Keep it safe.' She spoke these words in hushed tones. Then, reverting to her normal voice, she asked me if I would like to go to the opera. She had been given tickets by her boss. She worked at that time in the city. She thought it was something by Mozart, but could not remember. *The Marriage of Figaro* was the only opera I had seen. I told her this. 'Would you mind seeing it again?' she asked.

'No, I'd love to come,' I said.

'That's good,' she said, and gave me a slip of paper on which she had already written the date, and the time I was to be at her flat. I smiled to myself at the preparation she had made before issuing the invitation. And I puzzled in my mind about her, trying to reconstruct her as she might have been, a shy girl, awkward, unsure of herself, thirty or more years before. And this sense of an earlier Alice, unmarked, unblemished, untangled in the net of devotion that so completely held her now, was

198

emphasised when the moment came to say goodbye to us both, and she kissed me on the cheek, and then reached up towards his shoulder, slightly on the tips of her matronly feet, to be kissed in turn by him, a kind of soiled rapture in every fibre of her solid, reliable frame.

III

'You're in league against me. The pair of you.' Laurie sat in the armchair beside the gas-fire which she had put on. She had a brooding, crumpled look about her. She seemed to me suddenly so old and pitiful. The bruises in the face were echoed in the dowdy look of her clothes, a brownish tweed skirt, a faded blue jumper, and a flowered shapeless pinafore. She had on bedroom slippers. 'Well, you can clear out. It's my house, and I don't want you.' She began to roll a cigarette.

I held back. There was nothing I could say. I was of no account in her eyes, only an extension of him, and one that mocked at her. In contrast with her hostility, an element of tempered steel in their relationship, my own less questioning devotion was a force that undermined: I could claim, with some justice, that my love was stronger; he could certainly rely on it as such.

He moved into the centre of the room, under the single light. 'I . . . ' he seemed to be gritting himself against his own anger. 'I didn't mean to hit you.'

She grunted. 'I'm used to it.' She was preoccupied with the little wisps of tobacco, the flimsy rectangle of paper. 'I'm not having it any more. It's my life here. My life.' She licked the thin line at the edge of the paper and folded it over. For some reason she had abandoned the rolling machine which earlier she had hurled across the room. Now she stuck the end of the uneven thin little cigarette between her lips. Speaking through it she said, 'I've been all my life here. Since my first marriage, bringing up my daughter. Then you come barging in, breaking things up and taking over. You're a bully, George. You always want it your way. Well, this time it's not going to be like that.' She had allowed one match to burn out. Now she lit another and a thin wisp of smoke rose up from the curling end of paper which flared minutely before the tobacco itself caught. 'It's going to be different.' She spoke with a coolness that could not be challenged. There was nothing to argue over. These were statements of fact, the terms of a treaty over which his veto rights were negligible. She did not even look at him, but stared ahead of her, occasionally glancing at the fire, occasionally turning her eyes towards me. Eventually, my presence by the door seemed to provoke some consideration of my position in the new order of things. She gestured vaguely in my direction. 'And he'll have to move down here somewhere. I've a tenant for that top room, a friend of Esther's. We need the money. And with him gallivanting here and there he's more away than at home.'

Consideration of me rather than of him gave him back the powers of speech. 'Of course he'll move. First thing tomorrow. Do you hear that?'

I nodded.

'We'll reorganise down here. All be together. Sort things out. It will be better.'

I looked from one of them to the other, and counted over the few days that were left of the summer holiday. It was bad enough being in the same house if things were to be shaped from now on by the bleak emptiness of their present attitudes to each other. But to be in the basement, on top of them, seemed a much grimmer prospect.

I looked at my father. I was resentful all over again. 'If you're all right,' I said, 'I'll go to bed.' It was a statement, calmly stripped of the concern which, deep down, I felt, but which I shared with two women at least, possibly others. If he sensed it, he was equally circumspect, and just nodded. Under the circumstances he could not embrace me. His eyes, tired and listless, had lost their power to reach out and encompass me and the space in which I stood. I felt no longer that he was an overseer of my actions; quite the reverse: It was I who looked out for and around him, I who had brought him back, I who could now safely leave him and retire to bed. If he sensed this change he was circumspect about it, and just nodded.

Once again I climbed the stairs. There was no figure of Esther ahead of me, as there had been before; no prospect of comfort in conversation. At the top I hesitated, thinking for a moment or two whether or not I would knock on her door, but guessed that she would be asleep. Then I remembered what Laurie had said about her friend needing my room, and a little knot of resentment developed within me: even Esther was becoming an engine of inconvenience. Where could I turn?

IV

I saw his face before me, the expression of polite inquiry: 'Do you think it will help?' So much for my attempts to bring prayer to his aid. Yet I must try again. I knew it. A small leaflet, tucked into the pages of my Bible, gave references for different forms of spiritual help. The eighth chapter of Romans was offered to those 'seeking victory'; some verses from the first chapter of Joshua to those 'facing a crisis'; that part of the Sermon on the Mount, invoking the example of the lilies of the field, for those who were 'anxious'; other portions of scripture for the 'lonely', the 'tempted'; and for one 'afraid of the future' Psalm 37 was offered: 'and he shall give thee the desires of thine heart.' Oh, if this were true! In all of time, has it ever been true?

I was engulfed by the sense that these guidelines were for me. I toiled through them, gathering momentary comfort with the hunger of a starved man. The righteous and the wicked seemed to be arrayed before me; to the righteous was salvation offered; to the wicked the prospect of their seed being cut off and they themselves, like the fat of the lamb, being consumed away into smoke. Yet who were the righteous? Who the wicked? Was my father to be consumed away? Was I to inherit the land?

I tried to pray. I suppose I offered up prayers, and they meant something. But they did not seem to encompass the impending catastrophe which I sensed in the air. And I found myself kneeling and thinking and sorting out my judgments and feelings, having departed from the intense communion, the strain and stress of the hardest of all expressions of faith: prayer itself.

Thought was an indictment, undermining faith. My mind was an enemy to my belief just as my body had been, and would again be.

As I wrestled with these tangled feelings there came a knock at my door. I got up from my knees, closing the Bible and putting it on a table, and crossed the room. It was Esther.

'Oh, hello, Esther,' I said. 'Come in. I was going to knock, but I thought you'd be in bed.'

She stood outside the door. She was dressed as she had been earlier in the evening, but had let her hair out of its ponytail and was wearing nothing on her feet.

'I heard you come up,' she said. 'Come and have some coffee. Did you find him?'

'Yes,' I said. 'I was right. He was there.'

I told her some of the things I had learnt. Not all of them. I could not bring myself to mention the attempt at suicide, unconvincing as it had seemed. I wanted to preserve my own dignity, and saw myself doing it by preserving his. And though I had faith in Esther it was not strong enough for me to be wholly straightforward with her. She listened as I unfolded the scene with Alice; then she asked me about earlier times. It was a relief to retreat into the past, to evoke for her the strange and stilted occasions which Alice, my father and myself had enjoyed together from time to time. It was a

202

spreading back into a comfortable and, in its way, settled era, when the constancy of my father's love for me, and mine for him, had outweighed, with complete ease, the inconstancy of a succession of different bed-sitting rooms, of impoverishment, of dependence. She listened. She asked questions. Her curiosity made me happy.

'Will they be all right?' she said eventually. I realised she was talking about Laurie and my father. We had returned to the sober present.

'I don't know. I hope so.'

'There's no need to move out of the room tomorrow.'

'Are you sure?' I asked.

'My friend doesn't need to come for another week.'

'Who is your friend?'

'It's another student.' She looked into my eyes, seeing the worry there. 'Her name's Sue. She's at R.A.D.A., near to us. You'll like her.'

'I'll be going back when she comes.'

'But you'll come again, won't you?' When I didn't answer she went on: 'It'll be all right. You'll see.'

'Maybe,' I said.

'I'll look after George.'

'That's the trouble.'

'What do you mean?'

'Everyone looks after him. They all do. All the time. But it never seems to work.'

Chapter Ten

I

I went to meet Mr Porphyry at All Souls. There was little traffic, and few enough people. The August holiday month of indifferent weather, cold and wet on the whole, had come to a blustery end, and September had begun with softer weather, more gentle, more still. I had time to spare, and walked with slow deliberation from the Oxford Circus underground station up towards Broadcasting House. As soon as I came out his directions became superfluous, and I identified straight away the elegant cone and pillars, and the unfinished balustrade of Nash's church, that 'knee of a jointed doll' that links Regent Street and Portland Place.

Though the sun shone brightly there was a whiteness in its light that gave forth faint hints of approaching autumn, curiously welcome as the long weeks away from school came to an end.

I would be returning to Coppinger the following Thursday and I was looking forward to it. The events of the previous evening had left me deeply dissatisfied with myself. Too old to be my father's child anymore, too young for Esther, too uncertain to be any real help to anyone, I came on that Sunday morning to meet Mr Porphyry, at a church which was then something of a spiritual beacon in London, in doubt about even the most recent event in my life, the accepting of God's salvation. Even that, it seemed, had not worked. It had offered me no real or convincing comfort; it had provided none for Alice, my father, Laurie; and if witnessing meant anything, serving as a test or representing a mark of practical endeavour, then I was a most imperfect creature, that morning, as I walked slowly up towards the top of Regent Street.

One needed to be early. The All Souls turnout was a good one, and Mr Porphyry parked his car at the beginning of Portland Place at about ten minutes to eleven. He said little as we went in. He seemed to know at least some members of the congregation, who were greeted with gruff brevity, and we took our places.

Something of the same vigour, the compelling energy, that had embraced us all in the twilit library of Ambleside Hall, filled the open, sunlit splendour of Nash's church. It gave to zeal a formality, to emotion a calmness, to faith a certain logic, that prescribed for me a direction that was to outlast Coppinger, and carry me some years onward in the hunt for purpose. And having fumbled the first test, the transition from the experience of God's grace, on the lake shore, to its attempted expression in Alice's flat and with Laurie, and coming home with my father, I was relieved when John Stott, or whoever it might have been, lifted my spirits for me by taking, from one of the epistles, some now forgotten example of obstruction, where truth is nonplussed, and faith fails to work out its purposes.

It gave to Mr Porphyry the encouragement he needed. After the delays and conversations leaving the church, he drove me to the Russell Hotel. We sat down in the main restaurant and ordered the table d'hôte Sunday lunch, a conventional enough feast of grapefruit and roast pork and trifle.

'So you found him with Alice?' he said. 'As you suspected. And was he drunk?'

'He was sleeping it off.'

'Oh. I see. And have you told me about this person, Alice?'

I reminded him of previous conversations.

'Ah, indeed. I do remember. She works in the city.'

'That's right, Mr Porphyry.'

'I think you told me she's been a friend for some time. Did you not think, once, that they might get married?'

I wondered to myself, was he confusing Alice with Ursula? What did he really remember? What right had I to expect him to grasp and understand so abnormal a web of relationships, where people could be summoned up, as it were, from the past, to perform acts of rescue, motions of love, when needed? He had absorbed what I had told him about my life before the advent of Laurie in the form of anecdote, firmly related to a set of rules which she had changed. The change, in his eyes as in the eyes of others, like Merchant, was not entirely satisfactory; after all, it had justified the scholarship which had brought us together. But now the past was reasserting itself as a present reality, and a benevolent one that could be said to challenge him. It had obscured the simple, direct light of salvation, it had checked the flow of words and feelings absorbed at Ambleside Hall, it had forced upon him the need to recognise names, like Alice and Ursula, as real people walking back into a drama that was already overfilled with the essential ingredients of tension, conflict, passion, pity. I mention Ursula not because she played any part at that time. She did not. But in his perception of my father—always an imperfect one, unsupported by direct experience of him—she was as real as Alice.

What does that mean? Little enough, really. How could I tell him that there was no one in the wide world like Alice? How could I convey her humanity side by side with her humble availability? She, who abased herself before my father, gave him money with which to drink, and resigned herself to each painful farewell as he set off back to Laurie or to some other woman, could she be presented to Mr Porphyry with any of the saintliness I believe she possessed? What concept of goodness could he possibly have that would embrace and absorb her? How could he recognise that unbroken thread of salvation, so different from any salvation he had ever encountered, which she offered to my father?

'And are there . . . um . . . other women like Alice? Is this person, Ursula, like her, or different?'

I smiled at him. He seemed a great way off. 'Different,' I said.

'Would she have helped?'

'She might have done. I did think he might have gone to her.'

'Instead of Alice?'

Again I smiled, perhaps a little sheepishly, certainly with a sense that I was apologising for my father.

This time he smiled back at me. 'Rum do,' he said. While I had been talking he had been tackling the food on his plate. Now he paused. 'You've told me about Alice. You've told me about Ursula. She's the one with the sister and the niece, family on the south coast where you spent Christmas?'

I nodded.

'Any others?'

I shook my head guiltily, unwilling to contend with any further revelations.

'That's a relief. He's certainly a bit of a lady's man, your father. I hardly know what to make of it all. Will it last now? The return home?'

'I think so. I don't really know.'

He finished his lunch, and sat back in his chair looking at me, the faraway, remote expression in his pale blue eyes giving life and distant concern to his craggy features.

'You'd better eat up,' he said. 'I'm coming between you and your lunch. I won't ask any more questions.' He went on talking, however. 'I'm overjoyed about Ambleside Hall. You now have something to which you can apply the power of prayer. You may not believe it, but that day at Coppinger, when we tramped diligently round the school, I had a firm conviction of the Lord's hand being upon you. God does indeed move in a mysterious way.' He nodded once or twice, his clear untroubled eyes conveying to me the sense of spiritual confidence he felt. 'Your difficulties will lessen with the help that will come to you. We must join in prayer for guidance.'

For a moment I thought that he was preparing for action suitable to his words there and then, and I finished the scraps of my lunch hurriedly, not quite knowing what would follow. But it was not so precipitate, and our conversation veered away on to more general topics, including the approaching Coppinger term.

I felt that I had really failed in any efforts I had made to convey to him the naked brutality of my father's anger, the cold bitterness of Laurie's exercise of her power, the endless compassion of Alice, and, important for myself, though hardly touched on with him, the restrained companionship with Esther. He had partial understanding that a crisis was shaping itself before my eyes, and, through me, in front of him. But he could not enter it, and he could not solve it, and the part of it most relevant to him was the clash that tested my faith. The events provoked prayer more than they demanded understanding. And, though I was grateful to him for his precise grasp of the details, I realised that this capacity in him was incidental to his real purpose, which was to place all the events on the plane of prayer and spiritual expectation. There came to me, through him, the odd realisation that faith manifests itself when the trials are accepted as trials. Too great an endeavour at psychological insight is a partial betrayal of the answers that are laid out for us in the pages of scripture, and in that wisdom combined with inspiration which men like Wilfred Cochrane commend.

It did not end there. It would be unfair to suggest that Mr Porphyry only had prayer and spiritual sustenance to offer. He took no pudding, and sat in silence while I ate up the trifle. He watched me all the time, a thoughtful frown on his face. When I had finished I looked up at him and smiled. 'That was very good,' I said. 'Thank you very much.'

He smiled briefly. 'And you return to school on Thursday?'
'Yes.'

'Would you . . .?' He paused. 'Would you like to be free of all this trouble in Chelsea? Would you like to have an alternative place to come to in the holidays?'

I stared at him, trying to understand. 'I don't really know what you mean, Sir.'

'If you needed a room, you know, there is one in the flat.'

'It's very kind of you, Sir.'

'But I meant something more . . . that perhaps you would prefer to make it your home.'

I felt immeasurably proud of what seemed to be an honour he was conferring upon me. From the lofty authority of all the things I knew about him he had already come down in friendship to my level, so that my pride was not contained in that. Nor was it in any spiritual benefits, for these had been carefully nurtured through the agency of other people. It was his life he was opening out to me, no less. I grasped none of the detailed implications of what he was offering. I simply knew, by instinct, that this was some great gift held out to me with no real hindrance, no condition, none of the impediments with which pity or benevolence can mar affection and prevent it from becoming love. In so far as I ever understood, in its full sense, that Christian love that is contained in the word Charity; in so far as I ever fully and completely believed in it, then it was in this manifestation. I did not know how to answer him. I was overwhelmed.

I think he understood this. He said: 'You need only think about it. Everything will be all right until you go back to school.'

More than half my lifetime divides me from those days. The compression of events which then crowded in, to defy and reverse his prediction that everything would be all right, to make into an eternity of experience the gap between that Sunday lunchtime and my return to Coppinger a few days later, has distorted memory. So, too, has the range and compass of Mr Porphyry's careful and consistent interest in me. As to my father he had already reached there the confines of his understanding. He had learnt enough, now knew more than enough, and wished, if he could, to detach me from at least some of the threats which he saw hovering over my head. Perhaps in reaching one set of confines he imposed upon himself, unwittingly, another: he set, in effect, a limitation upon his understanding of me. But it was done for Charity, and I loved him for it.

The 'mysterious way' in which God had moved, had brought together, in the space of twenty-four hours, one crisis and the answer to that crisis; he had himself engineered the process that had brought me to my knees, in Wilfred Cochrane's room at Ambleside Hall, at the start of a new spiritual life, and he had done so because of the things he had learnt about me from Merchant during the deliberations over who was to win the scholarship offered in his name. How could he doubt God's hand in such a conjunction of events? What more did he need to understand of the invisible forces that were there to challenge and test my spiritual strength? How could he possibly know that these events were the slight tug of wind in the trees that precedes the hurricane?

II

'I want this part to be savage,' the conductor said. 'We really are in the wilderness now. I want you to laugh him to scorn. I want you to shoot out your lips. And, when the tenor comes in after this chorus, remember: his heart has been broken; "He looked for some to have pity on him, but there was no man." O.K.? Let's take the chorus right through from the beginning. Basses?' He tapped with his baton, and then held out his hand in a gesture of restraint towards the pianist, as he waited for the rustling of scores to quieten.

I had watched Esther with undiminished concentration

during the long evening practice which was now coming to an end. She had seemed, on the second occasion, slightly unwilling to bring me. There may have been difficulty with the conductor; there may have been other reasons. But I had insisted, holding her to a vague promise made to me on the night I had gone to Alice and found my father there. And though she had suggested that I bring a book, in case I should be bored, I had not opened it.

To say I was captivated by Esther is true in a sense. Yet all sorts of qualifications are necessary. I never kissed her, though I wanted to, finding her infinitely desirable. And partly because of this, and presumably the unacceptability of an eighteen- or nineteen-year-old student having a fifteen-year-old schoolboy as a boyfriend, our affections for each other stuck in the indeterminate channel of companionship.

We were not together that much. She did have other friends. But when we were, there was a breathless admiration on my part for the passion with which she seemed to attack her own life. All her energies were narrowed down to music and study, and no doubt endless debates with fellow students as well, of which I had no first-hand knowledge. That she found room for me at all seems a puzzle now. I think it perhaps had something to do with Laurie and my father, with their uncertain relationship and with the capacity he had to draw in and involve people in his greedy and haphazard fashion, sparing no thought at all for the aftermath. Only this could explain Esther's presence on the night I discovered my father had walked out. But I do not think it was much more than affection for him. Like so many women, she was a little moved by his passionate intensity, different in its kind, but similar in its force, to her own. And this vague feeling was echoed in the interest she took in me.

On that night she was dressed, as so often with her, in black. Her thin jersey, low at the neck, revealed her throat and the swelling of her full breasts. She wore a neckband of black velvet, and with her hair pulled back behind her ears it emphasised the exposed, naked look of her. And, when she was singing, the vibrancy of her approach to the music, her attack, her concentration, suffused the tissue and bone and muscle, so that it seemed that her flesh tingled with the clear soprano sound of her voice.

It was that which I loved; what she did, the way she did it; and these, for me, constituted what she was. I did not know her in all her moods. That there were softer, sweeter, more uncertain sides to her character only really occurred to me later, after we had parted, and after I had heard from her that last and fateful time. In reality I hardly knew her at all. But I knew what she did: I read in her lips now the determination of her young life, more clearly formed than my own, more advanced, possibly narrower. I was captivated by the way she drew back her lips on the 'Surely, surely He hath borne our griefs . . .' In her eyes, in her face, in the swelling of her cheek, in her throat, there was scorn now, even venom. She really did shoot out her lips: 'He trusted in God,' she sang, 'that he would deliver him; let Him deliver Him, if He delight in Him.'

At this tangy, salt point in 'Messiah' the conductor ended the rehearsal. He was pleased with what they had done, and fixed times for their next encounter. With a stab I realised that I would be back at Coppinger by then, and that I would not see the full performance.

Esther glowed with the effort she had put into what she had been doing and was consciously happy as she came towards me, smiling and swinging her handbag into which she had dropped the score. How I wished, at that moment, that I was older and more assured, more confident and commanding than I in fact felt, or could possibly be. It was a wonder that it was to me she came at all, our leaving together made me feel proud.

'How is everything?' she asked.

'Will you let me know if it goes wrong, Esther? Will you write and tell me?'

'Is it no good?' She was surprised by the urgency of my question. I felt I had to tell her the truth.

'I don't know what will happen. When I found him with Alice she told me he had tried to commit suicide.'

She stopped and turned, staring at me in the soft, September evening light. 'What did he do?'

'Took pills.'

'Just recently?'

'Yes. He's been to Alice before, to get money. When he was drunk, when she shut him out.'

She slipped her arm into mine. 'Let's go and have some coffee.' We were near to a place called the Troubadour. Those were the early days of coffee bars, and to me they were rarer territory than pubs.

She did not ask me any more about the taking of the pills. But she wanted to know about Alice.

'It was really better before he married, wasn't it?'

'It was,' I said. 'Yes.'

'What will happen to you now?'

'It'll be all right.' I thought of Mr Porphyry.

'But will they?'

'He came back,' I said. I did not want to explore the question any further. It disturbed the new sense I had of my own prospects.

It was already dusk when we left and took the bus back to Chelsea. Getting off in King's Road we turned down Flood Street. We must have been quite close behind them before we recognised Laurie and my father. Esther, when she did so, quickened her pace in order to catch them up. But I put out my hand, took hold of her arm, and restrained her. I cannot pretend any sophisticated reasoning. My sudden act of restraint was instinctive, curious, nothing more. We had to slacken pace quite a bit, and I realised it would be a momentary respite anyway; the house, though at the bottom end of the street, was not all that far away. Even in the dusk I could see that both of them had been drinking and both were the worse for it, he considerably so. He was debating, with her as audience, some weighty matter. It turned out to be the question of whether or not Churchill should go on leading the Conservative Party.

My father had a poor regard for Churchill. He gave him some credit for his management of the second world war, but reserved much deeper antagonisms against him for alleged mistakes over naval appointments during the first world war, which to some extent, and in different ways, had affected my father, though I never knew how. But, if he felt that Churchill was not entirely the right man to be leading the Conservative Party, his avowed socialism, which had only the haziest of links with his more general views on life, tended to make him think that the longer Churchill did lead the Conservatives the more damaging it would be for that party, and therefore helpful for Labour. This was the drift of their conversation. Its importance was secondary to the phenomenon of seeing the two of them, arm-in-arm in the late summer twilight, talking noisily and in an atmosphere of mild contention, as they made their way home from the White Hart. The words came drifting back to us, soft and easy on the warm night air, his mind and body in a sort of numb harmony, induced by the beer he had drunk.

'Of course Toynbee always used to say to me, "George, if you go on the way you're going you'll sink the ship. Take us all down with you. If that's what you want?" Well, of course that's not what I ever wanted. But one gets stubborn. Churchill's stubborn. Doesn't know when to go, so let him stay. Yes, let him stay on.'

'He's always been a good leader. You don't really know anything about it, George.'

He laughed. 'Don't be ridiculous, woman. I know it all. I've watched his whole career. I was under his command when Asquith was Prime Minister and he was at the Admiralty. Beatty, Jellicoe, I can tell you, we kept a close watch on Winston in those days.'

'He was a young man.'

'He was a stubborn man. Look at the Dardanelles.' He swung out his hand in a gesture that embraced the whole vista ahead of them, as though, somewhere at the end of Flood Street, across the embankment, and out in the swirling waters of the Thames, lay the Dardanelles. 'Total misunderstanding of the situation.'

'Well, I don't think it was total,' Laurie said.

My father paused, holding an unwilling Laurie back in her stride for a moment. 'Well,' he said, 'I'll tell you what I think. I think you're a stubborn old trout.'

'Oh, come on!' she said. They moved forward.

Of all the women in his life, Laurie was the only one who drank with him. Others might take a drink, might visit bars occasionally, and in their various ways endeavour to come to terms with his drinking habits. But Laurie was different; drink for drink she could and did match him, and she did it because she liked it. If he was into a heavy bout, then she would at first hold back, attempting to restrain him, and if that failed she would walk out. But if the pace was common between them they would move along together, and what Esther and I were now witnessing was the most uncommon outcome. I thought of it as wisdom on Laurie's part. It was not, of course. It was just that she liked to drink as much as he did. But I judged it from the perspective of Alice's profound distaste for drink altogether, and Ursula's dislike of bars because they were rather 'common'; and from this set of contrasts I derived a certain hope for the future. Inasfar as anyone can ever use the term about anyone else, they were happy together. I believed it then, and held back, just for a few moments, savouring the deep contentment that spread towards me from the indistinct image of their two figures, swaying slightly, animated in their conversation, and heading with confident deliberation towards home.

There was no enmity between them, just then. It struck me forcibly as we closed up behind them. If there had been dreams and ambitions, hopes, aims, achievements, they were set aside in the flat, bald reality of their mundane existence. They were a middle-aged couple coming home from the pub at dusk on a late summer's evening, in a London street. Behind them lay the indifferent past; ahead lay the narrow realities of the pavement, of her house, and the slow brown waters of the river. If it is true that most people in this world live out the whole of their lives in an atmosphere of quiet desperation, then in my father's case, as he stumbled slightly, grasped on Laurie's arm more firmly, and laughed out once more in the deep, late dusk of that mild night, this had to be seen as a respite. A moment of peace and calm had descended on their heads. Past failures were temporarily forgotten, and the mind's eye turned aside momentarily from the general atmosphere of crisis.

'Come on, you drunken old fool,' Laurie said. 'Pull yourself together. We must get ourselves home.' There was a good-natured tone of amusement in her voice as well.

'It's good to see them laugh,' Esther said.

I nodded.

They stopped, and my father turned. Slowly, uncertainly, he recognised us. 'Ho, Ho!' he said. 'Young love! So, Esther, you teaching him a thing or two, eh?'

'Don't be so ridiculous!' Laurie said. 'You old goat!'

'Not ridiculous. Never ridiculous. The feelings of the heart are never ridiculous, are they, Esther?'

She shook her head. We stood together now.

'Just been having a few drinks, Laurie and I. And setting England to rights.'

'And have you got things properly organised?' I asked.

He looked at me, opening his eyes wide and puckering up his mouth in a thoughtful, contemplative expression, as though, for a moment, he did have the dispensation of party favours in the cradle of his hands. 'Well, it's not been easy, I can tell you that. We've had to puzzle over things a bit. But I believe we've settled it all. Fergy Bremer was in the White

Hart. Of course he's a Tory through and through, is Fergy. Right through to his narrow backbone. Fond of Churchill. Thinks he's a hero. But I believe we set him straight, didn't we, luvvy?'

'You don't set anyone straight, you old fool,' she replied, laughing at him. 'They agree with you. You're persuasive. Some of them are frightened of you. Don't like to argue. But they're just the same afterwards. You realise that?' She seemed astonished at the idea that he might believe his own words and their impact on the casual acquaintances at the White Hart.

'Oh, no. They think I'm right, duckie. You misjudge things.' His voice was vaguely aggrieved.

Laurie turned. 'Come on. Let's get home.' She began walking, and we followed. Esther caught up with her and I linked my arm through my father's. We had the outward semblance of a family. There was a strange, elusive harmony in the incongruous conjunction of Esther's slim and fluid form, and my stepmother's dumpy, over-deliberate pace, they balanced each other, in a strange way. I looked at Esther's gleaming hair, falling from the tight ribbon at her head down between her gently sloping shoulders, then at my stepmother's skimpy curls and the black and undistinguished felt hat she wore. Their steps were so different; Esther's light and free, Laurie's over-emphatic as a result of the drink she had taken. Yet they paced each other with an even harmony. And we followed, coming home, my hand on his arm.

He was mumbling to himself. 'Sonny boy, you'll never know it all. You see, it all broke up; we thought it would come right, after the war. I was young then, keen as mustard, acting sub-lieutenant, waiting for it to be confirmed. There was nothing I could not do.' He stopped. 'Nothing. But then—' he paused, his hand raised to emphasise the point he wanted to make, his bloodshot eyes turned towards me, alive, battling against the confusion in his mind. Then the light in them seemed to fade, and he looked away again. 'The Geddes Axe.

It did for many. Not me. I was too good for that. But there were other things, old son, other things.'

III

How it could possibly happen the way it did happen I shall never know. When I told Alice, the following evening, I was conscious of a certain reserve in her reception of my account, and with it just the faintest hint of regret. It must have been slightly painful to her to learn of a reconciliation the possibility of which she had doubted, in spite of agreeing that my father did have to go back. But to be told of *happiness;* that was a different, deeper claim which she was unwilling to accept. I could but present the evidence. Even that was given in truncated form, as we travelled by taxi to Sadler's Wells' Theatre.

To my astonishment Philpotts was in the foyer with two friends. He turned and saw me as we entered together, and I explained to Alice who he was. He detached himself from the two young men he was with, and crossed over, clearly determined, I felt, on avoiding a general conversation involving all five of us. Though I introduced him to Alice he turned directly back to me, and she, for her part, stood aside to let us talk. It was a slightly chilly encounter. I could not escape the feeling that he was embarrassed.

'I got the Porphyry Scholarship,' I said.

'Dear, dear. Bad luck.'

'Oh, come on, Phillers, it's not that bad.'

He looked calmly at me: 'I think, probably, you'll survive it. What other disasters have you to report?'

'Comber's dead. Killed in Korea.'

'Oh. Any staff changes?'

'None this year.'

'It's time they got rid of some more of the deadbeats. I think probably Patterson should go.'

'Bennett's in love with his wife,' I said.

'How could you possibly know that?'

'I have my sources of information.'

'You must be careful not to spread scandal. Particularly not about women. She was pretty, wasn't she? A handful, I'd guess. Must get back to my friends. You'll like this Mozart. The girl singing Susanna is very good. Porphyry send you to Ambleside?'

'Yes.'

'Predictable results?'

I nodded and blushed.

'Thought so. It'll wear off. Can't keep the team waiting. You on the phone?'

He bowed briefly to Alice. 'Don't tell Porphyry you've seen me. Probably regards me as a bad influence. Probably am. Pray for me.' He returned abruptly to his friends.

I was faintly shocked, but Alice gave me no time to think about Philpotts. Once we were in our seats she reverted to what I had been telling her about the previous evening. She was curious about detail. How had Laurie looked? How drunk had my father been? What form did her inebriation take? What physical show of affection had there been between them? Had he been noisy? Had he laughed much?

Is there, about those we love, an infinite curiosity? Many years later I was to see, in another form, an interest on Alice's part in all the details of my father's life which became, at the end, really the only way left to her by which the abiding love, that had lasted for thirty years, could find expression. And it was pitiable how time crushed it mercilessly into its final narrow form. But, on the night of our outing, a revival of a tradition that had been unbroken before the marriage to Laurie, it was an altogether different matter.

Having absorbed from me the main facts, and as many of the details as I could remember, the subject was dropped. During the course of the rest of the evening my father was mentioned only marginally. She concentrated on my work, on the forthcoming term, on whether I would be made a monitor, and on the work I might be doing for the General Certificate. We talked only a little of Mozart, and inasfar as I can remember, and odd as it now appears to be, I seem to have been singularly unimpressed by either the Beaumarchais comedy or the music of that most perfect opera.

It was in a mood, then, of no specially heightened awareness, but one of general satisfaction and pleasure, that we drove by taxi back to Chelsea. Alice would normally have gone directly to her flat, and either asked me in for tea, or given me a carefully prepared sum of money, sending me on home in the vehicle. But some deeper longing in her, a determination to be near and possibly to see, an instinctive wish to scent the air that surrounded him, prompted her to say 'Flood Street' to the taxi driver.

As we passed along the King's Road from Sloane Square I looked out at the evening throng—a distinctly modest one in those days compared with what it was to become—expecting, perhaps, to see again, as Esther and I had the night before, the slowly moving figures of my father and stepmother. I almost wanted it, in order to demonstrate to Alice how they were together, and that my report had been an accurate one. But there was no sign of them. We turned into the relative quiet of Flood Street, and headed down towards the river.

The taxi driver did not need to be told where the house was. He was forced to slow down by two or three people standing in the street; and, when they failed to move, he stopped. I had a slightly uneasy feeling which began to grow rapidly as I noticed that their attention was on our own house. But it was Alice who alerted me fully to the situation when she laid her hand on my arm, and then suddenly gripped it with enormous strength and said to me: 'Please do exactly what I say.' Then with quite uncharacteristic speed she got out, told the taxi to wait, and led me across towards the pavement.

I heard my father, then. 'She's a fiend! She's a positive fiend! Look at her, the adulterated bitch! Look at her!'

He stood, two steps up towards the front door of the house, pointing along the railings towards the gate which led down a flight of steps to the area and to the door into the basement flat. Laurie was standing inside the gate at the top of the flight, staring back at him. It was as if a sustained growl, as of an enraged dog, was coming from deep within her throat. In fact, as he spoke, she was repeatedly saying to him, 'You! You! You!' but doing it in so low and growling a tone, and with so great an attenuation of the syllable, that it seemed to be just one single sustained note. It was of hatred unconfined.

Two or three people stood, in bemused curiosity, an embarrassed audience that lacked the volition to pass on, did not dare take any positive action, and could hardly bring itself even to obey the strident demands from my father that they should look at my stepmother. The street lamp bathed the scene in pale, yellow light. Alice pushed through, and stood in front of him, on the pavement, looking up into his face. He was dressed as I had first seen him that holiday, in trousers, vest and indoor shoes without socks. He had on the braces which he had been so carefully stitching at that first encounter. His rage concealed the extent of his drunkenness, but his focusing upon Alice seemed to overlook the possibility of my being there with her. I had, in any case, held back a bit, not having her confidence or courage, and being acutely embarrassed by it.

He stared at her, not clear at first why she was there. Then it seemed that for a moment there were tears in his eyes. His face, his cheeks, his mouth were puffed and plumped up with sudden emotion. 'You have to help me!' he said. He spoke though clenched teeth. 'She'll destroy me! She's insane! Look at her! Look at her eyes!'

One or two heads turned surreptitiously, and through the iron railings caught a glimpse of the dark, blackish pits of her eyes, fixed unblinkingly on him. But Alice did not look. She remained fixed calmly in an attitude of concentration in front

221

of him, oblivious of the crowd, of me, of the public arena in which this confrontation was taking place, most of all of Laurie.

'I'll help you, George. I'll help you. Come on.' She put out her hand.

'Don't you touch him.' It was Laurie. 'He's mine. Leave mine to me.'

Alice ignored her completely, her podgy hand still held out to him in a gesture of rescue. In my cowardice I had sidled a little closer, ready to help. A couple more people had joined us, and an odd additional window had been thrown up, adding to the size of the audience. Everyone was obediently quiet and circumspect. No one offered help; no one could quite work out what help was needed.

My father would probably have noticed me as well if Laurie had not spoken. But at her words he turned towards the railings surrounding the area and grasped two of the 'spearhead' spikes that lined the tops in his large and powerful hands. 'You've done enough, you fiend! Shut up! I'll kill you! I'll kill you! I'll kill myself!' He tried to shake the metal, but it was solid and firm. He looked down at his hands, clenched so hard around the iron that it seemed he was milking it for blood.

Alice put her foot on the first step, as if to approach him, but he turned on her: 'Stay away from me! Do you hear? There's nothing can be done!' He turned more fully towards her, letting go the railings, his face as angry against her, it seemed, as it was against Laurie. 'You're the same! You're the same!' He raised his fist. He shook and trembled. Then he turned back to the railings and again seized two of the spikes. He seemed for a moment to be dancing from side to side with rage; then I thought it was the fact that he was stumbling from drunkenness, which in part he was. But finally I realised, with awful, fatally delayed clarity, that he was preparing to make a preposterous leap over the railings and into the area below.

Alice had the same thought at the same time, and we moved

222

together. Both of us were too late. He lurched up and over, hitting back with one hand, which knocked Alice in the face and threw her, off balance, against me, and then, his bottom scraping across the points of iron, his right leg following on awkwardly behind, he slipped forward and down.

It was the braces that saved him. The stout, clumsy combination of leather and felt, stitched and cobbled with a relentless ferocity which at the time I had considered strong enough to harness a team of horses, now caught themselves on one of the metal prongs along the top of the railing, and held his whole massive body suspended the ten or so feet above the area into which he intended to hurl himself, with far from fatal, though certainly unpleasant, consequences.

He was caught as a winged insect might be caught against a coat of fresh paint, attached roughly at the shoulders, with arms and legs free. And he moved them as an insect might, with clumsy, awkward and slow gestures. His legs ran slowly through the invisible air; his arms flailed helplessly, like those of a blinded boxer. The sheer weight of his body was dragging him down inside his trousers, and he could not help himself.

His anger had increased, and his voice now rose to a shriek of rage and fear. 'Get me down!' he screamed. 'Get me down! Get me down!'

Laurie stood and stared at him, still groaning out her 'You! You!' She seemed quite impervious to the danger he was in, should the stitching or the leather fail. This can all have taken only a moment in time. And yet the abiding impression I have is of us all frozen into complete immobility, mesmerised by this giant and helpless creature, this pinned and wriggling specimen of human kind.

Alice was the first to move, closely followed by me. We went either side, and reached over for his two arms. He felt us and grabbed us, and I knew immediately that we would be unable to manage him on our own. The tone of his voice changed now. The screaming died down in his throat to a pitiable cry of flooded appeal. 'Get me down, for the love of sweet Jesus, get me down. And lay me to rest. And end all this.' He let his head fall forward slightly, and I must own, guiltily, that I thought it was quite dramatic. I was convinced he would die at any moment anyway, from strain, but I was not really surprised, in the acutely concentrated mixture of reactions I felt, to include a judgment on his 'performance'. and even, a moment later, the curious urge to laugh.

This was provoked by the taxi-driver. Up to then he had watched from his cab. He had assessed Alice, rightly enough, as a woman who would pay her fare, and to have a free show thrown in as well was a bonus. But seeing how things had developed he now appeared at my elbow and pushed his way through. 'Come on, now, guv'ner,' he said, 'Let's put it orf for a day or two. I've gotta get 'ome to me bed. We can't 'ave this kind of caper goin' on, can we?' He was a fattish man, not too tall, but with great strength in his arms. He stood on the low wall into which the iron railings were set, leaned over, and reached down to grab my father under one of his armpits. With a sudden heave the three of us hauled him back up, twisting him round sufficiently for him to get a foot on to the same narrow wall. Alice bunched her coat up, and placed it across the spikes, and we then half-pulled and half-lifted him back on to the steps.

'Thank you,' Alice said to the taxi-driver.

Laurie had not moved. She was silent now, her black, intense eyes, in the lamplight, fixed on us.

'Oh, sweet Jesus Christ!' my father said. Less blasphemously, and in silence, I echoed the words.

Alice was more practical. 'We'll get him into the cab,' she said. 'I shall bring him to Sloane Street.'

I looked once again at the house, and at the figure of Laurie on the steps. Still she did not move. She was staring at Alice, the small, black points of her eyes glowing with a bitter agony. The hatred that emanated from them was unconfined. It bathed all of us. It made me afraid. I was past shame. I felt no humiliation. But I did retain the stabbing sense of fear. She seemed to me a dangerous woman. Stripped of possession, she was plotting some terrible revenge.

We helped him down the steps, and into the cab. People began to move away in order to let the vehicle go. At no time in the whole episode had Alice once looked at Laurie. But now, as she settled back beside him, her hand on his arm, her eyes fixed on his haggard, defeated profile, I think I detected in her face an expression of mild, restrained triumph mingled with her concern. She would not have to consider Laurie again.

IV

'What will *you* do?' Alice asked.

I looked across the table at her. I was dazed with fatigue. 'I'll ring Mr Porphyry,' I said. 'I can stay with him.'

'You don't need to until the morning. You can sleep on the chair.' She pointed to the armchair beside the fire.

'What about you?'

'I won't sleep.'

It was much later. My father was in the other room. We had put him in there, and he had eventually fallen into a deep and noisy sleep, occasionally crying out in the darkness, and prompting Alice to go in and watch over him for long, solicitous minutes at a time. When she did so, I felt isolated from her and him, and it seemed that I heard voices. I was told, not for the first time, and now in mocking tones, 'Bear Witness!' There flooded back to me the stillness and the sanctity of that room in Ambleside Hall. I saw again the vision of goodness and power, but it was more faint, more distant. The experience, the belief in a new life, a new start, did not belong to these occasions, nor was that love comparable in its power to Alice's love. I straddled more than I could understand. Much more.

'What will happen?' I said.

'I don't know.'

'I was wrong, wasn't I?'

'What do you mean?'

'Thinking they were happy.'

She smiled at me so sweetly. It was as if she reached out to me across the room, bridging not just the space between us, but time itself. The time that was before, when she and I and he had enjoyed a less disturbed closeness that vaguely approximated to 'family life', and my fears for the time that would follow, so much of it so painful, were swallowed up and absorbed in the temporary victory. And the love she felt, the overwhelming compassion, richly fulfilled in her instinctive possessiveness towards the great pulsating form of flesh and bone that lay now upon the bed next door, her bed, in her flat, under her roof, in her absolute charge, spread out around her, and absorbed me as well. Then, softly, she spoke: 'You understand only part of it,' she said. 'You cannot understand it all. It is far worse, my dear, and far better, than you will ever know.' Then she paused. 'Try and sleep in the chair,' she said. 'You're as tired as he is.'

Chapter Eleven

I

I returned to school. I left on my own for the first time, and though I felt a stab of regret that my father did not come with me to Paddington Station, this feeling was engulfed in its turn by the more superficial sense of my own self-importance and independence, as I quietly found a seat in the Coppinger carriages, and opened a copy of *John Bull* to read the latest instalment of the Victor Canning novel which was then running in serial form. *Tender to Moonlight*? I forget. Nor does it matter. Even the gesture is insignificant. Yet I recall it as a small, considered sequence of actions that still evokes from the welter of the past the slow evolution of one's self-determination. Surrounded by younger boys, by fond or impatient farewells, it was as if I had become an elder of the tribe.

Self-determination was accompanied by determination. I was gathering myself for a whole range of activities: study, the exercise of authority, perhaps sport, new friendships, music. The fist of energy inside me was clenched tight, ready to punch out. I had wasted time, dissipated my substance, prevaricated.

What I felt then was put into practice. The tense isolation of that late summer journey through the ripening harvests of the Thames valley led me back to a sudden but convincingly sustained attack on work. The springs of independence were released, the large energies, which in earlier terms had been expended upon intellectual ephemera, were concentrated now on the labours that directly mattered. I grasped the fact, early that autumn term, that I was plunging towards the first terminal point, the following summer, when a real academic hurdle, later to seem so trifling, would loom up before me. A half-dozen or so ordinary level papers served, in effect, to warm one up. But the prospect of it, that September, somehow vitalised my lethargic attitudes and produced a transition towards diverse enthusiasms, over Austerlitz and the Battle of the Nile, over the industrial character of the Ruhr and the trading importance of Rotterdam, over simultaneous equations, the food properties of cod liver oil and the poetic ones of Alfred de Musset.

Chiefly my mind concentrated on literature. All of a sudden names like Jane Austen and Charles Lamb and John Keats assumed personality and force. One had withstood them long enough. Now, with real attraction, they sucked me into their living worlds.

Bennett played a large part in this. I conceived of him now as a man of passion, and linked him to an odd fraternity which included Esther and my father. He had, by the force of his spirit, things to teach me which were just as important as the significance of what Keats wrote or Jane Austen felt.

I had emerged, or so I thought at the time, fairly untouched from the final crisis of the holiday. I had gone to Mr Porphyry's flat early the following morning, bringing my things from Flood Street, and had stayed there that night, before returning to school the following day. I had seen my father briefly before going on to Paddington, and he had seemed chastened and melancholy under Alice's protective ministrations. He had simply said to me that he did not know what he would do; probably stay with 'good old Alice, a real brick' for the time being.

Mr Porphyry had talked about 'laying it all before the Lord in prayer', and I had tried to do so on several occasions, but without much feeling of success. He was greatly concerned. He tried to understand, and seemed profoundly conscious of the hand of God in guiding him over the scholarship. But he could not visualise the episode of the braces without feeling a measure of disgust. He concealed it well enough, but to him it was sordid, a naked affront to normal convention, and something from which a young boy should be protected.

Yet even if I had reservations about his attitude, and the gulf that divided the world to which he belonged, into parts of which he wanted to draw me, and the world to which I belonged, and about which I had wholly ambivalent feelings, back at Coppinger I had limited strengths on which to rely. Inevitably, with less onerous occasions for the trial and for the testing of God's patience and strength than those that had occurred at the end of the holiday, I reverted, with a fair measure of zeal, and a youthful enthusiasm for those absolutes we all sought, to dependence on the saving grace which I really believed God himself had bestowed upon me at Ambleside Hall. Side by side with the sudden burst into work, at the beginning of that autumn term, there ran also an almost violent immersion in Scripture. I understand it now as a propensity of youth: ploughing and furrowing for experience, we deploy our innocent, greedy energies on books, among people, in the realms of spiritual self-examination. But then it worked. In the unchallenged security of Coppinger faith flourished.

I talked with Pritchett, and we had long arguments. We had both been made house prefects, and we enjoyed the status without working too hard to exercise the responsibility. Without Lytton, and having decided to recruit no one else to the inevitably brief balance of our school friendship, which would come to an end with Pritchett's own departure to college at Christmas, we were thrown more intimately together. He resisted my convictions and my zeal. He was greatly interested in what I had to say about Mr Porphyry, questioning me quite closely about Ambleside Hall, and what the residue period of the scholarship involved. I held back from telling him about my meeting with Mr Porphyry on the Sunday, and his proposal that I should be given a means of escape from Flood Street. I had still not fully absorbed all the implications of that, though in my mind it had emerged in the form of a promised release only, a very partial view of what the change would really mean. Nor did I tell Pritchett about the attempt at suicide, the episode of the braces, the iron heroism of Alice.

The memory of the events, their meaning, were locked within me. And though no one at the time was closer to me than Pritchett, there was inevitably a barrier between us during those early weeks of the autumn term. A bit unwillingly, he became a forward in the first fifteen.

'A bit shaming, isn't it?' he said to me, when the announcement was made. 'After all we've been through together.'

'We did agree to put sport behind us.'

'It's for the sake of the school,' he said with mock seriousness.

'I thought we agreed to put that behind us as well.'

He sighed. 'It tugs at the heartstrings. *Homo in adjutorium mutuum genitus est.*' He recited the school motto with deep solemnity.

'Pritchett, you clown! Are you going back on everything?'

'I feel the tides of the past bearing down upon me. Like Faustus, I have so little time, so little time.'

I stared at him. 'This is serious,' I said. 'I shall have to reconsider my position. I think I may have to rejoin the choir.'

'No!' he said. 'Not that! Think of the temptation.'

'I have.'

We teased each other in vague attempts to resuscitate the atmosphere that had prevailed among the three of us, when Lytton had been at school in the summer. And sometimes it worked. But there was a pervasive sense of change.

I went on worrying about my father. Then there came a letter which to some extent set my mind at rest.

'My dearest Son: You must forgive me for all the trouble I cause you. I wish it could be otherwise. But life must go on, and I must struggle as best I may. I am still with Alice. She cracks my nerves at times, but she is a brick. I simply don't know what I would do without her. I'm starting work again. I hope it will turn out alright. There's plenty to be done. And it's good for me, getting out in the open, Autumn's the time for gardens.

'Work hard. But not too hard. Look after yourself. And write to me if you can, soon. I enclose a 5/- P.O. I wish it could be more, but money is tight just now. I'm off the drink. God Bless. Your loving Dad, G.'

I feel great waves of pity now, when nothing can be done. I did not feel them then. I read into his letter the hope, the slender hope, that it would turn out all right. I was re-assured by the fact that he was with Alice, that he was not drinking, that he had begun to work again. And I set it aside to answer at the weekend with no more than a general sense of relief that things were, in one of his own phrases, 'on an even keel' once more.

Did I, subconsciously, respond to a deeper revelation that lay within both his words and the events which had led to him being, once again, 'with Alice'? Or did I avoid any such conclusions? It is the most difficult question of all to answer. He was by nature a man engulfed by his passions. It gave to all that he did a vitality, a force, that even in its most simple forms, such as the occasion on which he had sat in the sunlight stitching his trousers, was memorable. Women loved him for it. And if there was fear, and indeed hatred, they all responded to the drive that was at the heart of his character. As for me, when I ask myself the unanswerable question about my own responses then, it is in the negative sense; I am endeavouring to see at what stage I really learned the object lesson which he had taught me, again and again: that I should

231

learn from his mistakes and be as unlike him as it is possible for the same flesh and the same blood to be.

The response we shared was a common one: to the force of the passionate heart in the pursuit of happiness. But the gulf that separated us, even then, was so much greater than I could hope to have comprehended at that time. Whatever may have been the cause—and I think that my father himself was the greater part of it—my own response to passion was inescapably that of an onlooker. And he had made this so. Watching him had long since removed from me any real desire to give my heart to anyone. Yet it had not removed the deep consciousness I had that the giving of the heart was the most profound act possible. He taught me, through the instability of the relationships he went through, how suspect was passion in terms of what lasts, what survives. 'Giving', when motivated by passionate love only, seemed to be a dangerous quicksand. And while I responded always with part of my emotions, I held back, judged, and found wanting, with another part which grew in size and in the degree of control it exercised over my course of action.

Side by side, there existed within me an exaggerated awareness of sensitivity with little actual sensitivity at all. I was conscious of the force of human passion, of what it could do, how it worked within people, where it led. I was curious to the point of obsession. And yet, even then, as far as my own feelings were concerned, I was ruthlessly non-committal. There were poems which told me to feel certain things; yet experience, so far, had betrayed their authority. The dynamic character of action, as expressed in the events of history, was perpetually paraded before me; yet it only served to underline my own passivity. And, in the spiritual life, there was always the evidence of certain generous sacrifices of faith to etch before my eyes the compulsive interest in myself which lay at the heart of all that I did.

I do not offer this as an excuse for the imperfections of my narrative, which is concerned with myself; yet looking into the development of my friendships with Mr Porphyry, with Lytton and Pritchett, or looking at the compromised and very partial affections that I expended upon Esther or Janet, I perceive in part the reason for the limitations that emerge. Within the hard rock of my experience all the energies over which I had control had been compressed into the creation of a single nugget of selfishness. Those among whom I moved had been pressed into my service; flesh, mind, spirit, had been spent by me as an actor might exhaust his command of emotions, first in front of a mirror, then in rehearsal, then before an audience, but rarely, if ever, performing them to the full in his own life. And the expressing of all this, the undergoing of these experiences, really concerned only me. I was gallivanting within the soft walls of my own consciousness, using people to feed experience, using emotion to endorse the object-lessons given me by my father, but giving nothing whatsoever in payment. More than just learning that passion on its own is a quicksand, I had come to the conclusion, in observing him, that a passionate nature, without direction and purpose, without restraints of judgment and cerebral caution, will flounder and destroy. Seeing this in him, and not yet recognising in myself any of the possible tasks or ambitions that might kindle within me the appropriate fires to burn up those comparable fuels of nature that I possessed, I held back, and turned in upon myself.

Why Bennett began to draw me out I shall never know, though he did tell me, later, of the promise he perceived in me; but more than anyone else at that time he was responsible for my awakening to the joys and compulsions of work. With Lytton, other boys also had left, and those who moved on in my own year constituted a smaller, more intimate band. Certain lessons became more discursive; certain masters more intrusive; the borders between 'work' and 'play' were smudged and less certain; and one's attitudes to members of staff increasingly relaxed.

I stayed behind in the library one day to be given back

some work by Bennett. It was the end of class, and there was no urgency about moving on. The occasion was uncontrived; the others had gone, and we were left together.

'Why do you think he wrote it?' Bennett asked. He was sitting at the head of a long table in the centre of the room; I was two or three places down, facing towards the window.

'What was he really trying to do?' He clenched his fist. He was a big man, with big expressive hands which he used a great deal during his teaching.

'It's his response to nature, isn't it?' We had just recently embarked upon the first book of *The Prelude*. Flashing skates catching the starlight, and elfin pinnaces, were much in our minds; and during the lesson, in answer to a question from Bennett, I had used my own very appropriate experiences on the shores of Blea Tarn, in a slightly edited form, to demonstrate at first hand my understanding of the personification of that sombre and threatening spirit that overwhelmed the poet.

'But is there not something more?' he asked.

'Well, it's what happens to him that matters, isn't it?' I was looking out of the window where the sun fell on distant fields.

'What did you tell us about that small lake round which you walked?'

'I said it was the whole atmosphere. Overwhelming.' I turned to look at him. The intensity of his expectation flashed in his dark brown eyes. His hands, held up before him in a gesture that I can only think of as sacramental, since he was searching out and demonstrating some spiritual force, were quite immobile.

'Go on.'

'I don't understand.' I frowned at him. I felt both privileged and disturbed.

'Who was overwhelmed?' His hands were still raised, his eyes still fixed upon me.

'I was.'

234

'And if the same things happened the next day, the cloud over the edge of the fell, the still surface of the water, just as you described it, but no one there, what then?'

His voice had become quieter, and he now laid his hands flat on the table in front of him, on either side of the neat pile of his books. He was leaning forward, watching me.

'I suppose nothing, Sir. It wouldn't matter.'

'So where did the important things happen?'

I felt enveloped by the force of his argument, the waves of expectation flowing from him with each question.

'I suppose in my head, Sir.'

He smiled, and looked down. The book on top of the pile was his own copy of the poem, or of such portions of it as were set for our study that year. He began to lift the cover, as though intent on pursuing this additional brief lesson with a further snatch of reading. But then he let it fall and stood up, contenting himself with a brief quotation, almost to himself: 'until we recognise a grandeur in the beatings of the heart.'

I stood up as well. 'It doesn't need to be threatening, does it, Sir?'

'Oh, no. It does not need to be Nature at all. It can be many things.'

It was as if I had forgotten who Bennett was. Now I remembered. 'Like love?' I asked.

He looked across at me, swiftly, sternly, his forehead puckered by a frown. 'Yes,' he said. 'Like love. Among others, it is one of the passions that build up our mortal souls. But it is now lunchtime,' he went on, picking up his books and setting off down the length of the library, his gown swinging out behind him, 'and if you don't hurry, you'll be late.'

II

Her lips, warm and soft and wet, parted against mine, and I pressed my body closer to hers. Once more I had the sense of losing myself, of being engulfed in the full contours of her flesh. It attacked my physical equilibrium. It was dizzying in its compulsion. It was real, absolute, delicious.

I was swept back into Janet's arms after my return to Coppinger that autumn with all the urgent determination I was applying to work and to experience generally. The secret fulfilment of physical desire was as much part of those days as all the other interests and preoccupations. And it had the same intensity. They were breathless, often silent encounters. Our concern was with the body, with texture, sensation, the moisture of close proximity. We did not speak much; and when we did it was for respite, soon abandoned for the more compelling ripples of her laughter, welling up from inside her soft body, the touch of her hands, her breath sweet and warm, lips always willing and tender.

Time, which softens so many things, softens guilt. And the layers of experience we acquire, notably about sex, but about intellectual accomplishment, belief, physical experience of all kinds, mock not only our past innocence, but our past guilt as well. At the time, great clouds of shame hung over me. Shame at what? To touch, to kiss, to embrace, to caress? What shame should there be in that, save only the shame attached to motive? We simulated with a false flagrancy the act of sex; yet even this confession, made from a point in time that renders even the reference to one 'act of sex' pointless, will identify how small was the justification for the guilt I then felt.

Yet there it is: desire, fulfilment, shame, guilt. My embraces with Janet alternated with silent agonisings on my knees about my faith and spiritual purpose. Guilt intensified belief. Yet it failed to lessen the activities which fed the guilt. My youthful energy fuelled my desire, my capacity for work, my hunt for remedies, my urgent response to absolutes.

That Janet liked 'snogging', and more, gradually became something of a burden to me. I had not, in any sense, thought out or resolved how the life of the spirit, which genuinely pre-occupied much of my time, could flourish side by side with the life of the flesh, which did the same, or indeed with the life of the imagination into which I was being more and more firmly drawn. But each occasion raised shadows which steadily grew. Perhaps it is inevitable that the earliest and most burning convictions with which faith fills us are of a Pauline character: 'I know that in me (that is, in my flesh,) dwelleth no good thing.' The shadow of guilt is lengthened by Paul's equation of sin with flesh. And in the night, creeping away in the darkness, avoiding the board that squeaked just inside her door, I was often monumentally weighed down by the sense of transgression of vows that had so recently been made. And I would fling myself down at my bedside, my hands still scented with the odour of her body, to pray for I know not what. Had the Spirit, so recently implanted in me, fled away? Could I be forgiven, and sin again? Could I pray for the strength to resist, believe in my own prayer, and yet, when the time came again, not resist?

'They that are in the flesh cannot please God.' Oh, you Damascus Saint, what burdens you impose upon youth! Secretly hating and loving at the same time that severe saint, that comprehender of all loves in their different forms of splendour, restraint, guilt, I pursued the vigorous course of 'learning' to which I have given slight indication, and within which Janet played her part.

It was from her that I first heard mention of the Franklin Affair, as it came to be known at Coppinger. She had been curiously reticent, after our return from the summer holiday, about Mrs Patterson, and the possibility of something going on between her and Bennett that might have confirmed the words Pritchett and Lytton and I had heard from beneath the floorboards in the chapel. And there had been no direct attempt to discover more. We had simply accepted the absence of any confirmation, and for my part I had gone on in the clear conviction that the words heard represented an association which seemed to be confirmed by the frequency with which they were to be seen together.

They were such small encounters; the innocuous and legitimate meetings between a house tutor and a housemaster's wife. Talking together after meals in the central dining room, meeting by accident in the open ground of the school in the autumn sunshine, sitting together at school functions and with Patterson as well: these were the threads of evidence which, coupled with that first overheard conversation, confirmed the pattern of their love affair. Naturally, I took Janet up wrong one night when she said: 'There's going to be trouble in Patterson's house.'

'Is she going to leave?'

'Of course not. It's nothing to do with that.'

'What is it, then?'

'Do you know Franklin?'

'Yes,' I said. 'Not well.'

'What's he like?'

'I don't like him much.'

'But what's he *like*?' She seemed almost impatient with my subjective judgment. She wanted facts that would reveal his character.

'He's tough. It was never expected he would be a monitor. He always gave trouble to the seniors. What's he done?'

'I don't know,' Janet said. 'Mr Patterson came to see Dad. Said he was having trouble with Franklin, and Merchant was on to him. Then they went off to the study to talk.'

'Was it something serious?'

'It seemed to be. Some kind of carry-on between Franklin and other boys. Some of the younger ones in the house. He'd had a couple.'

'Patterson? Drinking?'

'Yes. A bit.'

'Because of Mrs Patterson?'

'I suppose.'

'It is Bennett, isn't it?'

238

'Yes.'

'What'll happen?'

'Don't know.'

'Who does? Who knows about it?'

'Not many people. Yet.' She looked at me, frowning. 'You like him, don't you?'

'Yes. He's a good teacher. He's really the best. He never wastes time. He gives you the real stuff, then leaves you to fill in the details.'

'He's good-looking.'

'Mrs Patterson thinks so.'

'She's not bad herself.'

'No. But there must be something more.' I looked into Janet's eyes. I imagined, rather than saw, the sultry glow, that so easily quenched fire of being desired. What was the force in Bennett that compelled us forward into work?

We fell to kissing again, and no more was said.

III

I rejoined the choir. Parker seemed to have mellowed. In reality, the change was in me rather than in him. No longer his leading treble, I had come back as a bass, and more senior, and the treatment was different.

Like the month of September itself, in that year, the events were confused and stormy, and I tell them with a sense of purpose and order that is dictated by the distance of the perspective and my own sense now of where they were to lead me, rather than with any exact reference to the real ordering of what happened. Joining the choir was just one link forged in the chains that bound me then, and still today jangle and jar in my memory. A new and younger treble had taken Kessner's place; Kessner, unlike myself eighteen months earlier, had moved directly into the small group of three altos. The new boy's name was David Wickham. He was in Patterson's house. His first solo that autumn term was early on, about the third Sunday, and he sang it with surprising strength and confidence.

Afterwards, outside the chapel, I stood with Pritchett. David Wickham came past us; and perhaps remembering the warmth that such remarks had kindled in me, in my own time, I called out to him: 'That was a fine bit of singing, Wickham.'

He stopped and turned his head, a slight smile on his lips. 'Thanks,' he said, looking up to me. 'I'll do better, though.' He paused, laughed, and moved on.

I can still see him now, caught in that moment of stopping, his head turned towards me, dark hair falling over his angular, rather broad features. He was slightly sallow, as if he had lived in India during his early years. There was a sparkle in his eyes, and his essential manner, to be more clearly defined later, one of positive impertinence. His reaction to my brief words of praise was quite different from what my own would have been, and left me slightly flummoxed.

'Cheeky, isn't he?' Pritchett said.

'Yes. I suppose he is. Young brat!'

'You've got to remember your position.'

'Have I? What do you mean?'

Then he looked at me, questioning: 'You taken by him?'

'Wickham?'

'Yes.'

'He sang well,' I said, slightly confused by Pritchett's words.

'I know less than you do about such things,' said Pritchett. 'But I would have said that he sang very well indeed. There is a tone in his voice, a forcefulness, something that cannot be stopped, like our nightingale.'

I nodded, surprised at Pritchett's perception. 'You'll not hear it again,' I said.

He shook his head. 'There's something I like about that boy,' he said. 'He'll get on.'

'He's new this term,' I said. 'And very young. What makes you so sure?'

'I have a feeling.'

'Is it based on anything?'

'I'm well informed. Worried, too, a bit.'

'Oh?'

'Yes. I hope—' Pritchett paused.

'What do you hope?'

'I hope he's not the object of Franklin's attentions.'

'What do you mean?'

'There's trouble brewing in that house. Bates without Marriot has no real control.'

'What about Patterson?'

'They say he's not well.'

'What does that mean?'

'Drink.'

We stood, wise, deliberative sixteen-year-olds, on the crest of the hill, with the early autumn wind blowing gustily towards us from the west, winnowing its way through the bent grasses, turning and twisting the still green leaves of the trees, creaking the branches, disturbing hair and dress with its far-off, gentle, but insistent warnings of the coming cold of winter. Clouds scudded in the blue sky, and the groups of people gradually began to thin out.

'What is Franklin doing?' I asked.

'Some elaborate form of tyranny,' said Pritchett. 'It involves fear, and certain sexual complicity from younger boys that I find distasteful.'

'And you think young Wickham may be part of this?'

'I don't know. I hope not. Merchant will be on to it soon enough. He has been seen talking with several boys from the house, and if there are indiscretions I rate highly the penetration of our headmaster.' He gave a short and humourless laugh, then looked away into the distance.

'Will Franklin be expelled?'

'Probably.'

'How do you know all this?'

'I have not been subject to the preoccupations that have

weighed upon your shoulders, young man. I have contemplated the world around me, and have observed the clouds gathering in certain quarters. The storm will soon break.'

I felt concern for Wickham; his alert confidence disturbed me. I shared Pritchett's distaste for the unspecified coercions exacted upon others by the gaunt and threatening figure of Franklin, and a stab of anxiety that Wickham himself might be embroiled. There was implicit in the clear, true timbre of his voice a sweet innocence that I no longer felt I could claim for myself, and it stirred within me uncertain longings. Somehow I felt that it would protect Wickham. He was too confident and assertive; he seemed to know too well what lay ahead of him. And although he did not in fact know, and although the eventual cycle of events was to prove tragic in the end, the Franklin Affair itself did not touch upon him.

It gathered pace slowly enough, in spite of Pritchett's personal sense of a storm building up. Merchant pursued his investigations during the early part of that same week. Once again in Janet's arms I learned of Patterson's difficulties, his dependence on the Gaffer, his inability to control the situation in his house. Then, on the Thursday, to a shocked assembly of the boys in Patterson's house, which the whole school heard about in the space of the following day, Merchant announced the expulsion of Franklin, and beat two other senior boys in front of their colleagues. No school announcement was made, but the headmaster made an evening tour of each house and gave a solemn talk to fifth and sixth form boys about what had been going on. Merchant was not entirely explicit, which may seem merciful enough, but in reality was conducive to greater speculation and the exercise of dark imaginings. It seemed to us that the 'unnatural affections' against which St Paul had breathed out his fiery condemnations had clearly taken on a form in Patterson's house that involved group gratifications of orgy-like dimensions. That was how I pondered them in those strange, unreal days, while I tussled with my own problems of purity, faith, passion and work.

IV

In the wake of Franklin's expulsion, Merchant sent for me. I went to him in considerable trepidation, for I carried a burden of guilt that was not entirely divorced from the unnamed acts for which Franklin had been expelled. Could he, by probings and conversations, have learnt, as he had learnt in the case of the other boy, of my nocturnal visits to Janet's bedroom? Of my quite genuine sense of sin? Of the effect this was having on my work and attitude? Morose at that time, and solitary, had my features revealed all too plainly the life of sin which I so desperately wanted to hide?

One can live over many lives in the compressed moments of expectations that lead towards a momentous encounter. Having invested Merchant with these great and omniscient powers of observation and deduction, having assumed an authority in respect of Janet which was quite impossible, by the time I actually went to his study I was thinking of myself as totally doomed, and wondering just what kind of confession might possibly save me from the disaster I was being called on to face, a disaster comparable to Franklin's.

Merchant was in a relaxed mood, and this made things worse. He even asked me to move a chair across from the side of his study, and sit down. School folklore about this being him at his most dangerous, probing with subtlety and kindness to bring about one's downfall, had established sinister connotations for Merchant when he smiled that were mythical, but compelling. He asked me about Porphyry and the scholarship. 'I have had other preoccupations,' he said, 'and they have prevented me speaking to you until now, much as I wanted to. Did all go well?'

I told him what I had done.

'And what did you make of our Mr Porphyry? Did you get on with him?'

'I think so, Sir.'

'It's hard to tell, isn't it?'

'What, Sir?'

'Whether you're getting on well with someone or not. It can be a puzzle. One looks into another person's eyes and fails to comprehend what there is behind them.' He paused, and looked calmly, benevolently into my eyes. I felt that the soiled sheets of my sin were clearly visible to him; and I had no such confidence in the inscrutability of my gaze. Nevertheless, and for all the papery trembling that I felt going through me, churning my stomach, turning my bowels to water, I returned his calm gaze, and waited for the blow to fall.

'And what happened at Ambleside Hall?'

The voices in my head cried to me, 'Bear Witness!' But other voices intervened: 'Hypocrite! Fraud! Lecher! You have become vain in your imagination, lustful and unclean, and your foolish heart is darkened!' I looked down at my hands, and felt my cheeks redden slightly. Then I looked up at Merchant. There was a kindly expression in his eyes. Where was he leading me? 'It was a great experience, Sir.' I said.

'Just that? An experience?'

'Well, more really. It's a different approach to things. It's . . . it's more complete, more total.'

He nodded slowly, then repeated my words: 'Different approach . . . more complete . . . more total . . . hm.'

I felt now that the time was ripe for the great axe to fall, and I had become calmer. Whatever I was there for lay in the bowl of human action. I had done what I had done, been what I had been, and if there were penalties to be paid I would pay them and move on.

Merchant cleared his throat. 'I have called you to see me because of the Franklin business. His two associates in the affair will be leaving at the end of this term. Patterson's house will be seriously depleted of senior boys and I want to move you there. You were made a house prefect this term. Normally I would want to see how you got on for a term, but in the

244

circumstances I would propose making you a school monitor in three weeks' time, at half-term, and moving you over at the beginning of next term as a school prefect, the only one, I'm afraid, that Patterson would have, since Bates is also leaving to go and study with Pritchett.' He looked calmly across his desk at me, waiting for a reply.

I felt a flood of relief. 'Thank you, Sir.'

'You agree?'

'Yes, Sir. Of course.'

'Good.' He examined for a moment or two his pale, elegant hands. Then he looked up at me again. 'Do you correspond with Mr Porphyry?'

'I wrote to thank him,' I said. 'He replied, and I have written since.'

'And you'll be seeing him at Christmas, of course.'

'Well, the scholarship. . . .'

'Yes. It goes on. I had forgotten.'

'He was very kind,' I said. I wondered whether I should mention the offer that Mr Porphyry had made. Instead, I asked; 'Has he written to you, Sir?'

'What do you mean?'

'About me? About the scholarship?'

'Not specifically.' There was something guarded about Merchant's references to Mr Porphyry. I was puzzled, and waited, watching his eyes, then looking down at his hands on the desk, the fingers loosely intertwined.

'You'll be sorry to leave Mr Forrest, I expect.'

'You've talked to him?'

For just a moment a strange expression crossed Merchant's face. He was puzzled, uncertain. Then it cleared. 'Oh, yes. It was Mr Forrest talked to me. He discussed it first with Mr Patterson, and then put your name forward.'

The air between us was suddenly still. In my mind I faltered. Into a few seconds was compressed a host of feelings. Thoughts chased and challenged each other.

Is it thus that we learn inscrutability? In that sudden instant a panoply of motives was laid bare. From Merchant, the idea was one thing; from the Gaffer, quite another. If by agreement between him and Patterson, how much was known, and how much had been said? How well did the Gaffer know his own daughter? How well did he know me? What had he said to Patterson that had not been said to Merchant? They were of a different vintage; had been together at Coppinger before the headmaster's appointment, and in becoming, with time, the only two whose appointments preceded the arrival of Merchant, had been drawn together in a friendship that was in part echoed by Janet's affection for Mrs Patterson.

The room remained very still. Merchant looked at me not really expecting any reply, but possibly waiting for some reaction. I could think of nothing more I needed to say to him. He was clearly not the only figure involved in what was becoming the final shape and structure of my last years at Coppinger. I was already firmly committed, and could not step backwards. Merchant cleared his throat. 'I do not wish you to speak about this to anyone. And when I announce your promotion, I want it to be just that. No mention of a move to Patterson's house. That will only become known at the end of term. Is that clear?'

I nodded. 'Yes, Sir.'

'And can you do it?'

'I think so, Sir.'

'Very well. You may go.'

Though I had a sense of relief that my encounter with the headmaster was to my own obvious benefit, I left him with a persistent feeling of uncertainty. Mentally, my step faltered. Dimly, ahead of me, there lay dark territory. Once more in my ears there echoed the unforgettable passion of Bennett's words: 'I love you. I love you.' Then Mrs Patterson's: 'No! No!' Then Janet's report of Patterson himself seeking Forrest's help. And then the breaking of the storm clouds of the Franklin episode over the heads of us all. These threads and knots ran through the comb of my mind, catching, jarring, jolting; all in the space of those few moments, as I sat silent before Merchant's desk, and watched his careful precise hands where they rested on the clean blotting paper in the leather-cornered writing folder, did there unravel before my mind's eye the material for a further act in the drama? I did not know it; and much of it lay well into the future; yet even then I had a sense of foreboding induced by the complexities that were implicit in what Merchant had said. Things were not entirely as they seemed. The ground was shifting, the foundations were insecure. And even now, when none of it really matters any more, I sometimes wonder if that decision, presented to me that September afternoon for my approval— an approval so enthusiastically given, and in such ready agreement with the way I then felt—was not really the worst possible one for all of us.

Chapter Twelve

I

It was October. Days followed each other without any perceptible change, warm, dry, filled with sunshine. Though we were moving into autumn, and there had been occasional cold winds across the hills to give warning of the fact, the colours on the trees, the very stillness of the leaves themselves, offered a fragile but resolute changelessness to that particular turning point in the year's life and in my own. I love it best. Time pivots on the brink of change; the wind holds its breath knowing that all will soon tumble; and woodland vistas, seen close or at a distance, clothe in the softest and finest veils trees that will soon be stripped naked by winter. Much of my feeling for that particular season I associate in my mind with that year; with the high, unchanging skies towering up above the wolds; with the intermittent patchwork of sunlight spread across broad landscapes of field and woodland; with the sudden shock of scale as the eye focused upon a distant ploughman, in tiny isolation in the midst of a vast, unchanging scene, turning the yellow-gold stubble into dark brown earth again, still as likely behind horses, in those days, as on the seat of a tractor.

It did change, of course. All too swiftly the leaves on oak and elm and maple browned and wrinkled, and then fell;

the days shortened; rain and wind occasionally speeded up the slow transition towards winter. But, in the tide of human events that year, it was an interlude of Nature's sovereignty over everything.

I told no one of what Merchant had said. I did not confide in Pritchett; and I said nothing to Janet. I began to avoid her, making excuses about work and the possibility of our being found out. Forrest himself, strangely enough, said nothing, and it seemed almost as if an elaborate game was being played out, with nobody quite knowing all the rules. It alarmed me that I was able, with relatively little difficulty, as I then thought, to withdraw into a form of isolation. Like the leaves on the trees, I was held in fragile suspension, waiting for the frail, resinous link to be broken, waiting for the sudden gust of wind that would determine my future. I did not really know what was happening inside me, but I felt a degree of command, of strength, of independence that was entirely new. If I felt any regrets at all about this new disposition of feelings, they concerned Pritchett. And once or twice, in the early part of October of that year, I endeavoured to recover with him the carefree insolence that had marked us out in the days when Lytton was still at Coppinger. But it did not work. The points of reference were wrong. I could not involve Pritchett in my new-found enthusiasms, one of which was for romantic poetry, another for Bismarck: it simply washed over him, just as his more technical interests in architecture did over me. We had no heart for mischief. Responsibility lurked around the corner. And in his case the days of his schooling were strictly numbered. Because he and Bates, the ineffective head of Patterson's house who had come rather badly out of the Franklin affair, were both going to the same place after leaving Coppinger, they were much together; though I asked Bates a certain amount about the house, I did not tell him that I was to be moved there, and my curiosity had an odd ring about it that added to the pattern of detachment that was emerging.

Nor can I pretend that my uncertain faith, my faint voices,

my pursuit of revelation, was unaffected by the coldness of attitude that was in such marked contrast to the golden warmth of the season. I read scripture: but it was academically done, a pursuit from reference to reference of strange and obscure allusions; particularly those dealing with the awful iniquities of the flesh. And if at times I was to be found in the school chapel, sitting and staring up at the beamed roof, it was in a mood of hard and fiery isolation of spirit, as if, like some monk destined for work or service, I had to prepare myself by emptying my mind of feeling, and yet was unwilling to do so in too great a hurry.

For two or three weeks I heard nothing from my father, and that, too, had caused me no upset, or none that I detected. I did not reply to Mr Porphyry's letter, and heard from no one else.

I worked, for the first time, with real enthusiasm and with a certain consistency. The earlier, more youthful curiosity, disparate and uneven, was yoked now to themes which gave purpose and often a genuine thrill as ideas and discoveries which had once seemed useless coalesced with work that had conclusive targets.

Then, quite suddenly, in the space of a few days, four letters came for me, breaking in, not upon my peace of mind, for there was a certain fury in my isolation, but upon the fixed form it had taken. Warm days, late in the month, had pushed temperatures up into the seventies; but after that they fell, and it was then that the letters came. I give from them what is relevant, and I give it in the order of its coming.

The first was from Alice. 'Your father,' she wrote, 'has gone back to Flood Street. I am sure he will write to you soon, but I thought it my duty to drop you a line. I' (she wrote 'have', replaced it) 'had misgivings, but think perhaps it will be for the best. I looked after him as well as I could. And you know, my dear, I will always be here to help both him and you. Do try and come and see me at Christmastime. My love, Alice.'

In the mood I was in at that time this first letter, which

came on its own, made little impression. It was his life, his choice. He had told me, often enough, that he could never marry Alice. And for all the violence and venom of his relationship with Laurie, I could accept, having seen it at close quarters, if only for a brief space of time, that the stimulation gave him what he used to call 'life'. So that his return, and presumably a reconciliation after the terrible confrontation over the steps of the house at nightfall, came only as a partial surprise, and one that could be readily absorbed at the distance I then was from the events.

But it did not end there. In fact, it did not work. And my father wrote next, a brief and hurried scrawl on a paper torn from a duplicating book. 'My Dear Old Son, Things haven't worked out. I'm leaving London. Must get started somewhere new. Away from it all. Everything fresh. It will be better. I'll not be a bother to you. I know I've embarrassed you in the past. It won't happen again. We'll keep in touch. When I have my life organised and running smoothly, I'll write again. Don't worry. Do look after yourself. Keep wrapped up against the cold. Work hard. Play hard. I've written to your Mr Porphyry. Told him to look after you. A better influence on you than I am. More stable, more reliable. God bless. G.'

On the same day, in the afternoon, there came a letter in an unfamiliar hand from Chelsea. It was from Esther. She was the last person he had seen. 'I met him on the steps when he was leaving,' she wrote 'and he asked me to tell you that everything would be all right. He was going to the Cotswolds, but not near you. I'm afraid I didn't catch the name of the place, but he said something about "Manor Farm". He said he would write. Dear old George. He was unhappy when he left here. Don't be hard on him. Love, Esther.'

It was a Wednesday afternoon, after games. I took the letters, and walked up to the mainly deserted school buildings on the top of the hill. I sat outside, on a low wall. From an open window came the faint and uncertain notes of the French horn. It was Danby practising. From where I sat on the far

251

side of the main school, I could look down at the valley, and the course of the river there, marked by willows and poplars, where it wound its way through the rich, flat meadows. Only a few months before I had stood beside it, in the moonlight. It had seemed then that I stood firmly on the earth's floor and revelled in its lush, fertile promise. Now the summer was over, the harvest gathered. The crop in the field where we had tramped beside the dusky poppies at dawn had been reaped. The yellow stubble had gone under the plough. The trees beside the road from which had flown the sudden owl were tinted with yellow and brown.

'He was unhappy when he left here. Don't be hard on him.' Was there ever a time, I wondered, when he had been happy? What malevolent force drove him to blight all his own opportunities? What passion now directed his heavy tread towards these gentle hills and valleys? I felt pity for his troubled heart, and wanted to go to him. But where? And how?

It was pity, and a faint stab of conscience that I felt. He had said in his letter that I was not to worry, and though it may seem strange, even heartless, I obeyed the injunction. At least, that is what I believed I was doing. Perhaps, subconsciously, quite different reactions were taking place, and under the surface a tide of concern was welling up which explains what followed. I assumed he would do as he had said, and start all over again. I treated Esther's letter as information and did not bother to reply. She already belonged to a past that in terms of place and people was left behind. Dry-eyed, sitting on the school wall, staring down into the river valley, I reasoned out these things, and decided to wait and see what would happen. Slowly, a bit tentatively, Danby was trying out a passage from one of the Mozart horn concertos. He had taken to practising hard, and Parker spoke of him occasionally in admiring tones, to the effect that he would make something of his music. I felt, sitting there, a stab of jealousy. I possessed no comparable accomplishment, and such a possession was assuming importance. Danby had once been a close friend, and as trebles in the choir we had sung together. Now, we had drifted apart; he into the narrow confines of his music; and me? Where had I got? Where?

Still I did not understand. I was the seed at the heart of my own selfishness, feeding and giving growth to its protective, immunising layers. Whatever the circumstances of previous months and years may have been, however they compared with the conditions under which others of my age had grown up, they had created a blanket of tissue around any sense of feeling I had. Dimly, I perceived the barriers which I had constructed. One by one, with a callous determination, I had dealt with everyone in terms of their usefulness to me, and had then cast them aside. Lytton, Pritchett, Janet, Alice, Esther, even Mr Porphyry: ciphers for different forms of attachment.

I pared them to a particular shape and form with the knife of my own ruthless nature. If I sought friendship, it was there; the gratification of desire, and it was available; the monitoring of my spiritual responses, freely given; the endless burden of coping with my father, taken from me. What had *I* done? The best that can be said of me was that I had preserved a capacity for natural concern on behalf of him. The more truthful answer was that I had preserved the concern for myself.

The fourth letter came a day or two later, and was from Mr Porphyry. He talked of having had 'a most disturbing letter from your father. His actions are all the more perplexing, in that he seems to have a genuine love for you. I will, of course, do all I can. You have a place here to come to. Be assured of that. But we must pray for guidance over him, and seek it in Scripture (Ephesians 5 v. 18–19). Read also Galatians 3 v. 26–29.'

I did as he suggested. But being 'Abraham's seed' did not really offer me the appeasement of my natural concern for this bewildered and unhappy man, tramping the lonely roads, as I saw him, up to the deserted farmhouse and the empty byre where he had elected to start his life all over again.

II

I told nothing of how I felt. I spoke to no one. I seemed to walk under those high October skies as if I inhabited a deserted landscape. At every opportunity I would escape into the countryside around the school in order to be alone. I missed games, avoided school events, became increasingly recalcitrant. I tried to recall the past summer, with its warm, sensuous experiences. How distant it all seemed. The soft promises of June had produced only an indifferent harvest. I tried to recall the bell-like notes of the nightingale, but could not. In the mind it was possible to assemble the ingredients of that summer's night; but the sensations were lacking. The edifice of my isolation was cracking, and yet the direction in which it was seeking to fall was the only thing that I was totally unable to define. Somewhere, not far away, under the same vaulted skies of autumn with their ever more transitory and fitful shafts of sunlight, shallow across the changing trees and fields, was my father. And bit by bit, unwilling and slow in my reading of the messages that seemed to grow out of the season, seemed almost to breathe out of the hedgerows among which I pursued my solitary and pensive rambles, I came to an understanding that he needed me. I was his God, he mine. His letter had been a crying out from a wilderness of huge, indeed endless proportion; a prayer, a supplication, that folded in on itself, but nevertheless required from me some action. While I could look up into those Cotswold skies, that autumn, and read into their spreading glory and their soft and subtle light a sweet benevolence, his own reaction, to almost precisely the same vistas, was one of quiet agony. It must be. Bit by bit, this came to me, making me ashamed of my own self-pity. Bit by bit I fumbled my way out of thickets of unselfishness and perceived the silent appeal of his aching, torn heart.

I expected further word to come from Alice. Often enough he had referred to her as his 'lifeline'; and in all his tribulations, no matter where, no matter with whom, he had maintained contact with her. But when another letter came, a week or so later, the information was terse and negative. She had 'found out' about his departure, but did not know where he had gone. There was reproach in the tone of her words, subtle innuendoes, and I felt myself to be in receipt of part of it, as if, somehow, I had contributed to his departure.

The regular order of life at school is mainly punctuated by two things: the summonses of authority, and the messages that come from the outside world. And it was fair to say, in those indeterminate days, when I did not know what I wanted nor what was happening, that I would have been as happy without the interruptions as I was with them. They told me an indifferent story; they shed no glow of importance, no focus of envy, upon my status at Coppinger. Sensitive as well-made barometers to the climate of crisis that could at any moment bring down storms upon one's head, other boys noticed irregularities of behaviour, queried the summonses I had received, seemed sometimes to be in possession of second sight so delicate were the perceptions of things being amiss. Danby was one boy in my class who asked me what I was worrying about; Horridge was another; Pritchett had noticed, but had given up referring to my odd detachment. Then, one afternoon, I was again called from class.

I was wanted by Merchant. It was quite late. The October light was fading in a sky that held much colour. Leaves were being blown in the wind. I remember putting on an expression of slight irritation, and coupling it in my mind with the conscious and reproving thought that enough had already been said about my move to Patterson's house, and that no further conversations were required. Deep down, however, I suspected it was not that.

It was not yet night, though classes at that time were quite late in the evening. Lights had been turned on in classrooms, but the school passages were still in darkness, and I walked through the shadows, from one to another of the pools of yellow, filtering through the glass panes of doorways, along with the low hum of teaching and learning, until I came to Merchant's study. I knocked and went in. He looked up briefly from the papers on which he was working.

'Mr Porphyry came down today for a meeting of the Trustees. He wants to see you. He's in the library.'

'Is it about my father?' I said.

'Yes.'

'Has he spoken to you, Sir?'

'Yes.'

I felt a shiver of vague irritation.

'Is there some——?'

'You'd better go. He's returning to London tonight.' Merchant waved his hand in a gesture of dismissal.

I found Mr Porphyry in the library. He was holding his hat and a briefcase, and his rolled umbrella was looped over his arm. Not all the library lights were on, and he was at the far end, eyeing critically a large Pellegrini, 'The Angels warning Lot to Leave Sodom'. It had been bequeathed to the school by a member of the Llewellyn family, and it occurred to me that Mr Porphyry may have known it in another place. He heard me and turned, his eyes endeavouring to pierce the gloom at my end of the long, book-lined room, and I hurried towards him, apprehensively, and wishing I had answered his letter. I felt conscious of being in his debt. He had offered me security, at one level had given me 'new life', and he now stood as a bulwark against the apparent collapse of the rather uncertain situation I still called 'home'.

'I should have answered your letter,' I said. 'I'm sorry.'

'It doesn't matter. It's of no importance. Have you heard from your father? Where is he?'

I shook my head. 'I don't know.'

'I see.' He paused. His face was without expression, his pale, explorer's eyes focusing sadly upon me.

256

'I heard from Alice,' I said. 'But she didn't know either.'

'I am deeply concerned for you,' he said. 'This can't go on.'

I looked back at him without answering. I did not want in any way to extend the distance between us, yet his words seemed unable to comprehend the normality of what he found. This, that could not 'go on', was no better and no worse than other situations in which I had found myself. As a trustee he must have known of worse instances of what social workers would describe as parental indifference, negligence, delinquency. Whatever was special extended beyond the simple sequence of events which surrounded the bizarre image of my father hanging by his braces from the spikes of a set of iron railings.

I shrugged my shoulders. 'He'll turn up,' I said.

Very briefly, in a peremptory and dismissive tone, he laughed. 'So he should, the blighter! How dare he behave like this!' The light of bewildered anger, even bitterness, blazed for a moment in the remote blue eyes, but then was brought under control again.

My inclination was to laugh, in my turn, at Mr Porphyry for his way of expressing distaste and dismissal. At the same time I was conscious of real anger; for the first time in my experience of him he was letting go, beating in futile resentment at a waywardness which he regarded as evil.

'He had to go,' I said. 'He had to.'

'But it's perfectly disgraceful. I mean, there have to be certain standards.' His face was stern now. A faint flush of colour had gathered over his cheekbones.

I smiled faintly. It was a non-committal indication of vague agreement. He believed, from it, I think, that I shared his righteous anger. But it was by no means as strong as that. I was seeing him and my father balanced against each other in the scales of my judgment, and I suppose, subconsciously, I was beginning to make decisions. There seemed some ancient wisdom, some deeply natural perversity, in the

I   257

way in which my father had behaved. Lost, somewhere, but only temporarily under the scudding autumn winds, he yet held around himself, like a tattered cloak, an aura of paternal dignity and authority, almost of majesty, that made Mr Porphyry's strictures, legitimate and well-judged though they might have been, faintly ridiculous.

I looked away from him at the large, dark canvas he had been inspecting when I came in. The angels had supercilious expressions on their faces. The principal among them, directing his calm gaze into the eye of the ageing, balding Lot, who seemed to cringe away from God's message, had a sensuous, spoilt mouth and indifferent, heavy-lidded eyes. Impressive and self-important though he seemed, he was doing no more than delivering a message.

'I have been in touch with Wilf, with Commander Cochrane. He was in London this week, at a mission. We talked about you. He sends you greetings, in Christ. I'm overjoyed at what he tells me about you. You must realise you are chosen. You are among those that wait upon the Lord.'

I stood mute before him. In the oddly uncertain light of the library, where only some of the ceiling lights had been switched on, leaving bays of books and window alcoves in darkness, I felt that the conversation we were having was incongruous. I had reservations about waiting upon the Lord. I read into his words a faint threat.

'But my father,' I said. 'I must find him.'

'You have another Father now, a spiritual Father.'

'I know, Mr Porphyry. It's true. But what about my own father? Perhaps he needs me.'

'That's as may be. You said yourself, a moment ago, he'd turn up.'

Resolve had grown within me even as we had talked. My own attitudes were changing, then and there. It would not be altogether unattractive to go on the way I had gone in the past, following my father's doomed rampagings through life, feeding on his experience, and using my sense of duty as a

258

defence against other demands. One of these was Mr Porphyry's insistent pursuit of spiritual responses. In later years I was to admire him for priorities which, at that time, seemed threatening. Just then, however, his sense of purpose, his limited perspectives, so zealous in the service of one Father, so blind to the needs of another, marked for me a point of rejection. I could not see myself as part of his invisible cohort dedicated to the salvation of the world.

He may have sensed this. He said: 'I have already told you there is a room in my flat. You can always come. Come at Christmas.'

I thought to myself, 'In my Father's house. . . .'

In the painting on the wall behind his shoulder the angel's wings, sprouting out from the back of Pelligrini's very human, very sensual messenger from on high, seemed ridiculous.

I did not answer. The bell rang to bring class to an end, in fact to terminate evening school. Mr Porphyry was curiously still, a figure in repose. The affection I felt for him, on top of the sense of debt and obligation, was very real. But it was finite, having a precise perspective, and for the present I saw no purpose in prolonging or making more complex something of which I seemed already to have the measure. And so, amid the noise of emptying classes, the beat of shoes on the passage-ways, the strident cries of boyish voices in the echoing building, we parted.

III

On the Saturday of the week in which I had received the four letters, Pritchett came back from a rugby match against Blockley school, and the next morning, after chapel, he told me he had seen my father.

'Where?' I said.

'In Blockley.' He seemed to hesitate.

'In Blockley? What was he doing?'

'Just standing.'

'Just standing? Are you sure it was him?'

'Not altogether.' Pritchett frowned. 'Pretty sure. I have met him, you know. More than once.' There was a faint truculence in his determination.

'And he was just standing. Did you speak?'

'He was . . . he was pushing a bicycle through the street. The school bus had stopped. It was before the game, and we couldn't get out. Ferraby was just buying himself cigarettes.'

'Did he see you?'

Again, Pritchett looked unsure of how he should answer me. 'Well, I think he did. He can't have mistaken the bus, anyway, with the crest on the side. He stopped and looked up. He seemed about to lean his bicycle against a tree and come over. But then he turned and hurried away.'

'How did he look?'

'Well,' Pritchett paused. He seemed troubled. He looked at me for a moment, and then his words came out rather quickly. 'He was wearing old clothes, as far as I could see. He looked a bit sad. Could it have been him?'

I paused, looking calmly back into Pritchett's vaguely discomforted eyes. 'I don't know,' I said. 'I don't know where he is, at the moment. He may be visiting friends there.'

'Is that right? You have friends in Blockley? You never told me.'

I ignored his questions. 'How do you get to Blockley?' I asked.

'It's a good way. Over beyond Moreton in the Marsh.'

For a moment or two I considered taking Pritchett into my confidence and showing him the letters. But already at that time too much had built up between us that had not been shared, and the degree of explanation that would be necessary seemed to outweigh the possible help he might be to me.

We stood together looking out over the playing fields, silent, perhaps both of us a bit embarrassed. It was a still, warm day, and normally we would have strolled round the playing fields together or gone into the school library to read papers and magazines. But at that moment I had the desire to be alone, and confused with it was the feeling that I should find a map of the district, see exactly where Blockley was, and look for a 'Manor Farm'.

'I'm going to the library,' I said. 'I want to look something up.' And without any suggestion that he should accompany me, I walked away.

That afternoon the Gaffer sent for me. He had Patterson in his study with him, the two of them vaguely like conspirators.

'I've been meaning to have a word with you about this proposal that you should move to Mr Patterson's house,' Forrest said. 'I understand you're quite happy about it.'

'Yes, Sir.'

'You'll be a loss to us here. But I know Mr Patterson's in need of you.'

Patterson said: 'Absolutely. We've had troubles, and no mistake. The house has been going through a difficult patch. You'll be a welcome addition.'

I looked carefully at his weather-beaten face. In the stillness of the room, with both of them more or less concentrating on me, the waves of tension quite normal to the situation seemed to distort and fracture vision, and the capacity to measure and absorb distance. I had the strange feeling that I was locked into a cube of heavy air which contained both these men and myself. And there developed, quite rapidly, that strange sensation where each movement we made was enormously laboured, pushing through the strong liquid-like resistance of an atmosphere that had been charged and weighted by feelings and thoughts that were, in different degrees, distortions of the truth. I had felt the same way before; and have felt it many times since, an ugly, cloying, unreal imprisonment. In it, both Forrest and Patterson appeared different. Forrest's features, generally mobile, his eyes, fluid and alert, were fixed. And looking at Patterson I felt that I was suddenly seeing his face for the first time. Up to then I had looked upon him as a composite form, a 'character' in the school, a residue from the earlier, post-war days, with no great qualifications to teach, but with a certain dedication, his character heavily imbued with loyalty. He wore his ragged gown, threw chalk at inattentive pupils, ran sports, organised cricket, and had other attributes, mildly eccentric in their form. But on that late October afternoon, standing between them in the sunlit room, it was as if I saw, behind the mask of a day to day familiarity, a real face for the first time; heavy, long jaw; weak mouth; a broad and furrowed forehead; and hunted eyes, a little bloodshot, and uncertain about meeting mine.

He talked obliquely about the events in his house. He stressed the need for confidentiality. He struck me as pompous and unsure, a curious but not unreal combination.

'I need your help,' he said. 'I need your commitment to my house.' He looked at Forrest. 'It will be a wrench for you.'

Forrest nodded, but did not speak. He was relaxed, even contemplative. Patterson, in contrast, seemed strained and uneasy. I stared at his face, one that I would come to know so well. And it seemed then so fearfully naked that I had to turn away towards the Gaffer's more relaxed features.

What I was detecting I did not quite know. But, perhaps conscious that the interview was somehow failing in its purpose, my own housemaster said, 'That'll be all, now. Don't let the move disrupt your work.'

'No, Sir,' I said. 'I won't do that.'

I went on standing there, conscious of certain thin skeins of deception that wrapped round us, intensifying the clotted stillness of the room.

Forrest looked at me, an expression of inquiry in his eyes now, as if he wondered why I had not already departed.

'May I ask you something, Sir?' I said.

'Of course.'

I felt nervous. 'Was it your idea I should move?'

There was a pause. Then Patterson spoke. 'No. It was mine. I asked for you.' He looked directly at me, only for a moment or two, then at Forrest. Again there was a pause.

'I was not happy about it,' Forrest said. 'No one likes losing senior boys. But in the circumstances I thought it was best for the school.'

'Thank you, Sir.'

I left them together. If I felt within me a sense of that layering of motive, that duplicity in human actions, that steadily grows in its proportions with the passage of the years, I could not entirely condemn either Forrest or Patterson for what they were doing, nor why, since I also believed at the time that I concealed, at least from the former, dark matters just as deceitfully. But the burden seemed unusually heavy.

Being a Sunday afternoon I was free to walk out, and did so, picking blackberries along a deserted stretch of unmetalled road that led to one of the school's farm complexes. I could not shake off the sense of oppression, the faint agitation of guilt, and the belief that I was isolated. I could have spoken to Janet. She would have been light-heartedly sympathetic, making little of the move, dismissing my suspicions, and suggesting that we should still go on seeing each other. But already that had more or less come to a conclusion, and this fact prevented my confiding in her. Similarly, with Pritchett, an end had been reached to the kind of intimacy that was necessary if I were to explain the background to my feelings about Forrest and Patterson and Merchant. I felt dry-eyed and hard. A gnarled nugget of resentment had lodged somewhere inside me; indeterminate in its targets, it simply left me dissatisfied and cut off. And all I could think of, as I looked with desultory interest at the late harvest of fruit on the heaped brambles in the hedgerow, was my father's brave simplicity of heart as he set out once more in his life to salvage it from disaster, and make it all new once again. He represented nature unconfined; proud, solitary man, walking the earth not far from me with bewildered steps, saved from catastrophe or collapse by the assurance instinct gave him. I could imagine wild anger, gentle affection, passionate love,

263

rage, despair, pity, dread. But I could not, and did not read, in the picture of his heart that memory resurrected before me, deception or treachery, or plots, or schemes, or strategy. There was about him, in all his rages and wild anger, his own sort of innocence, his own version of simplicity. Failure that he might have been, unhappy man that he was, the flooding tide of nature in his being, that strove with a pitiful lack of success to control and harbour his energies and resources, was still the only milk of human kindness that I understood or wanted. The very fact that he had made no attempt to come to me moved my heart, and stirred within me a longing to see him again. He would have answers. I knew he would. For me, he always had answers.

IV

I was lucky, that Monday morning, in having periods of free study. I slipped away after breakfast, missing chapel, and was on the road heading north-west from the school, not long after eight. I had in my pocket the map I had taken from the school library, but hardly needed to use it, since I had virtually memorised the route I was to take. It followed the most minor roads of all until it reached the A44 to Moreton in the Marsh, and after that it was straightforward enough.

The night had brought the first frost of the year, and patches of grass were lightly dusted with its whiteness. It was clear, and the morning sunlight, slanting low across the gentle hills, woods and fields, soon warmed me as I walked and ran and walked again on a journey that I had measured out to be twelve miles or so, and which I fully expected I would have to complete on foot.

It was not the case. Shortly after reaching the main road a small, dusty black Morris came to a halt beside me in response to my appeal for a lift. I knew I was taking a risk, but felt it was justified.

'You'm from the 'Omes, then?'

'From Coppinger. Yes.'

'They were known as 'Omes in my time.'

'Changed since,' I said. 'It's more a school now.'

'Everythin' changes. Mostly stays same, though. Tha's the way. Ah.' He ruminated over the steering wheel, his heavy form leaning forward, his eyes wrinkling up against the sharp reflections of light from the frosty landscape. He stared along the straight, deserted road. 'You'm runnin' away then? 'Ad enough?'

'No,' I said. 'I have a free day. I'm off to try and find a farm near Blockley. Do you know it? Blockley, I mean?'

'Maybe.'

We started to climb, and the engine in the Morris laboured somewhat. Eventually, with much revving, he changed down. The hot inside of the car, heady with the smells of warm oil and dust and leather, was penetrated by a more intense whine from the engine.

'Are you just going to Moreton in the Marsh?' I asked. 'Or further?'

'Well, now, it so 'appens I'm going further. I've got to get to Chippin' Campden. Road goes through Blockley. I could leave you there.'

'Thanks very much,' I said. We topped the rise, and when the car engine seemed on the point of collapse in third gear, he gritted his teeth, and changed into fourth. 'Have you come far?' I asked.

''Ooky,' he said. 'I've a son over 'Ooky way. 'Ad to go and see 'im. Matter o' business. Stayed the night. Don't like drivin' much.' He stared grimly ahead along the road. The car was moving at about thirty-two miles an hour. 'What name did you say in Blockley?'

'I didn't say a name,' I replied. 'I don't know the name. It's just the farm. It's called Manor Farm. That's where my father is. I think.'

After a pause he opened his mouth and said 'Ah.' Then: 'Manor Farm, eh? And you'm not running away?'

265

'Why do you ask again?' I ventured.

'I wonder your father'd find work at Manor Farm.'

'Why is that?'

He gripped the steering wheel more tightly. 'It's a strange place, that's why.'

I looked sideways at him. His wrinkled, weathered face betrayed no particular emotion. If anything, he seemed to be smiling to himself.

Momentarily, his correct assumption that I was 'running away', an action that was not altogether out of the ordinary at that time in Coppinger's history, made me afraid. What had I done? Upon what had I embarked? And what would be the consequences? I would need to remain calm and level-headed, and it jolted me slightly into an awareness of the unknown territory into which I had departed by leaving the school that morning without permission. I felt I needed to act out my calmness upon this faintly suspicious man who was helping me on my way.

'Who owns it?' I asked him. 'The farm, I mean.'

'Name o' Toynbee. Mrs Toynbee. Widow woman.'

I was arrested by the name. Toynbee? Could it be that 'dear old Toynbee', my father's guide, mentor and friend in the thirties and early forties, had left as a legacy a widow to whom my father had now turned? Or was it just coincidental?

We drove, with considerable labourings of the engine, up through the village of Bourton-on-the-Hill, and turned off for Blockley.

V

She looked at me. 'You're his son, then?'

'Yes,' I said.

'You've come from Coppinger?'

'Yes.'

She did not react with any warmth or welcome. No smile

266

softened her features. If anything, a slight look of resignation came into her eyes, as if I represented an intrusion, the first, into a brief and secret idyll. 'And you want to see him?'

The question seemed superfluous, even idiotic. I stared at her, waiting for her to say that I could not. Eventually I asked her, 'Where is he?'

She pointed along the front of the house where the driveway turned out of view. 'You'll find him working by the greenhouses.'

'May I go up to him?'

She seemed completely bemused, unable to determine anything. She lowered her arm and again paused before nodding slowly and saying, 'Yes. I suppose you can. You'll find your way.'

'He is all right, isn't he?'

'Oh, yes,' she said. 'He's all right.'

She seemed to me undistinguished, distant, unimportant. In a narrative which in part endeavours to untangle and understand the quest in his own life for a happiness which I think he never found, Mrs Toynbee represented the beginning of something different for him, a strange new succession of what the world would call love affairs. Brief in their duration, wholesome in their affections, pregnant with yearnings and dreams to begin with, they were wholly and utterly doomed, one after the other. The term 'love affair' embraces so much, generalising and even trivialising events and encounters which stretch from the simple, innocent passions of youth to the always final but never complete loves of our maturity. For him, the dependency of his life upon his love was total; and it did not work. In witnessing the beginning, and slowly realising the fact as I stood there in that strange suspension of will and action, face to face with the present object of his own search for salvation, I was seized by foreboding. She did not matter. Nothing that she said mattered, nor the place, with its sign on the gate, 'Plants for Sale', and its unkempt appearance into which already I could see evidence of the intrusion of his firm and reorganising hand. It did not matter. What they thought together, and felt, and hoped for, and planned was doomed. But inside him was something that I wanted, a spark, a flame, a fire, and that was not doomed.

Suddenly I was conscious of wasting upon her time and feeling that I could ill spare.

'I'll find him by the greenhouses, then?'

'Yes,' she said, and stared at me, a bleak, pinched look in her face upon which the sharp autumn sunlight fell. 'You'll find him.'

I followed her instructions. I walked up through outbuildings to where three greenhouses stretched across the even, upward curve of the wold. Beyond them, she had said, I would find him working at a fresh plot of ground.

Again, I had a sense of neglect. Cold frames were empty. There were weeds. Portions of seed beds were dug over, and raked. But the pervasive sense was of a past activity, perhaps of numerous hands, that would require considerable labour and attention to bring back again. The morning sunlight in the still and frosty air reflected sharply from the surfaces of glass, the warm brickwork and the white-painted wood. And as I rounded the last corner it bathed in golden light the tilled earth that curved upward in an even sweep towards where the high wolds spread out to the west. With the contrast in weather, all of the summer, with all that it seemed to stand for, the lushness and the promise, the unfulfilled and heady desires which I associated with the valley floor below Coppinger, with Janet's form emerging from the still dark waters of the stream that night in June, now seemed lost for ever. This was different, harder territory; the north-west corner of that part of the county, the last high edge of sandstone. And what one looked out on was really the gathering of winter. Out there under the cold fire of the October sun, was the wilderness where nightingales do not sing.

My father was twenty yards away, facing towards me, a hoe in his hands, the blade of it moving sharply through the earth in quick, energetic thrusts. He was puffing some kind of tune through his lips, the humming note combining oddly with the spent breath, and the melody making irregular and uneven the frequency and the shapes of the white puffs of air coming out of his mouth. As I came into view he stopped and looked up, standing perfectly still. His face was frowning. He had taken the sun since I had last seen him, and looked fitter than he had been in Chelsea. In just a few weeks he had assumed a leaner, sparser appearance. His mouth was open, as if he was going to frame some question, some challenge. It was even as if he was holding his breath, and I suddenly realised that the sun directly behind my back, low still in the sky, and full in his eyes, was blinding him. The frown closed down into a wrinkling of the eyes that slowly penetrated the glare.

'Is that you, old son?' His voice was almost a whisper.

I walked forward to the edge of the bed on which he was working. 'Yes. It's me,' I said. 'I came over to see you.'

'Have you the day free?'

I shook my head. 'I just came,' I said. 'I had to see you.'

'How did you know? How did you find out?' His words were spoken softly, in a tone of relief.

'A friend saw you in Blockley. Saturday afternoon.'

He frowned. 'But how——?'

'Esther wrote and told me the name of the farm. I got a lift.'

He stared at me. He had cast aside a woollen cardigan, and was dressed in a faded blue shirt and his trousers, with the massively stitched and cobbled braces holding them up. He had brown shoes on, but no socks, and in spite of the frosty morning looked warm from the work. He had struck an attitude of contemplation and pause, one knee bent slightly, and his right arm and hand reaching out and resting on the hoe. 'And you just came over? Like that?'

'Yes.'

'And they let you?'

I looked down at the ground. 'What are you putting in here?' I asked.

'Oh, my God,' he said. 'What have you done?' He clenched the fist of the slack hand which had been hanging down by his side, and brought it up and across his body, pressing it into his chest as though it might ease some great and throbbing pain there. 'I'm no good,' he said, shaking his head. 'I've messed things up.'

I thought of all the 'messing up' that seemed to be going on around me, and could not see that his actions, ameliorated a little by his confession, were that much worse than the deceits and transgressions of others. I shook my head at him 'No,' I said.

'I have, old son. The whole bang shooting match. It's all gone. Must start again.'

'But you have started again.'

He looked at me. A queer, sad smile played over his face. He stared round at the ground he had already reclaimed, and I followed his gaze, examining the evidence of his brief duration in that place. Then our eyes again met.

'It was no good,' he said.

'I know.'

'It wasn't Laurie,' he said. He shook his head. He was frowning at the sunlight still. Then he added: 'It was me.' Again he looked down. The tone in his voice was one of sadness, without hope. The good, rewarding earth in which his bewildered eyes searched for answers that did not come, mocked him at that stage. He was still too violent, too impetuous a man to settle for the small redemption it could offer him. One day, what little portion of happiness there would be in the remaining years of his life would come from the soil, and from his patient wrestling with it; but that was not yet. It lay around him, inert, passive, mocking the short span of his time there.

Did he want me to contradict him? At first, I could not. We are too brutal in our youth; the whole of life's action is so black and so white. I wanted comfort, and in wanting it gave it. But I felt as I stood there that I could not go against his own wisdom, in which I had always believed. For what seemed endless moments we stood, opposite each other. The burden of action seemed to rest on me. He was lost in sad contemplation of the earth at his feet. I was lost in the vain hunt for some crumbs of comfort I could offer. What stood in the way of finding them were his own words: 'It was me.' He was right; yet I needed to pretend otherwise. Was he asking me to contradict him? Was he asking me to raise him up? Was he reaching out across that little space of sunlit ground for some kind of endorsement of his shabby acts? Was he calling in a modest account he held with my affection at a time when the thin and spartan nature of his fresh start stared threadbare in his eyes?

'Father,' I said. Then I paused. It was the first time I had called him that. It was to become a new way of addressing him from then on, and it arrested his attention. He looked up slowly. 'You mustn't believe it was only you. You mustn't. It was her as well. Esther says it. Alice says it. I say it.' I looked into his eyes. His face was pinched by defeat.

Again, for long moments, we stared at each other. Then, slowly, his expression cleared. 'You're a good old son,' he said. 'You don't know what this means to me, your coming here, finding me out in this place. You just don't know.' He shrugged his shoulders in a funny, half-embarrassed gesture. He grasped the hoe, and moved to the edge of the bed, poking at odd clumps of earth, breaking them down.

I did not answer him again. We stood there together, that short patch of earth between us, in the still bright sunlight of that October morning, under the high freckling of thin and intermittent white cloud that gave to the great dome of blue that lay beyond an even greater sense of infinity. There was no further need for words. I would go back. We would both go on. Nothing would change. We were pledged to each other. We were pledged to the inescapable past, and to the people of that past. But it was secondary. There was no freedom to run towards. Our freedoms were in our own hearts. He looked again into my eyes, and there was on his face that same queer, sad smile, softening his features, making gentle and bearable once again the turmoil through which we had gone.

If our natures differed, and of course they did, then part of the difference lay in the quantities of unhappiness to which fortune had made us each heirs. And though the balance was wrong, horribly unfair, weighted in my favour, as time would show, and greatly against him, yet between us, across that small patch of tilled earth which he would seed or plant before once more passing on, there existed evenness of sorts, a lever between us for which the fulcrum, immovably fixed, was our common blood.

Did he, with his awful life, buy for me a better one? All the occasions on which we start out again are doomed. Nature folds in upon herself with each season, so that new years are beginning and old years ending both in and out of the calendar year's story. The ground is seeded in autumn also, and there are harvests in the springtime of the year. Nothing could reinforce or strengthen further the invisible bonds that held us. I could turn and walk away, and it would be the same between us. The months of that summer had ruffled the surface of our love, changing and altering its balance and depth, but having no impact on its foundation. I would be back at Coppinger by lunch. He would be at his work. And from our shoulders would have lifted, if only for the present, and if only in part, that burden the weight of which, pressing down in its vague and undefined form, had brought me across the borders of three shires of England to stand before him, seeking reconciliation, finding partial redemption.